THE MISADVENTURES OF SHERLOCK HOLMES

EDITED BY
SEBASTIAN WOLFE

A CITADEL PRESS BOOK
Published by Carol Publishing Group

First Carol Publishing Group Edition 1991

Copyright © 1989 by Sebastian Wolfe and Xanadu Publications Ltd
Introduction copyright © 1987 by Sebastian Wolfe

A Citadel Press Book
Published by Carol Publishing Group
Citadel Press is a registered trademark of
Carol Communications, Inc.

Editorial Offices	Sales & Distribution Offices
600 Madison Avenue	120 Enterprise Avenue
New York, NY 10022	Secaucus, NJ 07094

In Canada: Musson Book Company
A division of General Publishing Co. Limited
Don Mills, Ontario

Published by arrangement with Xanadu Publications Ltd

Manufactured in the United States of America
10 9 8 7 6 5 4 3 2

Carol Publishing Group books are available at special discounts
for bulk purchases, for sales promotions, fund raising, or
educational purposes. Special editions can also be created to
specifications. For details contact: Special Sales Department,
Carol Publishing Group, 120 Enterprise Ave., Secaucus, NJ 07094

ISBN 0-8065-1245-8 (cloth)
ISBN 0-8065-1235-0 (paper)

Contents

INTRODUCTION

Ever since Sherlock Holmes attained his first great popularity in the 1890s he has been imitated, parodied and burlesqued by admiring or envious writers, and in the century or so that has passed since then there have been literally thousands of non-canonical stories, not to mention a huge body of scholarly work on Holme's origins, tastes, habits, dwellings, dressing-gowns and so forth, that in sheer mass is rivalled only by research on Shakespeare and his writings. As H.R.F. Keating has observed, Holmes is a true myth, whose image is familiar to virtually every inhabitant of English-speaking countries throughout the world. And *still* those letters go to 221B Baker Street, where the Abbey National Building Society employs a secretary full-time to deal with them.

Holmes was not the first Great Detective and, as a host of friendly critics have pointed out, his detecting does not always stand up to the closest scrutiny, but he is assuredly the Greatest of all the Great Detectives, without whom no series calling itself *The Great Detectives* could possibly be worthy of the name – hence this specially-commissioned collection of Sherlockian stories (there being little point in reprinting the original adventures, which are readily available elsewhere and surely known by heart by all but the most recent devotee of the mystery story).

The distinctions between parodies, pastiches and burlesques are not very clear, so suffice to say that I have included plenty of all three: burlesques such as the ones by Robert L. Fish and the late John Lennon go straight for the belly-laugh, but to read a whole book of them would be like dining exclusively on cranberry sauce, so I have balanced the menu with parodies – gentler satires such as the ones by Ardath Mayhar and Maurice Baring – and pastiches, by which I mean fully-fledged stories inspired directly (H.R.F. Keating) or indirectly (Anthony Boucher, H.F. Heard) by the great original. These are, I think, excellent tales in their own right, which can be enjoyed entirely on their own terms.

In the pages that follow we'll meet Sherlock Holmes in a truly staggering variety of disguises. Ellery Queen listed as long ago as 1951 some of the parody names – Thinlock Bones, Picklock Holes, Shamrock Jolnes, Sherlaw Kombs, Solar Pons and Holmlock Shears are just a few – and now we find Holmes appearing as a Martian bird, as a dog, as a time-traveller, as a fraud and as an abject failure . . . there are seemingly no limits to the inventiveness of Holmes parodists, and I for one have no complaints about that.

The only real problem has been choosing from this embarassment of riches, and in making this selection I have tried to go for less familiar stories (several are published here for the first time in this country, and one for the first time anywhere) in what I hope is a balanced and enjoyable bill of fare. In doing this I was greatly helped by Ronald Burt de Waal's *The World Bibliography of Sherlock Holmes and Dr. Watson* and by Ellery Queen's *The Detective Short Story*.

Finally I should perhaps explain that only as the contents of this book were being finalized, when it was too late to make changes, did I learn of the existences of an earlier volume with the same title, edited by Ellery Queen in 1944. I have not been able to locate a copy of this book – it was suppressed, I gather, by the Conan Doyle Estate – so any resemblances between that *Misadventures* and this one are necessarily coincidental.

SEBASTIAN WOLFE
London, 1989

The Martian Crown Jewels

POUL ANDERSON

The signal was picked up when the ship was still a quarter million miles away, and recorded voices summoned the technicians. There was no haste, for the ZX28749, otherwise called the *Jane Brackney*, was right on schedule; but landing an unmanned spaceship is always a delicate operation. Men and machines prepared to receive her as she came down, but the control crew had the first order of business.

Yamagata, Steinmann, and Ramanowitz were in the GCA tower, with Hollyday standing by for an emergency. If the circuits *should* fail – they never had, but a thousand tons of cargo and nuclear-powered vessel, crashing into the port, could empty Phobos of human life. So Hollyday watched over a set of spare assemblies, ready to plug in whatever might be required.

Yamagata's thin fingers danced over the radar dials. His eyes were intent on the screen. 'Got her,' he said. Steinmann made a distance reading and Ramanowitz took the velocity off the Dopplerscope. A brief session with a computer showed the figures to be almost as predicted.

'Might as well relax,' said Yamagata, taking out a cigarette. 'She won't be in control range for a while yet.'

His eyes roved over the crowded room and out its window. From the tower he had a view of the spaceport: unimpressive, most of its shops and sheds and living quarters being underground. The smooth concrete field was chopped off by the curvature of the tiny satellite. It always faced Mars, and the station was on the far side, but he could remember how the planet hung enormous over the opposite hemisphere, soft ruddy disc blurred with thin air, hazy greenish-brown mottlings of heath and farmland. Though Phobos was clothed in vacuum, you couldn't see the hard stars of space: the sun and the floodlamps were too bright.

There was a knock on the door. Hollyday went over, almost drifting in the ghostly gravity, and opened it. 'Nobody allowed in here during a landing,' he said. Hollyday was a stocky blond man with a pleasant, open countenance, and his tone was less peremptory than his words.

'Police.' The newcomer, muscular, round-faced, and earnest, was in plain clothes, tunic and pajama pants, which was expected; everyone in the tiny settlement knew Inspector Gregg. But he was packing a gun, which was not usual.

Yamagata peered out again and saw the port's four constables down on the field in official space-suits, watching the ground crew. They carried weapons. 'What's the matter?' he asked.

'Nothing . . . I hope.' Gregg came in and tried to smile. 'But the *Jane* had a very unusual cargo.'

'Hm?' Ramanowitz's eyes lit up in his broad plump visage. 'Why weren't we told?'

'That was deliberate. Secrecy. The Martian crown jewels are aboard.' Gregg fumbled a cigarette from his tunic.

Hollyday and Steinmann nodded at each other. Yamagata whistled. 'On a robot ship?' he asked.

'Uh-huh. A robot ship is the one form of transportation

2

from which they could not be stolen. There were three attempts made when they went to Earth on a regular liner, and I hate to think how many while they were at the British Museum. One guard lost his life. Now my boys are going to remove them before anyone else touches that ship and scoot 'em right down to Sabaeus.'

'How much are they worth?' wondered Ramanowitz.

'Oh . . . they could be fenced on Earth for maybe half a billion UN dollars,' said Gregg. 'But the thief would do better to make the Martians pay to get them back . . . no, Earth would have to, I suppose, since it's our responsibility.' He blew nervous clouds. 'The jewels were secretly put on the *Jane*, last thing before she left on her regular run. I wasn't even told till a special messenger on this week's liner gave me the word. Not a chance for any thief to know they're here, till they're safely back on Mars. And that'll be safe!'

'Some people did know, all along,' said Yamagata thoughtfully. 'I mean the loading crew back at Earth.'

'Uh-huh, there is that.' Gregg smiled. 'Several of them have quit since then, the messenger said, but of course, there's always a big turnover among spacejacks – they're a restless bunch.' His gaze drifted across Steinmann and Hollydɔv, both of whom had last worked at Earth Station and come to Mars a few ships back. The liners went on a hyperbolic path and arrived in a couple of weeks; the robot ships followed the more leisurely and economical Hohmann A orbit and needed 258 days. A man who knew what ship was carrying the jewels could leave Earth, get to Mars well ahead of the cargo, and snap up a job here – Phobos was always shorthanded.

'Don't look at me!' said Steinmann, laughing. 'Chuck and I knew about this – of course – but we were under security restrictions. Haven't told a soul.'

3

'Yeah. I'd have known it if you had,' nodded Gregg. 'Gossip travels fast here. Don't resent this, please, but I'm here to see that none of you boys leaves this tower till the jewels are aboard our own boat.'

'Oh, well. It'll mean overtime.'

'If I want to get rich fast, I'll stick to prospecting,' added Hollyday.

'When are you going to quit running around with that Geiger in your free time?' asked Yamagata. 'Phobos is nothing but iron and granite.'

'I have my own ideas about that,' said Hollyday stoutly.

'Hell, everybody needs a hobby on this Godforsaken clod,' declared Ramanowitz. 'I might try for those sparklers myself, just for the excitement –' He stopped abruptly, aware of Gregg's eyes.

'All right,' snapped Yamagata. 'Here we go. Inspector, please stand back out of the way, and for your life's sake don't interrupt.'

The *Jane* was drifting in, her velocity of the carefully precalculated orbit almost identical with that of Phobos. Almost, but not quite – there had been the inevitable small disturbing factors, which the remote-controlled jets had to compensate, and then there was the business of landing her. The team got a fix and were frantically busy.

In free fall, the *Jane* approached within a thousand miles of Phobos – a spheroid 500 feet in radius, big and massive, but lost against the incredible bulk of the satellite. And yet Phobos is an insignificant airless pill, negligible even beside its seventh-rate planet. Astronomical magnitudes are simply and literally incomprehensible.

When the ship was close enough, the radio directed her gyros to rotate her, very, very gently, until her pickup antenna was pointing directly at the field. Then her jets were cut in, a mere whisper of thrust. She was nearly

4

above the spaceport, her path tangential to the moon's curvature. After a moment Yamagata slapped the keys hard, and the rockets blasted furiously, a visible red streak up in the sky. He cut them again, checked his data, and gave a milder blast.

'Okay,' he grunted. 'Let's bring her in.'

Her velocity relative to Phobos's orbit and rotation was now zero, and she was falling. Yamagata slewed her around till the jets were pointing vertically down. Then he sat back and mopped his face while Ramanowitz took over; the job was too nerve-stretching for one man to perform in its entirety. Ramanowitz sweated the awkward mass to within a few yards of the cradle. Steinmann finished the task, casing her into the berth like an egg into a cup. He cut the jets and there was silence.

'Whew! Chuck, how about a drink?' Yamagata held out unsteady fingers.

Hollyday smiled and fetched a bottle. It went happily around. Gregg declined. His eyes were locked to the field, where a technician was checking for radioactivity. The verdict was clean, and he saw his constables come soaring over the concrete, to surround the great ship with guns. One of them went up, opened the manhatch, and slipped inside.

It seemed a very long while before he emerged. Then he came running. Gregg cursed and thumbed the tower's radio board. 'Hey, there! Ybarra! What's the matter?'

The helmet set shuddered a reply; 'Señor . . . Señor Inspector . . . the crown jewels are gone.'

Sabaeus is, of course, a purely human name for the old city nestled in the Martian tropics, at the juncture of the 'canals' Phison and Euphrates, Terrestrial mouths simply cannot form the syllables of High Chlannach, though

5

rough approximations are possible. Nor did humans ever build a town exclusively of towers broader at the top than the base, or inhabit one for twenty thousand years. If they had, though, they would have encouraged an eager tourist influx; but Martians prefer more dignified ways of making a dollar, even if their parsimonious fame has long replaced that of Scotchmen. The result is that though interplanetary trade is brisk and Phobos a treaty port, a human is still a rare sight in Sabaeus.

Hurrying down the avenues between the stone mushrooms, Gregg felt conspicuous. He was glad the airsuit muffled him. Not that the grave Martians stared; they varkled, which is worse.

The Street of Those Who Prepare Nourishment in Ovens is a quiet one, given over to handicrafters, philosophers, and residential apartments. You won't see a courtship dance or a parade of the Lesser Halberdiers on it: nothing more exciting than a continuous four-day argument on the relativistic nature of the null class or an occasional gunfight. The latter are due to the planet's most renowned private detective, who nests there.

Gregg always found it eerie to be on Mars, under the cold deep blue sky and the shunken sun, among noises muffled by the thin oxygen-deficient air. But for Syaloch he had a good deal of affection, and when he had gone up the ladder and shaken the rattle outside the second-floor apartment and had been admitted, it was like escaping from nightmare.

'Ah, Krech!' The investigator laid down the stringed instrument on which he had been playing and towered gauntly over his visitor. 'An unexbected bleasure to see hyou. Come in, my tear chab, to come in.' He was proud of his English – but simple misspellings will not convey the whistling, clicking Martian accent.

The Inspector felt a cautious way into the high, narrow room. The glowsnakes which illuminated it after dark were coiled asleep on the stone floor, in a litter of papers, specimens, and weapons; rusty sand covered the sills of the Gothic windows. Syaloch was not neat except in his own person. In one corner was a small chemical laboratory. The rest of the walls were taken up with shelves, the criminological literature of three planets – Martian books, Terrestrial micros, Venusian talking stones. At one place, patriotically, the glyphs representing the reigning Nestmother had been punched out with bullets. An Earthling could not sit on the trapeze-like native furniture, but Syaloch had courteously provided chairs and tubs as well; his clientele was also triplanetary.

'I take it you are here on official but confidential business.' Syaloch got out a big-bowled pipe. Martians have happily adopted tobacco, though in their atmosphere it must include potassium permanganate.

Gregg started. 'How the hell do you know that?'

'Elementary, my dear fellow. Your manner is most agitated, and I know nothing but a crisis in your profession would cause that.'

Gregg laughed wryly.

Syaloch was a seven-foot biped of vaguely storklike appearance. But the lean, crested, red-beaked head at the end of the sinuous neck was too large, the yellow eyes too deep; the white feathers were more like a penguin's than a flying bird's, save at the blue-plumed tail; instead of wings there were skinny red arms ending in four-fingered hands. And the overall posture was too erect for a bird.

Gregg jerked back to awareness. God in Heaven! The city lay gray and quiet; the sun was slipping westward over the farmlands of Sinus Sabaeus and the desert of the Aeria; he could just make out the rumble of a treadmill cart passing beneath the windows – and he sat here with a story which could blow the Solar System apart!

His hands, gloved against the chill, twisted together. 'Yes, it's confidential, all right. If you can solve this case, you can just about name your own fee.' The gleam in Syaloch's eyes made him regret that, but he stumbled on: 'One thing, though. Just how do you feel about us Earthlings?'

'I have no prejudices. It is the brain that counts, not whether it is covered by feathers or hair or bony plates.'

'No, I realize that. But some Martians resent us. We do disrupt an old way of life – we can't help it, if we're to trade with you –'

'*K'teh*. The trade is on the whole beneficial. Your fuel and machinery – and tobacco, yesss – for our kantz and snull. Also, we were getting too . . . stale. And of course space travel had added a whole new dimension to criminology. Yes, I favor Earth.'

'Then you'll help us? And keep quiet about something which could provoke your planetary federation into kicking us off Phobos?'

The third eyelids, closed, making the long-beaked face a mask. 'I give no promises yet, Gregg.'

'Well . . . damn it, all right, I'll have to take the chance.' The policeman swallowed hard. 'You know about your crown jewels.'

'They were lent to Earth for exhibit and scientific study.'

'After years of negotiation. There's no more priceless relic on all Mars – and you were an old civilization when we were hunting mammoths. All right. They've been stolen.'

Syaloch opened his eyes, but his only other movement was to nod.

'They were put on a robot ship at Earth Station. They were gone when the ship reached Phobos. We've damn near ripped the boat apart trying to find them – we did take the other cargo to pieces, bit by bit – and they aren't there!'

Syaloch rekindled his pipe, an elaborate flint-and-steel process on a world where matches won't burn. Only when it was drawing well did he suggest: 'It is possible the ship was boarded en route?'

'No. It isn't possible. Every spacecraft in the System is registered, and its whereabouts are known at any time. Furthermore, imagine trying to find a speck in hundreds of millions of cubic miles, and match velocities with it . . . no vessel ever built could carry that much fuel. And mind you, it was never announced that the jewels were going back this way. Only the UN police and the Earth Station crew could know till the ship had actually left – by which time it'd be too late.'

'Most interesting.'

'If word of this gets out,' said Gregg miserably, 'you can guess the results. I suppose, we'd still have a few friends left in your Parliament –'

'In the House of Actives, yesss . . . a few. Not in the House of Philosophers, which is of course the upper chamber.'

'It could mean a twenty-year hiatus in Earth-Mars traffic – maybe a permanent breaking off of relations. Damn it, Syaloch, you've *got* to help me find those stones!'

'Hm-m-m. I pray your pardon. This requires thought.' The Martian picked up his crooked instrument and plucked a few tentative chords. Gregg sighed.

The colorless sunset was past, night had fallen with the unnerving Martian swiftness, and the glowsnakes were emitting blue radiance when Syaloch put down the demifiddle.

'I fear I shall have to visit Phobos in person,' he said. 'There are too many unknowns for analysis, and it is never well to theorize before all the data have been gathered.' A bony hand clapped Gregg's shoulder. 'Come, come, old chap. I am really most grateful to you. Life was becoming infernally dull. Now, as my famous Terrestrial predecessor would say, the game's afoot . . . and a very big game indeed!'

A Martian in an Earthlike atmosphere is not much hampered, needing only a hour in a compression chamber and a filter on his beak to eliminate excess oxygen and moisture. Syaloch walked freely about the port clad in filter, pipe, and *tirstokr* cap, grumbling to himself at the heat and humidity.

He donned a spacesuit and went out to inspect the *Jane Brackney*. The vessel had been shunted aside to make room for later arrivals, and stood by a raw crag at the edge of the field, glimmering in the hard spatial sunlight. Gregg and Yamagata were with him.

'I say, you *have* been thorough,' remarked the detective. 'The outer skin is quite stripped off.'

The spheroid resembled an egg which had tangled with a waffle iron: an interesting grid of girders and braces above a thin aluminium hide. The jets, batches, and radio mast were the only breaks in the checkerboard pattern, whose depth was about a foot and whose squares were a yard across at the 'equator.'

Yamagata laughed in a strained fashion. 'No. The cops fluoroscoped every inch of her, but that's the way these cargo ships always look. They never land on Earth, you know, or any place where there's air, so streamlining would be unnecessary. And since nobody is aboard in

10

transit, we don't have to worry about insulation or airtightness. Perishables are stowed in sealed compartments.'

'I see. Now where were the crown jewels kept?'

'They were supposed to be in a cupboard near the gyros,' said Gregg. 'They were in a locked box, about six inches high, six inches wide, and a foot long.' He shook his head, finding it hard to believe that so small a box could contain so much potential death.

'Ah . . . but *were* they placed there?'

'I radioed Earth and got a full account,' said Gregg. 'The ship was loaded as usual at the satellite station, then shoved a quater mile away till it was time for her to leave – to get her out of the way, you understand. She was still in the same free-fall orbit, attached by a light cable – perfectly standard practice. At the last minute, without anyone being told beforehand, the crown jewels were brought up from Earth and stashed aboard.'

'By a special policeman?'

'No. Only licensed technicians are allowed to board a ship in orbit, unless there's a life-and-death emergency. One of the regular station crew – fellow named Carter – was told where to put them. He was watched by the cops as he pulled himself along the cable and in through the manhatch.' Gregg pointed to a small door near the radio mast. 'He came out, closed it, and returned on the cable. The police immediately searched him and his spacesuit, just in case, and he positively did not have the jewels. There was no reason to suspect him, of anything – good steady worker – though I'll admit he's disappeared since then. The *Jane* blasted a few minutes later and her jets were watched till they cut off and she went into free fall. And that's the last anyone saw of her till she got here – without the jewels.'

'And right on orbit,' added Yamagata. 'If by some freak she had been boarded, it would have thrown her off enough for us to notice as she came in. Transference of momentum between her and the other ship.'

'I see.' Behind his faceplate, Syaloch's beak cut a sharp black curve across heaven. 'Now then, Gregg, were the jewels actually in the box when it was delivered?'

'At Earth station, you mean? Oh, yes. There are four UN Chief Inspectors involved, and HQ says they're absolutely above suspicion. When I sent back word of the theft, they insisted on having their own quarters and so on searched, and went under scop voluntarily.

'And your own constables on Phobos?'

'Same thing,' said the policeman grimly. 'I've slapped on an embargo – nobody but me has left this settlement since the loss was discovered. I've had every room and tunnel and warehouse searched.' He tried to scratch his head, a frustrating attempt when one is in a spacesuit. 'I can't maintain those restrictions much longer. Ships are coming in and the consignees want their freight.'

'*Hnachla.* That puts us under a time limit, then.' Syaloch nodded to himself. 'Do you know, this is a fascinating variation of the old locked room problem. A robot ship in transit is a locked room in the most classic sense.' He drifted off.

Gregg stared bleakly across the savage horizon, naked rock tumbling away under his feet, and then back over the field. Odd how tricky your vision became in airlessness, even when you had bright lights. That fellow crossing the field there, under the full glare of sun and floodlamps, was merley a stipple of shadow and luminance . . . what the devil was he doing, tying a shoe of all things? No, he was walking quite normally –

'I'd like to put everyone on Phobos under scop,' said

Gregg with a violent note, 'but the law won't allow it unless the suspect volunteers – and only my own men have volunteered.'

'Quite rightly, my dear fellow,' said Syaloch. 'One should at least have the privilege of privacy in his own skull. And it would make the investigation unbearably crude.'

'I don't give a fertilizing damn how crude it is,' snapped Gregg. 'I just want that box with the Martian crown jewels safe inside.'

'Tut-tut! Impatience has been the ruin of many a promising young police officer, as I seem to recall my spiritual ancestor of Earth pointing out to a Scotland Yard man who – hm – may even have been a physical ancestor of yours, Gregg. It seems we must try another approach. Are there any people on Phobos who might have known the jewels were aboard this ship?'

'Yes. Two men only. I've pretty well established that they never broke security and told anyone else till the secret was out.'

'And who are they?'

'Technicians, Hollyday and Steinmann. They were working at Earth Station when the *Jane* was loaded. They quit soon after – not at the same time – and came here by liner and got jobs. You can bet that *their* quarters have been searched!'

'Perhaps,' murmured Syaloch, 'it would be worthwhile to interview the gentlemen in question.'

Steinmann, a thin redhead, wore truculence like a mantle; Hollyday merely looked worried. It was no evidence of guilt – everyone had been rubbed raw of late. They sat in the police office, with Gregg behind the desk and Syaloch leaning against the wall, smoking and regarding them with unreadable yellow eyes.

13

'Damn it, I've told this over and over till I'm sick of it!' Steinmann knotted his fists and gave the Martian a bloodshot stare. 'I never touched the things and I don't know who did. Hasn't any man a right to change jobs?'

'Please,' said the detective mildly. 'The better you help the sooner we can finish this work. I take it you were acquainted with the man who actually put the box aboard the ship?'

'Sure. Everybody knew John Carter. Everybody knows everybody else on a satellite station.' The Earthman stuck out his jaw. 'That's why none of us'll take scop. We won't blab out all our thoughts to guys we see fifty times a day. We'd go nuts!'

'I never made such a request,' said Syaloch.

'Carter was quite a good friend of mine,' volunteered Hollyday.

'Uh-huh,' grunted Gregg. 'And he quit too, about the same time you fellows did, and went Earthside and hasn't been seen since. HQ told me you and he were thick. What'd you talk about?'

'The usual,' Hollyday shrugged. 'Wine, women, and song. I haven't heard from him since I left Earth.'

'Who says Carter stole the box?' demanded Steinmann. 'He just got tired of living in space and quit his job. He *couldn't* have stolen the jewels – he was searched.'

'Could he have hidden it somewhere for a friend to get at this end?' inquired Syaloch.

'Hidden it? Where? Those ships don't have secret compartments,' Steinmann spoke wearily. 'And he was only aboard the *Jane* a few minutes, just long enough to put the box where he was supposed to.' His eyes smoldered at Gregg. 'Let's face it: the only people anywhere along the line who ever had a chance to lift it were our own dear cops.'

14

The Inspector reddened and half rose from his seat. 'Look here, you –'

'We've got *your* word that you're innocent,' growled Steinmann. 'Why should it be any better than mine?'

Syaloch waved both men back. 'If you please. Brawls are unphilosophic.' His beak opened and clattered, the Martian equivalent of a smile. 'Has either of you, perhaps, a theory? I am open to all ideas.'

There was a stillness. Then Hollyday mumbled: 'Yes, I have one.'

Syaloch hooded his eyes and puffed quietly, waiting.

Hollyday's grin was shaky. 'Only if I'm right you'll never see those jewels again.'

Gregg sputtered.

'I've been around the Solar System a lot,' said Hollyday. 'It gets lonesome out in space. You never know how big and lonesome it is till you've been there, all by yourself. And I've done just that – I'm an amateur uranium prospector, not a lucky one so far. I can't believe we know everything about the universe, or that there's only vacuum between the planets.'

'Are you talking about the cobblies?' snorted Gregg.

'Go ahead and call it superstition. But if you're in space long enough . . . well, somehow, you *know*. There are things out there – gas beings, radiation beings, whatever you want to imagine, there's *something* living in space.'

'And what use would a box of jewels be to a cobbly?'

Hollyday spread his hands. 'How can I tell? Maybe we bother them, scooting through their own dark kingdom with our little rockets. Stealing the crown jewels would be a good way to disrupt the Mars trade, wouldn't it?'

Only Syaloch's pipe broke the inward-pressing silence. But its burbling seemed quite irreverent.

'Well –' Gregg fumbled helplessly with a meteoric

15

paperweight. 'Well, Mr. Syaloch, do you want to ask any more questions?'

'Only one.' The third lids rolled back, and coldness looked out at Steinmann. 'If you please, my good man, what is your hobby?'

'Huh? Chess. I play chess. What's it to you?' Steinmann lowered his head and glared sullenly.

'Nothing else?'

'What else is there?'

Syaloch glanced at the Inspector, who nodded confirmation.

'I see. Thank you. Perhaps we can have a game sometime. I have some small skill of my own. That is all for now, gentlemen.'

They left, moving like things in the haze of a dream through the low gravity.

'Well?' Gregg's eyes pleaded with Syaloch. 'What next?'

'Very little. I think . . . yesss, while I am here I should like to watch the technicians at work. In my profession, one needs a broad knowledge of all occupations.'

Gregg sighed.

Ramanowitz showed the guest around. The *Kim Brackney* was in and being unloaded. They threaded through a hive of spacesuited men.

'The cops are going to have to raise that embargo soon,' said Ramanowitz. 'Either that or admit why they've clamped it on. Our warehouses are busting.'

'It would be politic to do so,' nodded Syaloch. 'Ah, tell me . . . is this equipment standard for all stations?'

'Oh, you mean what the boys are wearing and carrying around? Sure. Same issue everywhere.'

'May I inspect it more closely?'

'Hm?' *Lord, deliver me from visiting firemen!* thought Ramanowitz. He waved a mechanic over to him. 'Mr.

Syaloch would like you to explain your outfit,' he said with ponderous sarcasm.

'Sure. Regular spacesuit here, reinforced at the seams.' The gauntleted hands moved about, pointing. 'Heating coils powered from this capacitance battery. Ten-hour air supply in the tanks. These buckles, you snap your tools into them, so they won't drift around in free fall. This little can at my belt holds paint that I spray out through this nozzle.'

'Why must spaceships be painted?' asked Syaloch. 'There is nothing to corrode the metal.'

'Well, sir, we just call it paint. It's really gunk, to seal any leaks in the hull till we can install a new plate, or to mark any other kind of damage. Meteor punctures and so on.' The mechanic pressed a trigger and a thin, almost invisible stream jetted out, solidifying as it hit the ground.

'But it cannot readily be seen, can it?' objected the Martian. 'I, at least, find it difficult to see clearly in airlessness.'

'That's right. Light doesn't diffuse, so . . . well, anyhow, the stuff is radioactive – just enough so that the repair crew can spot the place with a Geiger counter.'

'I understand. What is the half-life?'

'Oh, I'm not sure. Six months, maybe? It's supposed to remain detectable for a year.'

'Thank you.' Syaloch stalked off. Ramanowitz had to jump to keep up with those long legs.

'Do you think Carter may have hid the box in his paint can?' suggested the human.

'No, hardly. The can is too small, and I assume he was searched thoroughly.' Syaloch stopped and bowed. 'You have been very kind and patient, Mr. Ramanowitz. I am finished now, and can find the Inspector myself.'

'What for?'

17

'To tell him he can lift the embargo, of course.' Syaloch made a harsh sibilance. 'And then I must get the next boat to Mars. If I hurry, I can attend the concert in Sabaeus tonight.' His voice grew dreamy. 'They will be premiering Hanyech's *Variations on a Theme by Mendelssohn*, transcribed to the Royal Chlannach scale. It should be most unusual.'

It was three days afterward that the letter came. Syaloch excused himself and kept an illustrious client squatting while he read it. Then he nodded to the other Martian. 'You will be interested to know, sir, that the Estimable Diadems have arrived at Phobos and are being returned at this moment.'

The client, a Cabinet Minister from the House of Actives, blinked. 'Pardon, Freehatched Syaloch, but what have you to do with that?'

'Oh . . . I am a friend of the Featherless police chief. He thought I might like to know.'

'*Hraa.* Were you not on Phobos recently?'

'A minor case.' The detective folded the letter carefully, sprinkled it with salt, and ate it. Martians are fond of paper, especially official Earth stationery with high rag content. 'Now, sir, you were saying –?'

The parliamentarian responded absently. He would not dream of violating privacy – no, never – but if he had X-ray vision he would have read:

'Dear Syaloch,

'You were absolutely right. Your locked room problem is solved. We've got the jewels back, everything is in fine shape, and the same boat which brings you this letter will deliver them to the vaults. It's too bad the public can never know the facts – two planets ought to be grateful to you – but I'll supply that much thanks all by myself, and insist that any bill you care to send be paid in full. Even if the Assembly had to make a special appropriation, which I'm afraid it will.

'I admit your idea of lifting the embargo at once looked pretty wild to me, but it worked. I had our boys out, of course, scouring Phobos with Geigers, but Hollyday found the box before we did. Which saved us a lot of trouble, to be sure. I arrested him as he came back into the settlement, and he had the box among his ore samples. He has confessed, and you were right all along the line.

'What was that thing you quoted to me, the saying of that Earthman you admire so much? "When you have eliminated the impossible, whatever remains, however improbable, must be true." Something like that. It certainly applies to this case.

'As you decided, the box must have been taken to the ship at Earth Station and left there – no other possibility existed. Carter figured it out in half a minute when he was ordered to take the thing out and put it aboard the *Jane*. He went inside, all right, but still had the box when he emerged. In that uncertain light nobody saw him put it 'down' between four girders right next to the hatch. Or as you remarked, if the jewels are not *in* the ship, and yet not *away* from the ship, they must be *on* the ship. Gravitation would hold them in place. When the *Jane* blasted off, acceleration pressure slid the box back, but of course the waffle-iron pattern kept it from being lost; it fetched up against the after rib and stayed there. All the way to Mars! But the ship's gravity held it securely enough even in free fall, since both were on the same orbit.

'Hollyday says that Carter told him all about it. Carter couldn't go to Mars himself without being suspected and watched every minute once the jewels were discovered missing. He needed a confederate. Hollyday went to

Phobos and took up prospecting as a cover for the search he'd later be making for the jewels.

'As you showed me, when the ship was within a thousand miles of this dock, Phobos gravity would be stronger than her own. Every spacejack knows that the robot ships don't start decelerating till they're quite close; that they are then almost straight above the surface; and that the side with the radio mast and manhatch – the side on which Carter had placed the box – is rotated around to face the station. The centrifugal force of rotation threw the box away from the ship, and was in a direction toward Phobos rather than away from it. Carter knew that this rotation is slow and easy, so the force wasn't enough to accelerate the box to escape velocity and lose it in space. It would have to fall down toward the satellite. Phobos Station being on the side opposite Mars, there was no danger that the loot would keep going till it hit the planet.

'So the crown jewels tumbled onto Phobos, just as you deduced. Of course Carter had given the box a quick radioactive spray as he laid it in place, and Hollyday used that to track it down among all those rocks and crevices. In point of fact, its path curved clear around this moon, so it landed about five miles from the station.

'Steinmann has been after me to know why you quizzed him about his hobby. You forgot to tell me that, but I figured it out for myself and told him. He or Hollyday had to be involved, since nobody else knew about the cargo, and the guilty person had to have some excuse to go out and look for the box. Chess playing doesn't furnish that kind of alibi. Am I right? At least, my deduction proves I've been studying the same canon you go by. Incidentally, Steinmann asks if you'd care to take him on the next time he has planet leave.

'Hollyday knows where Carter is hiding, and we've

20

radioed the information back to Earth. Trouble is, we can't prosecute either of them without admitting the facts. Oh, well, there are such things as blacklists.

'Will have to close this now to make the boat. I'll be seeing you soon – not professionally, I hope!

Admiring regards,
Inspector Gregg'

But as it happened, the Cabinet minister did not possess X-ray eyes. He dismissed unprofitable speculation and outlined his problem. Somebody, somewhere in Sabaeus, was farniking the krats, and there was an alarming zaksnautry among the hyukus. It sounded to Syaloch like an interesting case.

From the Diary of Sherlock Holmes

MAURICE BARING

Baker Street, January 1. – Starting a diary in order to jot down a few useful incidents which will be of no use to Watson. Watson very often fails to see that an unsuccessful case is more interesting from a professional point of view than a successful case. He means well.

January 6. – Watson has gone to Brighton for a few days, for change of air. This morning quite an interesting little incident happened which I note as a useful example of how sometimes people who have no powers of deduction nevertheless stumble on the truth for the wrong reason. (This never happens to Watson, *fortunately.*) Lestrade called from Scotland Yard with reference to the theft of a diamond and ruby ring from Lady Dorothy Smith's wedding presents. The facts of the case were briefly these: On Thursday evening such of the presents as were jewels had been brought down from Lady Dorothy's bedroom to the drawing-room to be shown to an admiring group of friends. The ring was amongst them. After they had been shown, the jewels were taken upstairs once more and locked in the safe. The next morning the ring was missing. Lestrade, after investigating the matter, came to the conclusion that the ring had not been stolen, but had either been dropped in the drawing-room, or replaced in one of the other cases; but since he had searched the room

22

and the remaining cases, his theory so far received no support. I accompanied him to Eaton Square to the residence of Lady Middlesex, Lady Dorothy's mother.

While we were engaged in searching the drawing-room, Lestrade uttered a cry of triumph and produced the ring from the lining of the arm-chair. I told him he might enjoy the triumph, but that the matter was not quite so simple as he seemed to think. A glance at the ring had shown me not only that the stones were false, but that the false ring had been made in a hurry. To deduce the name of its maker was of course child's play. Lestrade or any pupil of Scotland Yard would have taken for granted it was the same jeweller who had made the real ring. I asked for the bridegroom's present, and in a short time I was interviewing the jeweller who had provided it. As I thought, he had made a ring, with imitation stones (made of the dust of real stones), a week ago, for a young lady. She had given no name and had fetched and paid for it herself. I deduced the obvious fact that Lady Dorothy had lost the real ring, her uncle's gift, and, not daring to say so, had had an imitation ring made. I returned to the house, where I found Lestrade, who had called to make arrangements for watching the presents during their exhibition.

I asked for Lady Dorothy, who at once said to me:

'The ring was found yesterday by Mr. Lestrade.'

'I know,' I answered, 'but which ring?'

She could not repress a slight twitch of the eyelids as she said: 'There was only one ring.'

I told her of my discovery and of my investigations.

'This is a very odd coincidence, Mr. Holmes,' she said. 'Some one else must have ordered an imitation. But you shall examine my ring for yourself.' Whereupon she fetched the ring, and I saw it was no imitation. She had of course in the meantime found the real ring.

But to my intense annoyance she took it to Lestrade and said to him:

'Isn't this the ring you found yesterday, Mr. Lestrade?'

Lestrade examined it and said, 'Of course it is absolutely identical in every respect.'

'And do you think it is an imitation?' asked this most provoking young lady.

'Certainly not,' said Lestrade, and turning to me he added: 'Ah! Holmes, that is where theory leads one. At the Yard we go in for facts.'

I could say nothing; but as I said good-bye to Lady Dorothy, I congratulated her on having found the real ring. The incident, although it proved the correctness of my reasoning, was vexing as it gave that ignorant blunderer an opportunity of crowing over me.

January 10. – A man called just as Watson and I were having breakfast. He didn't give his name. He asked me if I knew who he was. I said, 'Beyond seeing that you are unmarried, that you have travelled up this morning from Sussex, that you have served in the French Army, that you write for reviews, and are especially interested in the battles of the Middle Ages, that you give lectures, that you are a Roman Catholic, and that you have once been to Japan, I don't know who you are.'

The man replied that he *was* unmarried, but that he lived in Manchester, that he had never been to Sussex or Japan, that he had never written a line in his life, that he had never served in any army save the English Territorial force, that so far from being a Roman Catholic he was a Freemason, and that he was by trade an electrical engineer – I suspected him of lying; and I asked him why his boots were covered with the clayey and chalk mixture peculiar to Horsham; why his boots were French Army service boots, elastic-sided, and bought probably at Valmy; why the second half of a return ticket from Southwater was emerging from his ticket-pocket; why he wore the medal of St Anthony on his watchchain; why he smoked Caporal cigarettes; why the proofs of an article on the Battle of Eylau were protruding from his breastpocket, together with a copy of the *Tablet*; why he carried in his hand a parcel which, owing to the untidy way in which it had been made (an untidiness which, in harmony with the rest of his clothes, showed that he could not be married) revealed the fact that it contained photographic magic lantern slides; and why he was tattooed on the left wrist with a Japanese fish.

'The reason I have come to consult you will explain some of these things,' he answered.

'I was staying last night at the Windsor Hotel, and this morning when I woke up I found an entirely different set of clothes from my own. I called the waiter and pointed this out, but neither the waiter nor any of the other servants, after making full enquiries, were able to account for the change. None of the other occupants of the hotel had complained of anything being wrong with their own clothes.

'Two gentlemen had gone out early from the hotel at 7.30. One of them had left for good, the other was expected to return.

'All the belongings I am wearing, including this parcel, which contains slides, belong to someone else.

'My own things contained nothing valuable, and consisted of clothes and boots very similar to these; my coat was also stuffed with papers. As to the tattoo, it was done at a Turkish bath by a shampooer, who learnt the trick in the Navy.'

The case did not present any features of the slightest interest. I merely advised the man to return to the hotel and await the real owner of the clothes, who was evidently the man who had gone out at 7.30.

This is a case of my reasoning being, with one partial exception, perfectly correct. Everything I had deduced would no doubt have fitted the real owner of the clothes.

Watson asked rather irrelevantly why I had not noticed that the clothes were not the man's own clothes.

A stupid question, as the clothes were reach-me-downs which fitted him as well as such clothes ever do fit, and he was probably of the same build as their rightful owner.

January 12. – Found a carbuncle of unusual size in the plum-pudding. Suspected the makings of an interesting case. But luckily, before I had stated any hypothesis to Watson – who was greatly excited – Mrs. Turner came in and noticed it and said her naughty nephew Bill had been at his tricks again, and that the red stone had come from a Christmas tree. Of course, I had not examined the stone with my lens.

The Anomaly of the Empty Man

ANTHONY BOUCHER

'This is for you,' Inspector Abrahams announced wryly. 'Another screwy one.'

I was late and out of breath. I'd somehow got entangled on Market Street with the Downtown Merchants' Association annual parade, and for a while it looked like I'd be spending the day surrounded by gigantic balloon-parodies of humanity. But it takes more than rubber Gullivers to hold me up when Inspector Abrahams announces that he's got a case of the kind he labels 'for Lamb.'

And San Francisco's the city for them to happen in. Nobody anywhere else ever had such a motive for murder as the butler Frank Miller in 1896, or such an idea of how to execute a bank robbery as the zany Mr. Will in 1952. Take a look at Joe Jackson's *San Francisco Murders*, and you'll see that we can achieve a flavor all our own. And when we do, Abrahams lets me in on it.

Abrahams didn't add any explanation. He just opened the door of the apartment. I went in ahead of him. It was a place I could have liked if it hadn't been for what was on the floor.

Two walls were mostly windows. One gave a good view of the Golden Gate. From the other, on a fine day, you could see the Farallones, and it was a fine day.

The other two walls were records and a record player. I'd heard of the Stambaugh collection of early operatic

27

recordings. If I'd been there on any other errand, my mouth would have watered at the prospect of listening to lost great voices.

'If you can get a story out of this that makes sense,' the Inspector grunted, 'you're welcome to it – at the usual fee.' Which was a dinner at Lupo's Pizzeria, complete with pizza Carus', tomatoes with fresh basil and sour French bread to mop up the inspired sauce of Lupo's special *calamari* (squids to you). 'Everything's just the way we found it.'

I looked at the unfinished highball, now almost colorless with all its ice melted and its soda flat. I looked at the cylindrical ash of the cigaret which had burned itself out. I looked at the vacuum cleaner – a shockingly utilitarian object in this set for gracious living. I looked at the record player, still switched on, still making its methodical seventy-eight revolutions per minute, though there was no record on the turntable.

Then I managed to look again at the thing on the floor.

It was worse than a body. It was like a tasteless bloodless parody of the usual occupant of the spot marked X. Clothes scattered in disorder seem normal – even more normal, perhaps, in a bachelor apartment than clothes properly hung in closets. But this . . .

Above the neck of the dressing gown lay the spectacles. The sleeves of the shirt were inside the sleeves of the dressing gown. The shirt was buttoned, even to the collar, and the foulard tie was knotted tight up against the collar button. The tails of the shirt were tucked properly into the zipped-up, properly belted trousers. Below the trouser cuffs lay the shoes, at a lifelike angle, with the tops of the socks emerging from them.

'And there's an undershirt under the shirt,' Inspector

28

Abrahams muttered disconsolately, 'and shorts inside the pants. Complete outfit; what the well-dressed man will wear. Only no man in them.'

It was as though James Stambaugh had been attacked by some solvent which eats away only flesh and leaves all the inanimate articles. Or as though some hyperspatial suction had drawn the living man out of his wardrobe, leaving his sartorial shell behind him.

I said, 'Can I dirty an ashtray in this scene?'

Abrahams nodded. 'I was just keeping it for you to see. We've got our pictures.' While I lit up, he crossed to the record player and switched it off. 'Damned whirligig gets on my nerves.'

'Whole damned setup gets on mine,' I said. 'It's like a striptease version of the *Mary Celeste*. Only the strip wasn't a gradual tease; just abruptly, *whoosh!*, a man's gone. One minute he's comfortably dressed in his apartment, smoking, drinking, playing records. The next he's stark naked – and where and doing what?'

Abrahams pulled at his nose, which didn't need lengthening. 'We had the Japanese valet check the wardrobe. Every article of clothing James Stambaugh owned is still here in the apartment.'

'Who found him?' I asked.

'Kaguchi. The valet. He had last night off. He let himself in this morning, to prepare coffee and prairie oysters as usual. He found this.'

'Blood?' I ventured.

Abrahams shook his head.

'Visitors?'

'Ten apartments in this building. Three of them had parties last night. You can figure how much help the elevator man was.'

'The drink?'

'We took a sample to the lab. Nothing but the best scotch.'

'Motive?'

'Gay dog, our Mr. Stambaugh. Maybe you read Herb Caen's gossip column too? And Kaguchi gave us a little fill-in. Brothers, fathers, husbands . . . Too many motives.'

'But why this way?' I brooded. 'Get rid of him, sure. But why leave this hollow husk . . . ?'

'Not just why, Lamb. How?'

'How? That should be easy enough to –'

'Try it. Try fitting sleeves into sleeves, pants into pants, so they're as smooth and even as if they were still on the body. I've tried, with the rest of the wardrobe. It doesn't work.'

I had an idea. 'You don't fit 'em in,' I said smugly. 'You take 'em off. Look.' I unbuttoned my coat and shirt, undid my tie, and pulled everything off at once. 'See,' I said; 'sleeves in sleeves.' I unzipped and stepped out of trousers and shorts. 'See; pants in pants.'

Inspector Abrahams was whistling the refrain of 'Strip Polka.' 'You missed your career, Lamb,' he said. 'Only now you've got to put your shirt tails between the outer pants and the inner ones and still keep everything smooth. And look in here.' He lifted up one shoe and took out a pocket flash and shot a beam inside. 'The sock's caught on a little snag in one of the metal eyelets. That's kept it from collapsing, and you can still see the faint impress of toes in there. Try slipping your foot out of a laced-up shoe and see if you can get that result.'

I was getting dressed again and feeling like a damned fool.

'Got any other inspirations?' Abrahams grinned.

'The only inspiration I've got is as to where to go now.'

'Some day,' the Inspector grunted, 'I'll learn where you

30

go for your extra-bright ideas.'

'As the old lady said to the elephant keeper,' I muttered, 'you wouldn't believe me if I told you.'

The Montgomery Block (Monkey Block to natives) is an antic and reboantic warren of offices and studios on the fringe of Grant Avenue's Chinatown and Columbus Avenue's Italian-Mexican-French-Basque quarter. The studio I wanted was down a long corridor, beyond that all-American bend where the Italian newspaper *Corriere del Popolo* sits catty-corner from the office of Tinn Hugh Yu, Ph.D. and Notary Public.

Things were relatively quiet today in Dr. Verner's studio, Slavko Catenich was still hammering away at his block of marble, apparently on the theory that the natural form inherent in the stone would emerge if you hit it often enough. Irma Borigian was running over vocal exercises and occasionally checking herself by striking a note on the piano, which seemed to bring her more reassurance than it did me. Those two, plus a couple of lads industriously fencing whom I'd never seen before, were the only members of Verner's Varieties on hand today.

Irma ah-ah-ahed and pinked, the fencers clicked, Slavko crashed, and in the midst of the decibels the Old Man stood at his five-foot lectern-desk, resolutely proceeding in quill-pen longhand with the resounding periods of *The Anatomy of Nonscience*, that never-concluded compendium of curiosities which was half Robert Burton and half Charles Fort.

He gave me the medium look. Not the hasty 'Just this sentence' or the forbidding 'Dear boy, this page *must* be finished'; but the in-between 'One more deathless paragraph' look. I grabbed a chair and tried to watch Irma's singing and listen to Slavko's sculpting.

There's no describing Dr. Verner. You can say his age is somewhere between seventy and a hundred. You can say he has a mane of hair like an albino lion and a little goatee like a Kentucky Colonel who never heard of cigars. ('When a man's hair is white,' I've heard him say, 'tobacco and a beard are mutually exclusive vices.') You can mention the towering figure and the un-English mobility of the white old hands and the disconcerting twinkle of those impossibly blue eyes. And you'd still have about as satisfactory a description as when you say the Taj Mahal is a domed, square, white marble building.

The twinkle was in the eyes and the mobility was in the hands when he finally came to tower over me. They were both gone by the time I'd finished the story of the Stambaugh apartment and the empty man. He stood for a moment frowning, the eyes lusterless, the hands limp at his sides. Then, still standing like that, he relaxed the frown and opened his mouth in a resonant bellow.

'You sticks!' he roared. (Irma stopped and looked hurt.) 'You stones!' (The fencers stopped and looked expectant.) 'You worse than worst of those that lawless and uncertain thoughts' (Slavko stopped and looked resigned.) 'Imagine howling,' Dr. Verner concluded in a columbine coo, having shifted in mid-quotation from one Shakespearean play to another so deftly that I was still looking for the joint.

Verner's Varieties waited for the next number on the bill. In majestic silence Dr. Verner stalked to his record player. Stambaugh's had been a fancy enough custom-made job, but nothing like this.

If you think things are confusing now, with records revolving at 78, 45, and 33⅓ rpm, you should see the records of the early part of the century. There were cylinders, of course (Verner had a separate machine for them). Disc records, instead of our present standard sizes, ranged anywhere from 7 to 14 inches in diameter, with curious fractional stops in between. Even the center holes came in assorted sizes. Many discs were lateral-cut, like modern ones; but quite a few were hill-and-dale, with the needle riding up and down instead of sideways – which actually gave better reproduction but somehow never became overwhelmingly popular. The grooving varied too, so that even if two companies both used hill-and-dale cutting you couldn't play the records of one on a machine for the other. And just to make things trickier, some records started from the inside instead of the outer edge. It was Free Enterprise gone hogwild.

Dr. Verner had explained all this while demonstrating to me how his player could cope with any disc record ever manufactured. And I had heard him play everything on it from smuggled dubbings of Crosby blow-ups to a recording by the original *Florodora* Sextet – which was, he was always careful to point out, a double sextet or, as he preferred, a duodecimet.

'You are,' he announced ponderously, 'about to hear the greatest dramatic soprano of this century. Rosa Ponselle and Elisabeth Rethberg were passable. There was something to be said for Lillian Nordica and Lena Geyer. But listen!' And he slid the needle into the first groove.

'Dr. Verner –' I started to ask for footnotes; I should have known better.

'Dear boy . . . !' he murmured protestingly, over the preliminary surface noise of the aged pressing, and gave me one of those twinkles of bluest blue which implied that surely only a moron could fail to follow the logic of the procedure.

I sat back and listened. Irma listened too, but the eyes of the others were soon longingly intent on foils and chisel. I listened casually at first, then began to sit forward.

I have heard, in person or on records, of all the venerable names which Dr. Verner mentioned – to say nothing of Tebaldi, Russ, Ritter-Ciampi, Souez and both Lehmanns. And reluctantly I began to admit that he was right; this was *the* dramatic soprano. The music was strange to me – a setting of the Latin text of the *Our Father*, surely eighteenth century and at a guess by Pergolesi; it had his irrelevant but reverent tunefulness in approaching a sacred text. Its grave sustained lilt was admirable for showing off a voice; and the voice, unwavering in its prolonged tones, incredible in its breath control, deserved all the showing off it could get. During one long phrase of runs, as taxing as anything in Mozart or Handel, I noticed Irma. She was holding her breath in sympathy with the singer, and the singer won. Irma let out an admiring gasp before the soprano had, still on one breath, achieved the phrase.

And then, for reasons more operatic than liturgical, the music quickened. The sustained legato phrases gave way to cascades of light bright coloratura. Notes sparkled and dazzled and brightness fell from the air. It was impeccable, inapproachable – infinitely discouraging to a singer and almost shocking to the ordinary listener.

The record ended. Dr. Verner beamed around the room as if he'd done all that himself. Irma crossed to the piano, struck one key to verify the incredible note in alt upon which the singer had ended, picked up her music, and wordlessly left the room.

Slavko had seized his chisel and the fences were picking up their foils as I approached our host. 'But Dr. Verner,' I led with my chin. 'The Stambaugh case . . .'

'Dear boy,' he sighed as he reached the old one-two, 'you mean you don't realize that you have just heard the solution?'

'You will have a drop of Drambuie, of course?' Dr. Verner queried formally as we settled down in his more nearly quiet inner room.

'Of course,' I said. Then as his mouth opened, '"For without Drambuie,"' I quoted, '"the world might never have known the simple solution to the problem of the mislaid labyrinth."'

He spilled a drop. 'I was about to mention that very fact. How . . . ? Or perhaps I have alluded to it before in this connection?'

'You have,' I said.

'Forgive me.' He twinkled disarmingly. 'I grow old, dear boy.'

Ritualistically we took our first sip of Drambuie. Then:

'I well remember,' Dr. Verner began, 'that it was in the autumn of the year 1901 . . .

. . . that the horror began. I was by then well established in my Kensington practice, which seemed to flourish as it never had under the ministrations of its previous possessor, and in a more than comfortable financial position. I was able at last to look about me, to contemplate and to investigate the manifold pleasures which a metropolis at once so cosmopolitan and so insular as London proffers to the unattached young man. San Francisco of the same period might perhaps compare in quality; indeed my own experiences here a few years later in the singular affair of the cable cabal were not unrewarding. But a man of your generation knows nothing of those pleasures now ten lustra faded. The humours of the Music Halls, the delights of a hot bird and a cold bottle shared with a dancer from Daly's, the simpler and less expensive delights of punting on the Thames (shared, I may add, with a simpler and less expensive companion) – these claimed what portion of my time I could salvage from my practice.

But above all I was devoted to music; and to be devoted to music meant, in the London of 1901, to be devoted to – but I have always carefully refrained from the employment of veritable and verifiable names in these narratives. Let me once more be discreet, and call her simply by that affectionate agnomen by which my cousin, to his sorrow, knew her: *Carina*.

I need not describe Carina as a musician; you have just heard her sing Pergolesi, you know how she combined nobility and grandeur with a technical agility which these degenerate days associate only with a certain type of light soprano. But I must seek to describe her as a woman, if woman she may be called.

When first I heard the tittle-tattle of London, I paid it small heed. To the man in the street (or even in the stalls) *actress* is still a euphemism for a harsher and shorter term, though my experience of actresses, extending as it has over three continents and more than my allotted three score and ten of years, tends to lead me, if anywhere, to an opposite conclusion.

The individual who stands out from the herd is the natural target of calumny. I shall never forget the disgraceful episode of the purloined litter, in which the veterinarian Dr. Stookes accused me of – but let us reserve that anomaly for another occasion. To return to Carina: I heard the gossip; I attributed it to as simple a source as I have indicated. But then the evidence began to attain proportions which the most latitudinarian could hardly disregard.

First young Ronny Furbish-Darnley blew out his brains. He had gambling debts, to be sure, and his family chose to lay the stress upon them; but his relations with

Carina had been common knowledge. Then Major Mac-Ivers hanged himself with his own cravat (the MacIvers tartan, of course). I need hardly add that a MacIvers had no gambling debts. Even that episode might have been hushed up had not a peer of so exalted a name that I dare not even paraphrase it perished in the flames of his ancestral castle. Even in the charred state in which they were recovered, the bodies of his wife and seven children clearly evinced the clumsy haste with which he had slit their throats.

It was as though . . . how shall I put it? . . . as though Carina were in some way a 'carrier' of what we had then not yet learned to call The Death Wish. Men who knew her too well hungered no longer for life.

The press began to concern itself, as best it might with due regard for the laws of libel, with this situation. Leading articles hinted at possible governmental intervention to preserve the flower of England from this insidious foreigner. Little else was discussed in Hyde Park save the elimination of Carina.

Even the memorable mass suicides at Oxford had provided no sensation comparable to this. Carina's very existence seemed as much in danger as though Jack the Ripper had been found and turned over to the English people. We are firm believers in our English justice; but when that justice is powerless to act, the Englishman aroused is a phenomenon to fear.

If I may be pardoned a Hibernian lapse, the only thing that saved Carina's life was . . . her death.

It was a natural death – perhaps the first natural action of her life. She collapsed on the stage of Covent Garden during a performance of Mozart's *Così fan tutte*, just after having delivered the greatest performance of that fantastic aria, *Come scoglio*, that a living ear has heard.

There were investigations of the death. Even my cousin, with an understandable personal interest, took a hand. (He was the only one of Carina's close admirers to survive her infection; I have often wondered whether this fact resulted from an incredible strength or an equally incredible inadequacy within him.) But there was no possible doubt that the death was a natural one.

It was after the death that the Carina legend began to grow. It was then that young men about town who had seen the great Carina but once began to mention the unmentionable reasons which had caused them to refrain from seeing her again. It was then that her dresser, a crone whose rationality was as uncertain as her still persistent terror was unquestionable, began to speak of unspeakable practices, to hint at black magic as among milady's avocations, to suggest that her utterance (which you have heard) of flights of notes, incredibly rapid yet distinct, owed its facility to her control and even suspension of the mortal limitations of time.

And then began . . . the horror. Perhaps you thought that by *the horror* I meant the sequence of Carina-carried suicides? No; even that lay still, if near the frontier, within the uttermost bounds of human comprehension.

The horror passed those bounds.

I need not ask you to envision it. You have beheld it. You have seen clothing sucked dry of its fleshly tenant, you have seen the haberdashers' habitation sink flabbily in upon itself, no longer sustained by tissue of bone and blood and nerves.

All London saw it that year. And London could not believe.

First it was that eminent musicologist, Sir Frederick Paynter, FRCM. Then there were two young aristocrats, then, oddly, a poor Jewish peddler in the East End.

I shall spare you the full and terrible details, alluding only in passing to the Bishop of Cloisterham. I had read the press accounts. I had filed the cuttings for their very impossibility (for even then I had had adumbrations of the concept which you now know as *The Anatomy of Non-science*).

But the horror did not impinge upon me closely until it struck one of my own patients, a retired naval officer by the name of Clutsam. His family had sent for me at once, at the same time that they had dispatched a messenger to fetch my cousin.

As you know, my cousin enjoyed a certain fame as a private detective. He had been consulted in more than one previous instance of the horror; but I had read little of him in the press save a reiteration of his hope that the solution lay in his familiar dictum: 'Discard the impossible; and whatever remains, no matter how improbable, must be true.'

I had already formulated my now celebrated counter-dictum: 'Discard the impossible; then if *nothing* remains, some part of the "impossible" must be possible.' It was thus that our dicta and ourselves faced each other across the worn and outdated naval uniform on the floor, complete from the gold braid on its shoulders to the wooden peg below the empty left trouser leg, cut off at the knee.

'I imagine, Horace,' my cousin remarked, puffing at his blackened clay, 'that you conceive this to be your sort of affair.'

'It is obviously not yours,' I stated. 'There is something in these vanishings beyond –'

'– beyond the humdrum imagination of a professional detective? Horace, you are a man of singular accomplishments.'

I smiled. My cousin, as my great-uncle Etienne used to remark of General Masséna, was famous for the accuracy of his information.

'I will confess,' he added, 'since my Boswell is not within earshot, that you have occasionally hit upon what satisfies you, at least, as the truth in some few cases in which I have failed. Do *you* see any element linking Captain Clutsam, Sir Frederick Paynter, Moishe Lipkowitz and the Bishop of Cloisterham?'

'I do not.' It was always discreet to give my cousin the answer which he expected.

'And I *do*! And yet I am no nearer a solution than . . .' His pipe clenched in his teeth, he flung himself about the room, as though pure physical action would somehow ameliorate the lamentable state of his nerves. Finally he paused before me, looked sharply into my eyes and said, 'Very well. I shall tell you. What is nonsense in the patterns shaped by the reasoning mind may well serve you as foundation for some new structure of unreason.

'I have traced every fact in the lives of these men. I know what they habitually ate for breakfast, how they spent their Sundays, and which of them preferred snuff to tobacco. There is only *one* factor which they all possess in common: Each of them recently purchased a record of the Pergolesi *Pater Noster* sung by . . . *Carina*. And those records have vanished as thoroughly as the naked men themselves.'

I bestowed upon him an amicable smile. Family affection must temper the ungentlemanly emotion of triumph. Still smiling, I left him with the uniform and the leg while I betook myself to the nearest gramophone merchant.

The solution was by then obvious to me. I had observed that Captain Clutsam's gramophone was of the sapphire-needled type designed to play those recordings known as hill-and-dale, the vertical recordings produced by Pathé and other companies as distinguished from the lateral recordings of Columbia and Gramophone-and-Typewriter. And I had recalled that many hill-and-dale recordings were at that time designed (as I believe some wireless transcriptions are now) for an inside start, that is, so that the needle began near the label and traveled outward to the rim of the disc. An unthinking listener might easily begin to play an inside-start record in the more normal manner. The result, in almost all instances, would be gibberish; but in this particular case . . .

I purchased the Carina record with no difficulty. I hastened to my Kensington home, where the room over the dispensary contained a gramophone convertible to either lateral or vertical recordings. I placed the record on the turntable. It was, to be sure, labeled INSIDE START; but how easily one might overlook such a notice! I overlooked it deliberately. I started the turntable and lowered the needle . . .

The cadenzas of coloratura are strange things in reverse. As I heard it, the record naturally began with the startling final note which so disheartened Miss Borigian, then went on to those dazzling *fioriture* which so strengthen the dresser's charge of time-magic. But in reverse, these seemed like the music of some undiscovered planet, coherent to themselves, following a logic unknown to us and shaping a beauty which only our ignorance prevents us from worshipping.

And there were words to these flourishes; for almost unique among sopranos, Carina possessed a diction of diabolical clarity. And the words were at first simply *Nema . . . nema . . . nema . . .*

It was while the voice was brilliantly repeating this

reversed *Amen* that I became *literally* beside myself.

I was standing, naked and chill in the London evening, beside a meticulously composed agglomeration of clothing which parodied the body of Dr. Horace Verner.

This fragment of clarity lasted only an instant. Then the voice reached the significant words: *olan a son arebil des men . . .*

This was the Lord's Prayer which she was singing. It is common knowledge that there is in all necromancy no charm more potent than that prayer (and most especially in Latin) *said backwards.* As the last act of her magical malefactions, Carina had left behind her this record, knowing that one of its purchasers would occasionally, by inadvertence, play it backwards, and that then the spell would take effect. It had taken effect now.

I was in space . . . a space of infinite darkness and moist warmth. The music had departed elsewhere. I was alone in this space and the space itself was alive and by its very moist warm dark life this space was draining from me all that which was my own life. And then there was with me a voice in that space, a voice that cried ever *Eem vull! Eem vull!* and for all the moaning gasping urgency in that voice I knew it for the voice of Carina.

I was a young man then. The Bishop's end must have been swift and merciful. But even I, young and strong, knew that this space desired the final sapping of my life, that my life should be drawn from my body even as my body had been drawn from its shell. So I prayed.

I was not a man given to prayer in those days. But I knew words which the Church has taught us are pleasing to God, and I prayed with all the fervour of my being for deliverance from this Nightmare Life-in-Death.

And I stood again naked beside my clothes. I looked at the turntable of the gramophone. The disc was not there.

Still naked, I walked to the dispensary and mixed myself a sedative before I dared trust my fingers to button my garments. Then I dressed and went out again to the shop of the gramophone merchant. There I bought every copy in his stock of that devil's *Pater Noster* and smashed them all before his eyes.

Ill though I could afford it, even in my relative affluence, I spent the next few weeks in combing London for copies of that recording. One copy, and one only, I preserved, you heard it just now. I had hoped that no more existed . . .

'. . . but obviously,' Dr. Verner concluded, 'your Mr. Stambaugh managed to acquire one, God rest his soul . . . and body.'

I drained my second Drambuie and said, 'I'm a great admirer of your cousin.' Dr. Verner looked at me with polite blue inquiry. 'You find what satisfied *you* as the truth.'

'Occam's Razor, dear boy,' Dr. Verner murmured, associatively stroking his smooth cheeks. 'The solution accounts economically for every integral fact in the problem.'

'But look,' I said suddenly. 'It doesn't! For once I've got you cold. There's one "integral fact" completey omitted.'

'Which is . . . ?' Dr. Verner cooed.

'You can't have been the first man that thought of praying in that . . . that space. Certainly the Bishop must have.'

For a moment Dr. Horace Verner was silent. Then he fixed me with the Dear-boy-how-idiotic! twinkle. 'But only I,' he announced tranquilly, 'had realized that in that . . . space all sound, like the Our Father itself, was reversed. The voice cried ever *Eem vull!* and what is that phonetically but *Love me!* backwards? Only *my* prayer was effective, because only I had the foresight to pray *in reverse phonetics.*'

I phoned Abrahams to say I had an idea and could I do some checking in the Stambaugh apartment?

'Good,' he said. 'I have an idea too. Meet you there in a half-hour.'

There was no Abrahams in the corridor when I got there; but the police seal was broken and the door was ajar. I went on in and stopped dead.

For the first moment I thought it was still Stambaugh's clothes spread out there. But there was no mistaking Inspector Abrahams' neat gray plainclothes – with no Abrahams in them.

I think I said something about *the horror*. I draw pretty much of a blank between seeing that empty suit and looking up to the far doorway and seeing Inspector Abrahams.

He was wearing a dressing gown of Stambaugh's, which was far too short for him. I stared at his grotesque figure and at the android parody which dangled from his hand.

'Sorry, Lamb,' he grinned. 'Couldn't resist the theatrical effect. Go on. Take a good look at the empty man on the floor.'

I looked. The clothes were put together with the exactly real, body-fitting, sucked-out effect which we had already decided was impossible.

'You see,' Abrahams said, 'I remembered the vacuum cleaner. And the Downtown Merchants' parade.'

I was back at the studio early the next morning. There was nobody from Verner's Varieties there but Slavko, and it was so relatively quiet that Dr. Verner was just staring at

44

the manuscript of *The Anatomy* without adding a word.

'Look,' I said. 'In the first place, Stambaugh's record player isn't equipped for hill-and-dale records.'

'They *can* be played even on an ordinary machine,' Dr. Verner observed tranquilly. 'The effect is curious – faint and with an odd echoing overlap, which might even enhance the power of the cantrip.'

'And I looked in his card catalog,' I went on, 'and he didn't have a recording of the Pergolesi *Pater Noster* by anybody.'

Dr. Verner widened his overblue eyes. 'But of course the card would vanish with the record,' he protested. 'Magic makes allowances for modern developments.'

'Wait a minute!' I exclaimed suddenly. 'Hey, I'm brilliant! This is one Abrahams didn't think of. It's *me*, for once, that solves a case.'

'Yes, dear boy?' said Dr. Verner gently.

'Look. You *can't* play an inside-start record backwards. It wouldn't work. Visualize the spiraling grooves. If you put the needle in the outside last groove, it'd just stay there ticking – same like it would if you put it in the inside last groove of a normal record. To play it backwards, you'd have to have some kind of gearshift that'd make the turntable spin backwards.'

'But I have,' said Dr. Verner blandly. 'It enables one to make extraordinary interesting experiments in sound. Doubtless Mr. Stambaugh had too. It woud be simple enough to switch over by mistake; he was drinking . . . Tell me: the spinning turntable that you saw . . . was it revolving clockwise or counterclockwise?'

I thought back, and I was damned if I knew. Clockwise, I took for granted; but if I had to swear . . . Instead I asked, 'And I suppose Captain Clutsam and the Bishop of Cloisterham had alternate counterclockwise gearshifts?'

'Why, of course. Another reason why such a serious collector as Mr. Stambaugh would. You see, the discs of the Fonogrammia company, a small and obscure firm but one boasting a few superb artists under exclusive contract, were designed to be so played.'

I stared at those pellucid azure eyes. I had no notion whether counterclockwise Fonogrammia records were the coveted objective of every collector or a legend that had this moment come into being.

'And besides,' I insisted. 'Abrahams has demonstrated how it was really done. The vacuum cleaner tipped him off. Stambaugh had bought a man-sized, man-shaped balloon, a little brother of those monster figures they use in parades. He inflated it and dressed it in his clothes. Then he deflated it, leaving the clothes in perfect arrangement with nothing in them but a shrunken chunk of rubber, which he could withdraw by unbuttoning the shirt. Abrahams found the only firm in San Francisco that manufactures such balloons. A clerk identified Stambaugh as a purchaser. So Abrahams bought a duplicate and pulled the same gag on me.'

Dr. Verner frowned. 'And the vacuum cleaner?'

'You use a vacuum cleaner in reverse for pumping up large balloons. And you use it normally for deflating them; if you just let the air out *whoosh!* they're apt to break.'

'The clerk' (it came out *clark*, of course) 'identified Stambaugh positively?'

I shifted under the piercing blueness. 'Well, you know identifications from photographs . . .'

'Indeed I do.' He took a deliberately timed pause. 'And the record player? Why was its turntable still revolving?'

'Accident, I guess. Stambaugh must've bumped against the switch.'

'Which projected from the cabinet so that one might

well engage it by accident?'

I pictured the machine. I visualized the switch and the depth to which one would have to reach in. 'Well, no,' I granted. 'Not exactly . . .'

Dr. Verner smiled down at me tolerantly. 'And the motive for these elaborate maneuvers by Mr. Stambaugh?'

'Too many threatening male relatives on his tail. He deliberately staged this to look oh-so-mysterious so nobody'd spot the simple fact that he was just getting the hell out from under. Abrahams has an all-points alarm out; he'll be picked up any time within the next few days.'

Dr. Verner sighed. His hands flickered through the air in a gesture of infinitely resigned patience. He moved to his record cabinet, took out a disc, placed it on the turntable, and adjusted certain switches.

'Come, Slavko!' he announced loudly. 'Since Mr. Lamb prefers rubber balloons to truth, we are conferring a signal privilege upon him. We are retiring to the other room, leaving him here alone with the Carina record. His cocksure materialism will surely wish to verify the effect of playing it in reverse.'

Slavko stopped pounding and said, 'Huh?'

'Come, Slavko. But first say a polite good-bye to Mr. Lamb. You may not be seeing him again.' Dr. Verner paused in the doorway and surveyed me with what seemed like genuine concern. 'Dear boy,' he murmured, 'you won't forget that point about the reverse phonetics . . . ?'

He was gone and so (without more polite good-bye than a grunt) was Slavko. I was alone with Carina, with the opportunity to disprove Dr. Verner's fabulous narrative once and for all.

His story had made no pretense of explaining the presence of the vacuum cleaner.

And Inspector Abrahams' theory had not even

attempted to account for the still-revolving turntable.

I switched on the turntable of the Verner machine. Carefully I lowered the tone-arm, let the oddly rounded needle settle into the first groove from the outer rim.

I heard that stunning final note in alt. So flawless was the Carina diction that I could hear, even in that range, the syllable to which it was sung: *nem*, the begining of the reverse-Latin *Amen*.

Then I heard a distorted groan as the turntable abruptly slowed down from 78 to zero revolutions per minute. I looked at the switch; it was still on. I turned and saw Dr. Verner towering behind me, with a disconnected plug dangling from his hand.

'No,' he said softly – and there was a dignity and power in that softness that I had never heard in his most impressive bellows. 'No, Mr. Lamb. You have a wife and two sons. I have no right to trifle with their lives merely to gratify an old man's resentment of scepticism.'

Quietly he lifted the tone-arm, removed the record, restored it to its envelope, and refiled it. His deft, un-English hands were not at their steadiest.

'When Inspector Abrahams succeeds in tracing down Mr. Stambaugh,' he said firmly, 'you shall hear this record in reverse. And not before then.'

And it just so happens they haven't turned up Stambaugh yet.

The Adventure of the Paradol Chamber

JOHN DICKSON CARR

NARRATOR *(reading)*: 'I find recorded in my notebook that it was after dark on a hot evening in August 1887. All day Sherlock Holmes had been moody and distraught. That evening he took up his violin. Leaning back in his armchair, he would close his eyes and scrape carelessly at the fiddle, which was thrown across his knee. Sometimes the chords were sonorous and melancholy. *(In pitch blackness, a few unearthly chords from violin.)* Occasionally they were fantastic and cheerful. *(Chords hop.)* I might have rebelled had it not been that he usually terminated them by playing in quick succession a whole series of my favorite airs.'

(Violin plays a few bars of Mendelssohn's 'Spring Song,' then fades. Lights slowly come up. HOLMES *and* WATSON *are sitting on opposite sides of stage, facing audience; table at* HOLMES's *side.* HOLMES *has violin across knee, bow in right hand; lighted pipe in mouth; eyes fixed glassily ahead.* WATSON *wears expression of ecstasy, hand in air as though it has been keeping time to music; copy of* Daily Telegraph *in his lap.)*

WATSON: My dear Holmes, your virtuosity is unrivaled. Pray continue!

HOLMES *(grim; on edge)*: I am in no mood for it, Watson. *(He puts down violin and bow on table; gets up.)* My mind is

49

tortured, *obsessed!*

WATSON *(amused)*: Surely not – again! – by Professor Moriarty?

HOLMES: He is the Napoleon of crime, Watson! You will find his spider trace, I dare wager, in that very newspaper. What is the first item on which your eye falls?

WATSON *(scanning paper)*: By Jove, Holmes, this *is* curious!

HOLMES: Quick, Watson, the item!

WATSON *(reading)*: 'Lord Matchlock, the Foreign Minister, collapsed in a faint as he was walking up Constitution Hill after leaving Buckingham Palace.'

HOLMES: Ah!

WATSON: 'We are happy to report, however, that Lord Matchlock's condition is not serious.'

HOLMES: I wonder!

WATSON: 'Messrs. Lestrade, Gregson and Athelney Jones, all of Scotland Yard, pronounce it a heat stroke. Lord Matchlock, on a hot day, was wearing a heavy frock coat, bombazine waistcoat, wing collar and Ascot tie, long flannel underwear, woolen socks, and Hessian boots. He therefore –'

(Violent reaction from HOLMES: WATSON *starts.)* My dear Holmes! What can be wrong with you?

HOLMES: *There's villainy here!*

WATSON *(taken aback)*: You jest, my dear fellow!

HOLMES: He was wearing no trousers, Watson! Lord Matchlock was wearing no trousers!

WATSON *(pause, stunned)*: Holmes, this is marvelous!

HOLMES *(waving it away)*: Elementary! But not uninstructive. Scotland Yard, of course, observed nothing.

WATSON: But why should Lord Matchlock, the Foreign Minister, have been walking up Constitution Hill without his britches?

HOLMES (*somber*): There lies our problem. If only . . .
(*Sharp knocking is heard off.*)
WATSON: A client, Holmes!
HOLMES: Perhaps even the answer to our problem. Come in!
(*Enter* LADY IMOGENE FERRERS, *in a state of restrained terror. She carries a paper parcel. In violent agitation, she looks from* HOLMES *to* WATSON: *finally chooses* HOLMES.)
IMOGENE: *You* are Mr. Sherlock Holmes! Every fiber of my woman's instinct tells me so! (*She rushes to seize* HOLMES *by the shoulders.*) Help me, Mr Holmes!
HOLMES (*austerely*): Pray compose yourself, madam. I shall do my best. A chair, Watson! (*He leads her to* WATSON'*s chair, and goes to his own.*) A cup of hot coffee, too, might be not unwelcome. I perceive that you are shivering.
IMOGENE: Alas, sir, it is not the cold which makes me shiver!
HOLMES: Not the cold? What then?
IMOGENE: It is fear, Mr. Holmes. It is terror! I am Lady Imogene Ferrers. My father is Lord Matchlock, the Foreign Minister.
WATSON (*bursting out*): They have stolen your papa's britches!
IMOGENE: I think you must be wizards, both of you! For I came here, Mr. Holmes, to show you . . . there! (*Rising dramatically, she opens the paper parcel and holds up in majesty a pair of trousers.*)
WATSON (*amazed*): Merciful heaven! Britches!
HOLMES (*exalted*): It is for these dramatic moments that my soul lives! Tell me, Lady Imogene: are they your father's trousers?
IMOGENE: No, Mr. Holmes! No! I had not thought, until this moment, that dear Papa was trouserless.

51

HOLMES: Ha! Then how came the trousers into your possession?

IMOGENE: This morning, Mr. Holmes, they were thrown from an upper window at Buckingham Palace. I saw them fall.

WATSON: Holmes, some fiend is snatching the britches from half London!

HOLMES: Good, Watson! But not, I think, quite good enough. May I see the evidence? *(She hands over the trousers.* HOLMES *scrutinizes them through a magnifying glass. Then to* LADY IMOGENE) Buckingham Palace, I think you said?

IMOGENE: Yes, Mr. Holmes. My father had gone there for a conference with the new French Ambassador, M. de Paradol, and Her Majesty the Queen. *(Faltering)* It – it concerned, I think, a secret treaty between France and Great Britain. Can you picture my dread – nay, my terror! – when I saw the trousers take wing from Her Majesty's window?

HOLMES: These are deep waters, my lady. Were you followed here?

IMOGENE: I hope not, Mr. Holmes! All day I have been riding in four-wheelers! And yet . . . *(Off, heavy and elaborate knocking)*

HOLMES: Quick, Watson! Make haste and hide the evidence! (HOLMES *hands the trousers to* WATSON, *who thrusts them inside his frock coat.* WATSON *turns and moves towards door.)*

WATSON: Holmes, this is no ordinary client! This is . . .

HOLMES: Speak out, man!

WATSON: *(stepping back to one side like a court chamberlain):* His Excellency the French Ambassador!

(Enter M. DE MARQUIS DE PARADOL: *top hat, frock coat, imperial beard. He swoops forward, center, removing hat, and*

adopts posture of immense dignity.)

PARADOL (*drawn up*): Messieurs! (*To* IMOGENE, *different tone*) Mademoiselle!

IMOGENE (*crying out*): You have come here, sir, about the hideous enigma at Buckingham Palace?

PARADOL (*fierce dignity*): I 'ave come 'ere, mademoiselle, to get *my pants!*

HOLMES: Are we to understand that Your Excellency's trousers have disappeared too?

PARADOL: No, no, no! Not deesappear. At Buckingham Palace, in de presence of Her Majesty de Queen, I 'ave remove my pants and throw dem out of de window!

WATSON: No!

PARADOL: But yes! All of a sudden I see – in a mirror! – six men in de masks and de false whiskers, which are creeping up on me to attack me. I cry: *Vive la France!* and do my duty. No pants.

IMOGENE: You performed this in the presence of Her Majesty?

PARADOL: I regret! She pushes a great cry and faints – boum! – on a gold sofa. And to you, mademoiselle, I weesh also to apologize.

IMOGENE: You owe me no apology.

PARADOL: I regret! It is I who have pinch the pants of your papa! I conk him on de onion wit a blackjack – *violà!* – because I must 'ave pants to follow *you.*

WATSON: The diplomatic service is sadly changed. But why should these wretches wish to purloin your britches?

PARADOL: You 'ave 'eard, perhaps, of the Paradol-Matchlock Treaty between England and France?

IMOGENE: The secret treaty! Yes!

HOLMES (*to Paradol*): And the secret treaty, I think, is in Your Excellency's trousers?

PARADOL (*staggered*): Quel homme! Quel homme

53

magnifique!

(As he speaks, HOLMES *takes the trousers from under* WATSON's *coat.)*

HOLMES: A secret chamber – two thin plates of copper – hides the secret treaty. May I return these valuables to Your Excellency? *(Bowing)*

PARADOL *(receiving trousers)*: Monsieur! In de name of my government, in de name of all France, I . . . *(He breaks off, staring; and begins to examine the trousers feverishly.)*

IMOGENE: You are agitated, M. de Paradol. Is the copper chamber not there?

PARADOL: The copper chamber, yes! But de treaty . . . is gone!

IMOGENE: *Gone!*

WATSON: *Gone!*

HOLMES: Have no fear, my dear sir. The secret treaty is still in *this* room. It has merely been abstracted by a thief and a traitor!

WATSON: Not Professor Moriarty?

HOLMES: Not Professor Moriarty, no. But his chief lieutenant – and the second most dangerous man in London – stands – here! *(He whips the false mustache off* WATSON, *who stands snarling.)*

IMOGENE: But that's Dr. Watson!

HOLMES: No, Lady Imogene. The real Watson lies bound and gagged in some den of infamy. May I introduce you to Colonel Sebastian Moran.

WATSON *(shouting)*: Curse you, Holmes! May you die of a bullet from my air gun!

PARADOL: But how – why did you suspect de wretch?

HOLMES: A very simple matter, I assure you. When he recognized a *new* French Ambassador, whose appointment has not yet been announced, I knew him for the villain he is. I gave him an opportunity to steal the treaty *(reaches into* WATSON's *inside pocket and produces impressive-looking document)* and he has done so.

PARADOL *(exultantly)*: The Adventure of de Paradol Chamber!

WATSON *(snarling)*: No, curse you! The Adventure of the Copper Britches!

The Adventure of the Conk-Singleton Papers

JOHN DICKSON CARR

NARRATOR: Crime marches on! . . . A long, thin silhouette emerges against the gaslight. Here is an unpublished record: 'In turning over my notes of some twenty years I cannot find any startling event on New Year's Eve except that which is forever associated with the Conk-Singleton Papers. On New Year's Eve of 1887, it is perhaps unnecessary to state, Mr. Sherlock Holmes did not wear a paper hat and blow squeakers at the Hotel Metropole. Far into the night, while the wind howled round our sitting room in 221B Baker Street, Holmes sat bending over a microscope . . .'

(SHERLOCK HOLMES *at microscope*, WATSON *immersed in a copy of H. Rider Haggard's* King Solomon's Mines)

HOLMES (*after a moment looks up and stares glassily out at audience*): It is spinach, Watson. Unquestionably, it is spinach!

WATSON: Holmes, you amaze me! What new wizardry is this?

HOLMES (*rising*): It means a man's life, Watson. The gardener was lying when he said he found Riccoletti's body in the gooseberry bushes. (*He rubs his hands.*) I think, perhaps, a note to our friend Lestrade . . .

WATSON (*jumps up*): Holmes! Merciful Heaven. I had forgotten!

HOLMES: Forgotten what?

WATSON: A note for you was delivered by hand this morning. You must forgive me. I was attending the funeral of my last patient.

HOLMES (*impatiently*): The letter, Watson! The letter! (WATSON *takes note from his pocket, hands it to* HOLMES, *who examines postmark, holds letter up to light, then opens with care and reads.*) 'There will call upon you tonight, at three o'clock in the morning precisely, a gentleman who desires to consult you about a matter of the deepest moment. Be in your chamber at that hour, and do not take it amiss if the visitor wears a mask.'

WATSON: This is indeed a mystery. What can it mean?

HOLMES: These are deep waters, Watson. If Porlock had not warned me about the Scarborough emeralds . . . (*Thoughtfully*) Three o'clock . . . (*Clock strikes three. Bong! Bong! Bong! Immediately followed by three loud raps on door in same tempo*)

WATSON: And that, if I mistake not, is our client now. (*Enter visitor dressed in evening clothes but covered with medals – decorations, stars, ribbons, etc.*)

VISITOR: Mr. Sherlock Holmes?

HOLMES: I am Mr. Sherlock Holmes. This is my friend and colleague, Dr. Watson.

VISITOR: You will forgive me, Mr Holmes, if I do not reveal my identity. I also wear plain evening dress so as not to be conspicuous.

HOLMES (*coldly*): You would be better served, My Lord, if Your Lordship removed the mask.

VISITOR (*staggering back*): You know me, then?

HOLMES: Who could fail to know Lord Cosmo Conk-Singleton, third son of the Duke of Folkstone and private secretary to the Prime Minister?

WATSON: You mean . . . Mr. Gladstone!

VISITOR (*finger at side of nose*): Sssh!

HOLMES (*same*): Sssh!

WATSON (*same to audience*): Sssssh!

VISITOR: The matter upon which I have come to consult you, Mr Holmes, is no ordinary one.

HOLMES: It seldom is. Pray be seated.

VISITOR (*sits*): It will be not unknown to you, Mr. Holmes, that for some time there has been – shall we say – disagreement between Mr. Gladstone and Her Gracious Majesty, Queen Victoria. I have here a diplomatic communication in Her Majesty's own hand, sent to Mr. Gladstone on December 15, 1886. You are empowered to read it. (*Hands important-looking document to* HOLMES.)

WATSON: These are deep waters, Holmes.

HOLMES: Her Majesty, I perceive, was not amused.

VISITOR: She was indeed (*hesitates*) somewhat vexed. (*Then suddenly amazed*) But how could *you* possibly know –

HOLMES: Her Majesty has twice underlined the word 'bastard.' And she has placed three exclamation points following her instructions as to what Mr. Gladstone should do with the naval treaty involving a certain foreign power. Surely our inference is obvious.

WATSON: Excellent!

HOLMES: But very superficial. (*Reading again*) 'Even that German sausage, my late husband, could have done better.' Hmm! Yes! But how do these diplomatic matters concern me?

VISITOR: Mr. Holmes, the Prime Minister has been poisoned!

WATSON: What?

VISITOR: On December 24th Mr. Gladstone received – apparently as a Christmas present from Queen Victoria – a case of Scotch whisky.

HOLMES: I see. And did the case indeed contain whisky?

VISITOR: Whisky, yes. But each bottle was most unhappily charged with two ounces of prussic acid!

WATSON: Merciful heaven! The man is dead!

VISITOR: No, Dr. Watson, no! *Dei gratia*, he still lives! The strength of the whisky neutralized the poison.

HOLMES *(blandly)*: Come, come, this is most disappoi – most interesting. Have you any proof, My Lord, that the Prime Minister drank this particular whisky?

VISITOR *(producing document)*: Here is a letter of thanks, in Mr. Gladstone's own hand, written on Christmas Eve. Pray read it aloud.

HOLMES: Will you oblige, Watson?

WATSON *(very dignified, clears throat gravely, and reads)*: December 24th, 1886. Illustrious Madam: How extremely kind of you to send me this case of whisky for Christmas! I have never tasted such superb whisky in my life. The whisky you have sent me for Christmas is superb. I keep tasting it and how kind of you to sen me thish wondrous whichkey which I keep tasting for Xmas. It really is mosh kind of you to keep sending me this whisky in cases which I kep tashing for whichmas. Hic! Dock, dickory dock, and kissmus.

VISITOR: Can there be any doubt, Mr. Holmes?

HOLMES: None whatever. Then it is your belief, My Lord, that Queen Victoria is the poisoner?

VISITOR: No, Mr. Holmes! *(Horrified)* A thousand times, no! But think of the scandal! It bids fair to rend asunder the fabric of the Empire! You must come down to Sussex and investigate. Will you come?

HOLMES: No, My Lord. I will not.

WATSON *(amazed)*: Holmes, this is unworthy of you! Why won't you go?

HOLMES: Because this man is not Lord Cosmo Conk-Singleton! *(Sensation.* HOLMES *produces revolver.)* Let me present you, Watson, to none other than Professor Moriarty.

WATSON: Professor Moriarty!

HOLMES: Your double disguise as a younger man, my dear Professor, deceived me for perhaps ten seconds. The note from Mr. Gladstone seems quite genuine. But the letter from Her Majesty is a manifest forgery.

WATSON: Forgery, Holmes?

HOLMES: Her language, Waston! Her language!

WATSON: You mean –

HOLMES: Queen Victoria, Watson, would never have written in so slighting a fashion of her late husband, Prince Albert. They intended the letter to lure me to Sussex while the Scarborough emeralds were stolen from Yorkshire, not knowing (HOLMES *produces emeralds from his pocket*) that Lord Scarborough had already given them to me for safekeeping!

VISITOR *(in a grating voice)*: One day, Mr. Holmes, you will try my patience too far!

(Curtain)

The Adventures of the Snitch in Time

AUGUST DERLETH AND MACK REYNOLDS

On an autumn afternoon of a year that, for manifest reasons, must remain nameless, there came to the attention of my friend, Mr. Solar Pons, a matter which was surely either the most extraordinary adventure ever to befall a private enquiry agent in or before our time, or an equally extraordinary misadventure, the *raison d'être* of which remains obscure even now, though it might have been born in the circumstances of the moment, for it was one of those days on which London was literally swallowed in a yellow fog, and we had both been confined to our quarters for two days, with no more incident than the arrival of an occasional paper and the unfailing complaint of our long-suffering landlady about Pons's spare appetite.

Even our warm and comfortable quarters, for all that a fire burned at the hearth, had begun to pall on us. Pons had exhausted the microscope; he had abandoned his chemistry set; he had ceased his abominable pistol practise; and for once there was not a single item of correspondence transfixed to the center of the mantelpiece by his knife. He had hardly stopped his restless wandering among the disorderly order of our quarters, and seated himself in his velvet-lined chair, holding forth on the points of difference between Stradivarius and Amati

61

violins, when he rose once more with his empty pipe in his hands.

He was at the fireplace, about to take the shag from the toe of his slipper, tackled below the mantelpiece, when suddenly, he paused. He stood so for a moment, in utter silence, his hawklike face keen with interest, his body seeming actually to lean forward as if to catch the sound that smote upon his ears.

'If I am not mistaken, Parker,' he said with unaccustomed gravity, 'we are about to have a most unusual visitor.'

I had been standing at the window looking out, and had just turned. 'Nothing has disturbed this fog for the past half hour,' I protested.

'My dear Parker, you are looking in the wrong direction. The footsteps are approaching from out there, and a little above.'

So saying, he turned to face the door with alert expectation in his gray eyes.

I had for some time been conscious of a curious sound, almost as of water sliding at regular intervals against the roof. Apparently this was what Pons had mistaken for the sound of footsteps. Almost at the same moment of this realization, a most peculiar assault was made on the door to our quarters. I had not heard the outer door; in truth, I had heard no step upon the stair. But now a kind of brushing sound broke in upon us; it began at the top of the door, and did not become a recognizable knock until it had descended to midpanel.

Being nearest the door, I moved to open it.

'Pray be cautious, Parker,' said Pons. 'And spare me your alarm. Unless I am in egregrious error, our visitor is from another world.'

I gazed at him, mouth agape. I had heard and marveled at his extraordinary deductions before, but this came from his lips with such calm assurance that I could not doubt his sincerity even while I could not accept his words.

'Come, Parker, let us not keep him waiting.'

I threw open the door. There, confronting us, was a strong, healthy man, bronzed by the sun, clad in a fantastic attire of such brilliant hues as to dazzle the eye. His footgear – a strange combination of sandal and slipper – must have made the curious slapping sounds I had at first mistaken for the dripping of water, but which Pons had correctly identified as footsteps, however alien to our previous experience.

Our visitor looked briefly at me and said, 'Ah, the famous literary doctor, I presume?' and smiled, as if in jest.

My astonishment at this manner of address, accompanied as it was with an almost insolent amusement, left me momentarily speechless.

'Come in, come in, my dear fellow,' said Pons behind me. 'Pray overlook Dr. Parker's rudeness. I perceive you have come a long way; your fatigue is manifest. Sit here and relieve yourself of the problem which brings you to these quarters.'

Our visitor walked into the room, inclining his head to acknowledge Pons's invitation.

'I hope you will forgive my coming without an appointment,' he said, in a somewhat stilted voice, accompanied by florid and Victorian gestures. 'I fear I had no alternative. Let me introduce myself – I am Agent Tobias Athelney of the Terra Bureau of Investigation, Planet Terra, of the Solar System League.'

Pons' eyes twinkled merrily.

'My dear sir,' I could not help interrupting, 'levity is all very well, but this is neither the time nor the place for it. Just where are you from?'

Our visitor had taken the seat to which Pons had waved him. At my words, he stopped short, took a small, violet-covered notebook from an inner fold of his robelike costume, and thumbed through it until he found the place he sought.

'Pray forgive me,' he murmured. 'If we were still using your somewhat fantastic calendar system, it would be the year 2565 A.D.'

Pons, who had been scrutinizing him closely, now leaned back, closed his eyes, and touched his fingertips together. 'So you represent yourself as a governmental agent of almost 700 years in the future, Mr. Athelney?' he said. 'A traveler in time?'

Our visitor grimaced. 'Not exactly, Mr. Pons. To my knowledge, there is no such thing as time travel, nor can such travel ever be developed. No, the explanation for my presence here is more elementary. We have recently discovered that the universe is not, indeed, one, but of an infinite number. We have learned that everything that possibly *could* happen *has* happened, *will* happen, and *is* happening. Given an infinite number of alternative universes, you can easily understand how this would be so. To illustrate, Mr. Pons, there are alternate space-time continua in which Napoleon won at Waterloo; there are still others in which Waterloo was a draw; and there are yet others in which the battle was never fought at all – indeed, in which Napoleon was never born!'

I flashed a glance of mounting indignation at Pons, but my companion's face had taken on that dream expression I had learned to associate with intense concentration. Surely it could not be that he was being deceived by this patent mountebank!

'Infinite other universes than this,' murmured Pons, 'containing other persons identical to myself, and to Dr.

Parker, here, who carry on their little lives in much the same manner as we do?'

Our visitor nodded. 'That is correct, Mr. Pons. There are still other space-time continua, in which there are no such persons as yourselves, never have been, and never will be.' He coughed almost apologetically. 'In fact, in this multitude of alternate universes, Mr. Pons, there are some in which you two are fictitious characters, the product of a popular writer's art!'

'Amazing!' exclaimed Pons, adding, with a glance at my dour face, 'and yet, not entirely incredible, would you say, Parker?'

'Preposterous!' I answered. 'How can you sit there and calmly accept this – this nonsense?'

'Dear me,' murmured Pons, 'let us not be too hasty, Parker.'

'I am sorry to have upset Dr. Parker,' said our visitor soberly, 'but it is from just such a universe that I have traveled to this. Approximately 700 years before my birth, in my space-time continuum, a series of stories dealing with Mr. Solar Pons and Dr. Lyndon Parker were written, presumably by Dr. Parker, and became the all-time favorites of the literature of deduction.'

'Let us assume all this is so,' said Pons. 'For what purpose have you come?'

'To consult you, Mr. Pons.'

'I fancied as much,' said my companion with a serene smile. 'Though it would seem a long chance indeed to consult a fictitious character.'

'*Touché!*' answered our client. 'But a fictitious character in *my* universe and 700 years before my time. But in *this* universe you are very real indeed, and the greatest detective of all time!' He sighed. 'You cannot imagine, Mr. Pons, the difficulty of first finding a continuum in which you were *real*, and then, on top of that, one in which you were contemporary.'

Pons sat for a moment in silence, stroking the lobe of his left ear. 'I submit,' he said at last, 'since patterns of crime and its detection continually evolve, you are haunting the wrong continuum, Mr. Athelney.'

'I think not, Mr. Pons, if you will hear me out.'

'Proceed.'

'One of our most scientifically advanced bands of criminals is named the Club Cerise, after the favorite color of its leader, Moriarty. They –'

'Moriarty!' exclaimed Pons.

'Yes, Mr. Pons. Moriarty. The name is familiar to you prehaps?'

'Indeed it is!' Pons was silent for a moment, his eyes closed. 'You know, Parker,' he said after a moment, 'I have always felt that one death at the Reichenbach was as false as the other.' He sat up in his chair, his gaze now intent on our visitor. 'Pray continue, Mr. Athelney! Where my illustrious predecessor could achieve but a stalemate, it seems that you offer me the opportunity for complete victory!'

'Well, then, Mr. Pons,' our visitor resumed, 'you will not be surprised to learn that Moriarty and his band have managed to escape retribution for some time, and it is in regard to their apprehension that I seek your assistance. The criminal method they have developed is based on the same discovery that allows my presence here. Moriarty and his Club Cerise have been making a practice of invading space-time continua in less developed eras than our own, and, utilizing our most advanced weapons and devices to assure their escape, have been despoiling these universes of their art treasures. Not long ago, for example, they went into a Twentieth Century universe and obtained a Da Vinci, a half dozen Rembrandts, and a priceless collection of Kellys.'

Pons' eyes widened a trifle. 'You are suggesting that the Irish have developed an artist of the stature of Da Vinci, Mr. Athelney?'

'Indeed, yes. A fellow named Kelly created a work of genius called *Pogo*, which appeared in hundreds of newspapers of his day. These were *Pogo* originals, including some of the very rare pre-strip drawings. With his fabulously valuable treasure, Moriarty and his band managed to return to our own space-time continuum. Obviously, we cannot punish them in our universe, since they have committed no crime there. Under ordinary circumstances, it would be possible to extradite them to the universe they plundered – but there are almost insurmountable complications.'

Pons smiled, still giving no evidence of being in the slightest troubled by the mad, ingenious account of our prospective client. 'I daresay "insurmountable" is the word to describe the problems attendant upon extradition of a group of criminals from a country which doesn't exist in the universe where the crime was committed. I submit that a Twentieth Century nation might be compelled to adopt extraordinary protective measures – if indeed these would be adequate – to deal with criminals seven centuries in advance of the police of that period.' But now he shook his head, with a gentle smile on his thin lips. 'But we must stop considering these ramifactions, or we shall soon find ourselves involved in the higher mathematics of space and time.'

'The importance of the problem is greater than might at first be evident,' continued our visitor. 'Given continued success on the part of Moriarty and his Club Cerise, there can be no doubt that other such bands will soon emulate them, and that eventually endless numbers of space-time pirates will give up other pursuits to devote themselves to the plundering of weaker continua with this type of snitch.'

'Snitch?' I repeated.

'Elementary, Parker,' murmured Pons impatiently. 'Obviously idiomatic for "theft".'

'The ultimate possibility will not have escaped you, Mr. Pons,' continued our client. 'Sooner or later, the increasing numbers of criminals would arrive in *this* space-time continuum and in *this* era.'

I could not be sure, but it seemed to me that at this suggestion a little color drained from Pons' cheeks. And, if a shudder went through that lean frame, he was again under perfect control within moments. He sat then in silence, his eyes closed, his head sunk to his chest with his fingertips gently tapping together.

Our visitor waited in silence.

Pons opened his eyes presently and asked, 'Pray tell me, Mr. Athelney – do you have income taxes in your world?'

Athelney groaned. 'My dear fellow, last year my taxes were unbelievably high. Bureaucracy runs rampant!'

'Capital, capital!' exclaimed Pons. 'Why not prosecute Moriarty for tax evasion?'

Our visitor shook his head dolefully. 'The criminals of our days are advanced, Mr. Pons. They *pay* their taxes.'

Once again Pons retreated into silence, taking time now to light up his calabash. But this time his silence was broken more quickly.

'I have some modest knowledge of British law, Mr. Athelney,' said Pons, 'but your laws may well differ. What type of social system prevails in your world and time?'

'It is usually referred to as Industrial Feudalism.'

'I am not familiar with the term, though I can guess its meaning. Pray elucidate.'

'In the same manner that Feudalism evolved from Chattel Slavery, and Capitalism from Feudalism, so Industrial Feudalism has evolved in our continuum from Capitalism. Ownership has contracted until a few princes of finance, a few industrial barons and lords of transportation completely control the government and practically all the wealth.'

'Do national boundaries still prevail.'

'Terra is united, but we have loose ties with the other planets of the Solar System.'

'Then doubtless you have tariff laws between the various planets.'

'Very rigid ones. Last month we apprehended some Martians smuggling duppl berries; they were given ten years.'

'I submit you have an obvious trap in which to take Moriarty and his Club Cerise, Mr. Athelney. They must pay import taxes on those art objects. Failure to do so puts them afoul of the law.'

Our client smiled broadly. 'I do believe, Mr. Pons, you have arrived at a solution to our problem.'

He came to his feet.

'I suggest your government pass such tariff restrictions as to make imports from other space-time continua prohibitive. Such a move, in view of the fact that the criminals of your time are so advanced as to pay their taxes, would in all likelihood prevent further depredations.'

Though our client was manifestly anxious to be off, he hesitated. 'I wish there were some way in which I could remunerate you, Mr. Pons. Unfortunately, we do not use the same system of exchange. All I can do is offer profound thanks in the name of my continuum.'

'There is surely remuneration enough implied in the promise that we will not be victimized here in our time and world by such as Moriarty,' said Pons. 'But, stay, Mr. Athelney – I perceive you are still troubled by some aspect of the matter.'

Our client turned from the threshold, to which he had walked. He smiled wryly. 'I fear, Mr. Pons, that this is but the initial step in our problem. Moriarty, when he learned I was to travel hither in search of the greatest detective of all time, took certain protective measures. He sent one of his own men to another space-time continuum to acquire the services of a most astute lawyer named Randolph Mason.'

'Pray be reassured,' responded Pons instantly. 'I can refer you to a rising young contemporary, who promises to be even greater, and is gaining a challenging reputation in the legal circles of his world. By an odd coincidence, not uncommon to fiction, he bears a similar family name. His given name, I believe, is Perry. My correspondents on the west coast of the United States have given me flattering reports of his talents. You will find him in Los Angeles, I believe. I commend him to your government. Good afternoon, Mr. Athelney.'

As soon as the door had closed behind our visitor, I turned to Pons. 'Should not one of us slip after him and notify the authorities of his escape?'

Pons walked to the window and looked out into the fog. Without turning, he asked. 'You thought him a lunatic, Parker?'

'Surely that was obvious!'

'Was it, indeed!' Pons shook his head. 'I sometimes think, Parker, that that happy faculty for observation which seems to come so readily to me encounters obstacles of demoralizing stubbornness in you.'

'Pons!' I exclaimed hotly, 'you cannot have been taken in by this – this mountebank and his hoax?'

'Was he both lunatic and mountebank, then?' asked

Pons, smiling in that superior manner which always galled me.

'What does it matter which he was? He was certainly one or the other.'

'If a mountebank, what was his motive? If a lunatic, how did he find his way here in this fog, which is surely as thick as any we have ever had? I fear some of us have an unhappy tendency to dismiss the incredible solely because it is incredible to *us*. Tell me, Parker, have you ever contemplated setting forth in the form of fiction these little adventures of mine in the field of ratiocination?'

I hesitated to answer.

'Come, come, Parker, it is evident that you have.'

'I confess, I have thought of it.'

'You have not yet done so?'

'No, Pons, I swear it.'

'You have spoken of your plans to no one?'

'No.'

'Our late client spoke of you as a literary doctor. "The famous literary doctor" were his exact words, I believe. If he were but a lunatic or mountebank, as you will have him, how came he then to know of your innermost hope and ambition in this regard? Or is there some secret communion between lunatics and mountebanks? I perceive, thanks to our Mr. Athelney, that, without regard to my wishes, you are destined to become a literary man at the expense of my modest powers.'

'Pons, I swear I have never put pen to paper,' I cried.

'But you will, Parker, you will. May I remind you of my distinguished predecessor's credo, that when all probable explanations have been shown false, the improbable, no matter how incredible, alone remains? This, I fancy, is one little adventure you will not be able to chronicle without a furtive blush or two.'

In this, at least, my companion was correct.

The Adventure of the Dog in the Knight

Robert L. Fish

In glancing through my notebook delineating the many odd adventures which I was fortunate enough to share with my good friend Mr. Schlock Homes in the early months of the year '68, I find it difficult to select any single one as being truly indicative of his profound ability to apply his personal type of analytical *Verwirrung*, which, taken at its ebb, so often led him on to success.

There was, of course, the case of the nefarious card-cheat whom Homes so cleverly unmasked in a young men's health organization in the small village of Downtree in Harts – a case I find noted in my journal as *The Adventure of the Y-Bridge*. It is also true that during this period he was of particular assistance to the British Association of Morticians in a case whose details are buried somewhere in my files but which resulted, as I recall, in a National Day being set aside in their honor. While it remains a relatively unimportant matter, the tale still is recorded in my case-book as *The Boxing-Day Affair*.

However, in general those early months were fruitless, and it was not until the second quarter of the year that a case of truly significant merit drew his attention. In my entry for the period of 15/16 April, '68, I find the case listed as *The Adventure of the Dog in the Knight*.

It had been an unpleasantly damp day, with a drizzle

compounded by a miasmic fog that kept us sequestered in our quarters at 221-B Bagel Street; but evening brought relief in the form of a brisk breeze that quickly cleared the heavy air. 'We have been in too long,' Homes said, eyeing me queryingly. 'I suggest a walk to clear away the cobwebs.'

I was more than willing. Homes had spent his day at the laboratory bench, and between the stench of his chemicals and the acrid odor of his Pakistanis, the room fairly reeked. For several hours we roamed the byways of our beloved London, our coat collars high against the evening chill, stopping on occasion at various pubs to ascertain the hour. It was eight o'clock exactly when we arrived back at our rooms, and it was to find a hansom cab standing at the kerb before our door.

'Ah,' Homes observed, eyeing the conveyance sharply. 'A visitor from Scotland Yard, I see!'

I was sufficiently conversant with Homes's methods by this time to readily follow his reasoning; for the crest of the Yard – three feet rampant on a field of corn – was emblazoned both on the door and the rear panel of the coach, clearly visible under the gas-lamp before our house, and the jehu sitting patiently on the box was both uniformed and helmeted. With some curiosity as to the reason for this late visit, I followed Homes up the stairs and into our quarters.

A familiar figure rose from a chair beside the unlit fireplace and turned to face us. It was none other than Inspector Balustrade, an old antagonist whose overbearing manner and pompous posturing had long grated upon both Homes's nerves and my own. Before we could even discard our outer garments he was speaking in his usual truculent manner.

'My advice to you, Homes,' he said a bit threateningly,

'is to keep your hands off the Caudal Hall affair. We have an open-and-shut case, and any interference on your part can only cause the luckless miscreant unwarranted and futile hope. In fact,' he continued, looking fiercer than ever, 'I believe I shall go so far as to *demand* that you leave the matter alone!'

Schlock Homes was quite the wrong person to address in such words and tones. 'Inspector Balustrade, do not rail at me!' said he sharply. He doffed his coat and deerstalker, tossing them carelessly upon a chair, striding forward to face the Inspector. 'I take those cases that interest me, and it is my decision alone that determines which they shall be.'

'Ah!' Inspector Balustrade's tiny eyes lit up in self-congratulation. 'I knew it – I knew it! I merely wished to confirm my suspicions. So they've been at you, eh? And, by the look of things, bought you! Lock, stock, and barrel!'

'Eh?'

'The lawyer chappies, that is,' Balustrade continued. 'Well, you're wasting your time listening to them, Mr. Homes. There is no doubt of the culprit's guilt.' He smiled, a sneering smile. 'Or do you honestly believe you have sufficient evidence to contradict that statement?'

'What I think is my affair,' Homes said, eyeing the man distastefully. 'You have delivered your message, Inspector, so I see little to be gained by your continued presence here.'

'As you wish, Mr. Homes,' Balustrade said with mock severity. He picked up his ulster, clamped his bowler firmly to his head, and moved to the door. 'But Dr. Watney here can bear witness that I did my best to save you from making a fool of yourself!' And with a chuckle he disappeared down the stairs.

'Homes!' I said chidingly, 'A new case, and you did not inform me?'

'Believe me,' he said sincerely, 'I know nothing of this. I have no idea what the Inspector was talking of.' He contemplated me with a frown. 'Is it possible, Watney, that we have inadvertently missed some items of importance in the morning journal?'

'It would be most unusual, Homes,' I began, and then suddenly remembered something. 'I do recall, now, Mrs. Essex borrowing the front page of the *Globe* to wrap some boots for the cobbler's boy to pick up, but if I'm not mistaken, the lad failed to appear. Let me get it and see if it can cast any light on this mystery.'

I hurried into the scullery, returning in moments with the missing sheet. I spread it open upon the table, pressing out the creases, while Homes came to stand at my side.

'Ah!' said he, pointing triumphantly. 'There it is!' He bent closer, reading the words half-aloud. '*Tragic Affair at Caudal Manor.* But where is the –? Ah, here it is, just beneath the headline.' He smiled in satisfaction at his discovery, and read on:

'"Late last evening an unfortunate incident occurred at Caudal Manor, the country estate in Kent of Sir Francis Gibbon, the 62-year-old Knight of the Realm. A small dinner party was in progress, at which the only guests were Sir Francis' sister-in-law, Mrs. Gabriel Gibbon, who is married to Sir Francis' younger and only brother and who has often acted at hostess for her bachelor brother-in-law; and a Mr. John Wain, a young visitor from the Colony of California, a chemist by trade, who is staying with Mr. and Mrs. Gabriel Gibbon as a house-guest. Mr. Gabriel, two years younger than his illustrious brother, was absent, having claimed he preferred to see his romance at the theatre rather than at home, and for this reason was spending his evening at the latest Boucicault offering in Piccadilly. Readers of the society news may recall that the beauteous Mrs. Gibbon, like Mr. Wain, was also a colonial from California at the time of her marriage two years ago.

'"The main course, chosen out of deference to their foreign guest, was frankfurters – called 'hot-dogs' abroad – which was also a favourite dish of his Lordship, Sir Francis. This course had already been consumed, washed down with ale, and a bitter-almond tart had also been eaten, when Sir Francis suddenly gasped, turned pale, and seemed to be having difficulty in his breathing and his speech; then, in a high nasal voice, he apologized to his guests for suffering from a stomach indisposition and stumbled out of the room. As quickly as the other two could finish their dessert, coffee, and brandy, and avail themselves of the fingerbowls, they hurried into the drawing-room to offer succor; but Sir Francis was sprawled on the rug in a comatose state and died before medical assistance could be summoned.

'"Mrs. Gabriel Gibbon was extremely distraught, and exclaimed, 'I didn't think my brother-in-law looked well for some time, and I often warned him that bolting down hot-dogs was bad for his heart condition, so I really cannot claim to be surprised by this sudden cardiac seizure, although I am, of course, quite heart-broken.' Her physician was called and offered her a sedative, but Mrs. Gibbon bravely insisted upon completing her duties as hostess, even demonstrating sufficient control to supervise the maids in the clearing and thorough washing and drying of the dishes, as well as the incineration of all the left-overs.

'"Students of Debrett will recall that the Gibbon family seat, Caudal Hall, was entailed for a period of ten generations by King George III, at the time the land, titles, and rights were bestowed on the first Gibbon to be knighted. The entailing of an estate, as we are sure our readers know, means that during this period the property must be passed on and cannot be sold or otherwise disposed of. With the death of Sir Francis, this condition has now ceased to be in effect, and Mr. Gabriel is now free to dispose of the estate as he chooses, or pass it on to his heirs in legal manner. Under the conditions of the original knighthood conferred on the first Gibbon, the title also continued for this period of ten generations, so Mr. Gabriel will only be entitled to be called Sir by his servants and those of his friends who dislike informality.'''

Homes paused a moment to remove a boot that blocked our vision of the balance of the article, and then leaned over further, staring in utter amazement at the portion of the column that had been revealed. In a startled tone of voice, he continued:

'''STOP PRESS: The police officials have just announced an arrest in the Caudal Hall affair, claiming that Sir Francis was the victim of none other than his guest, Mr. Wain, age 26, the American colonial. They point out that a chemist would have the necessary knowledge to administer a fatal potion in Sir Francis' food, and that despite the knight's known heart condition as testified to by his sister-in-law, they believe there is more to the matter than meets the eyes, and that the heart condition was at most only a contributory factor.

'''They note that Mr. Wain is left-handed and sat on Sir Francis' right, permitting his operative hand to constantly hover over his Lordship's food. They believe he took advantage of the fortuitous circumstance of a bitter-almond tart being served to pour oil of nutmeg, a highly toxic abortifacient, either onto the tart itself, or more likely onto the 'hot-dog' itself, in a dosage sufficient to cause Sir Francis his severe abdominal pain, and eventually his death. The police base their conclusion on the faint odor of nutmeg they discerned upon the lips of the deceased, although they admit it was difficult to detect because of the almost overpowering odor of the bitter-almond tart.

'"Whether Mr. Wain intended the dose to be fatal, the police say, is unimportant; he is nonetheless guilty of his victim's demise and shall pay the full penalty for his crime. They claim to have evidence that Mr. Wain is a revolutionary, propounding the theory that the American colonies are now independent, a viewpoint certain to have aroused the righteous wrath of so fine a patriot as Sir Francis Gibbon. Bad feelings could only have resulted, and it is the theory of the police that the dinner party developed into an argument which culminated in the tragic death of Sir Francis. Mrs. Gibbon's failure to remember any such quarrel is attributed to absent-mindedness, added to her concern over the success of the meal, which undoubtedly caused her to be inattentive. (Artist's sketches on Page 3)."'

'Fools!' Homes exclaimed in disgust, replacing the boot and rewrapping the package. 'Balustrade is an idiot!' He flung himself into a chair, looking up at me broodingly. 'We must help this poor fellow Wat, Wainey – I mean Wain, Watney!

'But, Womes – I mean Homes,' I said remonstratingly, 'it appears to me that they have a strong case against the young man. As a medical practitioner I admit that stomach pain is often found to be related to heart seizure, but still, one cannot rule out the possibility of other agencies.'

'Nonsense!' said Homes half-angrily. 'I can understand a young man's reason for harming a complete stranger, and I can even understand a chemist carrying about a vial of oil of nutmeg on the offhand chance he might meet someone to whom he wished to give stomach indisposition. But what I cannot lead myself to believe is that a university graduate would be so ill-informed as to honestly believe the American colonies are independent!' He shook his head. 'No, no, Watney, it is here that the police case falls down!'

He tented his fingers, staring fiercely and unseeingly over them through half-lidded eyes, his long legs sprawled before him. Minutes passed while I quietly sat down, remaining silent, respecting his concentration; then, of a sudden, our reveries were interrupted by the sound of footsteps running lightly up the stairs, and a moment later the door burst open to reveal a lovely young girl in her mid-twenties. She might have been truly beautiful had it not been for the tears in her eyes and the tortured expression on her face. Scarcely pausing for breath, she hurried across the room and knelt at Homes's side, grasping his two hands in hers.

'Oh, Mr. Homes,' she cried beseechingly, 'only you can save John Wain! In the first place, the scandal would be ruinous were a house-guest of mine to be found guilty of a crime; and besides, it would play havoc with the entire scheme!'

'You are Mrs. Gabriel Gibbon?'

'Yes, I will pay –' She paused, thunderstruck. 'But how could you have possibly known my identity?'

Homes waved the question aside with his accustomed modesty, preferring to return to the problem at hand. 'Pray be seated,' said he, and waited until she was ensconced across from him. 'I have read the account in the journal and I am also convinced that the police have made a grave error. Tell me,' he continued, quite as if he were not changing the subject, 'would I be correct in assuming that the cook at Caudal Manor is a fairly youngish woman? And unmarried, I should judge?'

'Indeed she is, but how you knew this I cannot imagine?'

'And did she recently have a quarrel with her fiancé?'

The young lady could only nod her head in stunned fashion.

'And one final question,' Homes went on, eyeing her steadily. 'By any chance did Mr. Wain complain at the table because his ale was not iced, as he was accustomed to drinking it?'

'He did, but –' The girl stopped speaking, coming to her feet and staring down at Homes almost in fear. 'Mr. Homes, your ability is more than uncanny – it borders on the supernatural!' Her eyes were wide. 'How could you possibly have known –?'

'There is nothing mystical in it,' Homes assured her gravely. 'In any event, you may return home with an untroubled mind. I assure you that Mr. Wain will join you – a free man – before many hours.'

'I cannot thank you enough, Mr. Homes! Everything I have heard and read about you is the truth!' Her lovely eyes welled with tears of gratitude as she left the room.

'Really, Homes,' I said shortly. 'I fail to understand any of this. What is this business of the unmarried cook and the warm ale?'

'Later, Watney!' Homes said, and picked up his greatcoat and deerstalker. 'At the moment I must go out and verify a few facts, and then see to it that poor Mr. Wain is freed. These colonials suffer sufficiently from a feeling of inferiority; incarceration can only serve to aggravate it.'

It was well past midnight before I heard Homes's key in

the door below, but I had remained awake, a warmed kippered toddy prepared against my friend's return, my curiosity also waiting to be assuaged. He clumped up the stairs wearily, doffed his coat and hat, and fell into a chair, accepting the toddy with a nod. Then, after quaffing a goodly portion, he put the glass aside, leaned forward, and burst into loud laughter.

'It would have done you good, Watney, to see Balustrade's stare when he was forced to unlock Wain's cell and usher the young man to the street,' he said with a grin. 'I swear for a moment there I thought the Inspector was going to physically engage me in fisticuffs!' He chuckled at the memory and finished his kippered toddy, visibly relaxing. 'And thank you, by the way, for your thoughtfulness in preparing this toddy for me. It was delicious.'

'You can demonstrate your gratitude in far better manner,' I said, possibly a trifle tartly, for it was well past my usual bedtime, 'by explaining this entire, complex, incomprehensible case to me, for none of it makes the slightest sense!'

'No?' he asked incredulously. 'I am rather surprised. I should have thought the medical evidence would have pointed you in the right direction. However,' he continued, seeing the look on my face and, as ever, properly interpreting it, 'let us begin at the beginning.' He lit a Pakistani.

'First, as you well know, Watney, I respect you quite highly as a medical man, but I have also made a study in depth of toxicology. You may recall my monograph on the Buster Ketones and the Hal-loids which had such a profound effect on early Hollywood comedies – but I digress. To me the evidence presented by the article in the morning journal was quite conclusive.'

His fine eyes studied my face, as if testing me. 'Tell me,

Watney, what precise toxicity results in the symptoms so accurately described by the writer in the journal?' He listed them on his fingers as he continued, 'One: stomach disorder. Two: dimness of vision – for you will remember that Sir Francis stumbled as he left the room, and yet, after living in Caudal Manor for all his sixty-two years, one must assume he could normally have made his way about blindfolded. Three: difficulty in speaking and breathing. And four: a nasal quality to his voice.'

Homes looked at me inquiringly. 'Well?'

'Botulism!' I said instantly, now wide-awake.

'Exactly! True, the symptoms are similar for hydro-cyanic poisoning, but with the knight consuming the frankfurter, botulism was clearly indicated. My questions to young Mrs. Gibbon regarding the ale and the cook merely confirmed it.'

'I beg your pardon, Homes?' I asked, completely lost once again.

'Let us take the ale first,' said he, his kindly glance forgiving my obtuseness. 'Certainly Mrs. Gabriel Gibbon, herself a colonial, would be aware that icing of ale is almost compulsory in the colonies, and would therefore be expected by her compatriot. The failure to do so on the part of a dedicated hostess, therefore, could only have been caused by one thing –'

'The absent-mindedness which the reporter mentioned?' I asked, eager to be of help.

'No, Watney! *The lack of ice!* Now, in a household the size of Caudal Manor, who has the responsibility for seeing that the supply of ice is adequate? Naturally, the cook. But an elderly cook with years of experience would never forget a matter as important as ice, particularly with a foreign guest expected. Therefore, the conclusion is inevitable that the cook was not elderly, but rather, on the contrary, young. Still, even young cooks who manage to secure employment in an establishment as noted as Caudal Manor are not chosen unless they are well-qualified; therefore, some problem must have been preying on the young cook's mind to make her forget the ice. Now, Watney, what problem could bother a young lady to this extent? Only one concerning a male friend; hence my conclusion that she had had a quarrel with her fiancé.' He spread his hands.

'But, Homes,' I asked, bewildered, 'what made you think of ice in the first place? Or rather, the lack of it? Merely the floe of ideas?'

'The botulism, of course, Watney! Lack of proper refrigeration is one of the greatest causes for the rapid growth of the fatal bacteria, and both Mrs. Gibbon and her friend Mr. Wain may count themselves fortunate that the organism attacked only the one frankfurter, or they might well have both joined Sir Francis in death!'

For several moments I could only gaze at my friend Mr. Schlock Homes with the greatest admiration for his brilliant analysis and masterful deductions.

'Homes!' I cried. 'You have done it again! Had it not been for your brilliant analysis and masterful deductions, an innocent colonial might have gone to the gallows for a crime due, in its entirety, to a hot-dog in the knight!' Then I paused as another thought struck me. 'But one thing, Homes,' I added, puzzled. 'What of the oil of nutmeg that the police made such a matter of?'

Homes chuckled. 'Oh, that? That was the easiest part of the entire problem, Watney. I stopped at the mortuary while I was out tonight and had a look at Sir Francis' cadaver. As I had anticipated, he had taken up a new after-shave lotion with a nutmet bouquet, and as soon as I can determine its name, I believe I shall purchase it as well.'

Due to the late hour when we finally retired that night, it was well past noon when I arose and made my way to the breakfast table. Homes had not arrived as yet, but I had no more than seated myself and reached for my first spoonful of chutneyed curry when he came into the room.

He greeted me genially and seated himself, drawing his napkin into his lap. In deference to his habits, I put aside my spoon for the moment and picked up the morning journal, preparing to leaf through it in search of some tidbit of news that might serve Homes as a means to ward off ennui. But I did not need to turn the page. There, staring at me from scare headlines, was an announcement that made me catch my breath.

'Homes!' I cried, shocked to the core. 'A terrible thing has happened!'

He paused in the act of buttering his kipper. 'Oh?'

'Yes,' I said sadly. 'Tragedy seems to have struck poor Mrs. Gibbon again!'

He eyed me sharply, his fish-knife poised. 'You mean –?'

'Yes,' I said unhappily, reading further into the article. 'It seems that early this morning, while taking his constitutional along Edgeware Road, Gabriel Gibbon was struck and killed by a car recklessly driving on the wrong side of the road. The police surmise the culprit may have been from the Continent, where drivers are known to use the wrong side of the road; but this is mere theory and unsupported by fact, particularly since the driver escaped and the description by the few witnesses is considered useless.'

'That poor girl!' said Homes, and sighed deeply.

'Yes,' I agreed. 'True, she will now inherit the Gibbon fortune, but this can scarcely compensate her for the loss of her loved one!'

'True,' Homes said thoughtfully. Then a possible solution came to him and he nodded. 'We can only hope that her friend Mr. Wain will stand by her in her hour of need, even as she stood by him in his! In fact, I believe he is enough in my debt for me to suggest it. A telegram form if you please, Watney –'

The Adventure of the Three Madmen

PHILIP JOSÉ FARMER

I

It is with a light heart that I take up my pen to write these the last words in which I shall ever record the singuler genius which distinguished my friend Sherlock Holmes. I realise that I once wrote something to that effect, though at that time my heart was as heavy as it could possibly be. This time I am certain that Holmes has retired for the last time. At least, he has sworn that he will no more go a-detectiving. The adventure of the three madmen has made him financially secure, and he foresees no more grave perils menacing our country now that our great enemy has been laid low. Moreover, he has sworn that never again will he set foot on any soil but that of his native land. Nor will he ever again get near an aircraft. The mere sight or sound of one freezes his blood.

The peculiar narrative which occupies these pages began on the second day of February, 1916. At this time I was, despite my advanced age, serving on the staff of a military hospital in London. Zeppelins had made bombing raids over England for two nights previously, mainly in the Midlands. Though these were comparatively ineffective, seventy people had been killed, one hundred and thirteen injured, and a monetary damage of fifty-three

86

thousand eight hundred and thirty-two pounds had been inflicted. These raids were the latest in a series starting the nineteenth of January. There was no panic, of course, but even stout British hearts were experiencing some uneasiness. There were rumours, no doubt originated by German agents, that the Kaiser intended to send across the channel a fleet of a thousand airships. I was discussing this rumour with my young friend, Doctor Fell, over a brandy in my quarters when a knock sounded on the door. I opened it to admit a messenger. He handed me a telegram which I wasted no time in reading.

'Great Scott!' I cried.

'What is it, my.dear fellow?' Fell said, heaving himself from the chair. Even then, on war rations, he was putting on overly much weight.

'A summons to the F.O.,' I said. 'From Holmes. And I am on special leave.'

'Sherlock?' said Fell.'

'No, Mycroft,' I replied. Minutes later, having packed my few belongings, I was being driven in a limousine toward the Foreign Office. An hour later, I entered the small austere room in which the massive Mycroft Holmes sat like a great spider spinning the web that ran throughout the British Empire and many alien lands. There were two others present, both of whom I knew. One was young Merrivale, a baronet's son, the brilliant aide to the head of the British Military Intelligence Department and soon to assume the chieftainship. He was also a qualified physician and had been one of my students when I was lecturing at Bart's. Mycroft claimed that Merrivale was capable of rivalling Holmes himself in the art of detection and would not be far behind Mycroft himself. Holmes' reply to this 'needling' was that only practise revealed true promise.

I wondered what Merrivale was doing away from the

War Office but had no opportunity to voice my question. The sight of the second person there startled me at the same time it delighted me. It had been over a year since I had seen that tall, gaunt figure with the greying hair and the unforgettable hawklike profile.

'My dear Holmes,' I said. 'I had thought that after the Von Bork affair . . .'

'The east wind has become appallingly cold, Watson,' he said. 'Duty recognises no age limits, and so I am called from my bees to serve our nation once more.'

Looking even more grim, he added, 'The Von Bork business is not over. I fear that we underestimated the fellow because we so easily captured him. He is not always taken with such facility. Our government erred grievously in permitting him to return to Germany with Von Herling. He should have faced a firing squad. A motor-car crash in Germany after his return almost did for us what we had failed to do, according to reports that have recently reached me. But, except for a permanent injury to his left eye, he has recovered.

'Mycroft tells me that Von Bork has done us and is doing us inestimable damage. Our intelligence tells us that he is operating in Cairo, Egypt. But just where in Cairo and what disguise he has assumed is not known.'

'The man is indeed dangerous,' Mycroft said, reaching with a hand as ponderous as a grizzly's paw for his snuff-box. 'It is no exaggeration to say that he is the most dangerous man in the world, as far as the Allies are concerned, anyway.'

'Greater than Moriarty was?' Holmes said, his eyes lighting up.

'Much greater,' replied Mycroft. He breathed in the snuff, sneezed, and wiped his jacket with a large red handkerchief. His watery grey eyes had lost their inward-turning look and burned as if they were searchlights probing the murkiness around a distant target.

'Von Bork has stolen the formula of a Hungarian refugee scientist employed by our government in Cairo. The scientist recently reported to his superiors the results of certain experiments he had been making on a certain type of bacillus peculiar to the land of the Pharaohs. He had discovered that this bacillus could be modified by chemical means to eat only sauerkraut. When a single bacillus was placed upon sauerkraut, it multiplied at a fantastic rate. It would become within sixty minutes a colony which would consume a pound of sauerkraut to its last molecule.

'You see the implications. The bacillus is what the scientists call a mutated type. After treatment with a certain chemical both its form and function are changed. Should we drop vials containing this mutation in Germany, or our agents directly introduce the germs, the entire nation would shortly become sauerkrautless. Both their food supply and their morale would be devastated.

'But Von Bork somehow got wind of this, stole the formula, destroyed the records and the chemicals with fire, and murdered the only man who knew how to mutate the bacillus.

'However, his foul deed was no sooner committed than detected. A tight cordon was thrown around Cairo, and we have reason to believe that Von Bork is hiding in the native quarter somewhere. We can't keep that net tight for long, my dear Sherlock, and that is why you must be gotten there quickly to track him down. England expects much from you, brother, and much, I am sure, will be given.'

I turned to Holmes, who looked as shaken as I felt. 'Surely, my dear fellow, we are not going to Cairo?'

'Surely, indeed, Watson,' he replied. 'Who else could

sniff out the Teutonic fox, who else could trap him? We are not so old that we cannot settle Von Bork's hash once and for all.'

Holmes, I observed, was still in the habit of using Americanisms, I suppose because he had thrown himself so thoroughly into the role of an Irish-American while tracking down Von Bork in that adventure which I have entitled 'His Last Bow.'

'Unless,' he said, 'you really feel that the old warhorse should not leave his comfortable pasture?'

'I am as good a man as I was a year and a half ago,' I protested. 'Have you ever known me to call it quits?'

He chuckled and patted my shoulder, a gesture so rare that my heart warmed.

'Good old Watson.'

Mycroft called for cigars, and while we were lighting up, he said, 'You two will leave tonight from a Royal Naval Air Service strip outside London. You will be flown by two stages to Cairo, by two different pilots, I should say. The fliers have been carefully selected because their cargo will be precious. The Huns may already know your destination. If they do, they will make desperate efforts to intercept you, but our fliers are the pick of the lot. They are fighter pilots, but they will be flying bombers. The first pilot, the man who'll take you under his wing tonight, is a young fellow. You may know of him, at least you knew his great-uncle.'

He paused and said, 'You remember, of course, the late Duke of Greyminster?'

'I will never forget the size of the fee I collected from him,' Holmes said, and he chuckled.

'Your pilot, Leftenant John Drummond, is the adopted son of the present Lord Greyminster,' Mycroft continued.

'But wait!' I said. 'Haven't I heard some rather strange

things about Lord Greyminster? Doesn't he live in Africa?'

'Oh, yes, in darkest Africa,' Mycroft said. 'In a tree house, I believe.'

'Lord Greyminster lives in a tree house?' I said.

'Ah, yes,' Mycroft said. 'Greyminster is living in a tree house with an ape.'

'Lord Greyminster is living with an ape?' I said. 'A female ape, I trust.'

'Oh, yes,' Mycroft said. 'There's nothing queer about Lord Greyminster, you know.'

'I have heard,' Merrivale said, 'that there is another feral man, that is, a human being raised by animals from infancy, in Africa at this time. I refer to the Indian baronet, Sir Mowgli of the Seeonee. He, as I understand it, was raised by wolves, not apes.'

'What is he doing in Africa?' Holmes said. 'India is his native land, and its central area his domain.'

'You haven't read the recent accounts of him in the *Times*?'

'No. I read only accounts of crimes and the agony column.'

I do not know why Holmes lied about this. It had long been evident to me and the readers of my accounts of his adventures that he reads almost everything in many London and some foreign journals.

'He is in central Africa with an American film company which is making a movie based on his life. He is playing himself as a boy of eighteen, though he is forty-three years old or thereabouts. His leading lady is the British actress, Countess Mary Anne Liza Murdstone-Malcon, better known under her stage name of Liza Borden.'

'Making a movie? During wartime?' I said. 'Isn't the baronet a major in the Army?'

'There are neither British nor German forces in that area,' Merrivale said. 'Major Sir Mowgli is on leave to make this film, which I understand contains much anti-German propaganda.'

Mycroft slammed his palm against the top of the table, startling all of us and making me wonder what had caused this unheard-of violence from the usually phlegmatic Mycroft.

'Enough of this time-wasting chitchat!' he said. 'The Empire is crumbling around our ears and we're talking as if we're in a pub and all's well with the world!'

He was right, of course, and all of us, including Holmes, I'm sure, felt abashed. But that conversation was not as irrelevant as we thought at the time.

An hour later, after receiving verbal instruction from Mycroft and Merrivale, we left in the limousine for the secret airstrip outside London.

II

Our chauffeur drove off the highway onto a narrow dirt road which wound through a dense woods of oaks. After a half-mile, during which we passed many signs warning trespassers that this was military property, we were halted by a barbed wire gate across the road. Armed R.N.A.S. guards checked our documents and then waved us on. Ten minutes later, we emerged from the woods onto a very large meadow. At its northern end was a tall hill, the lower part of which gaped as if it had a mouth which was open with surprise. The surprise was that the opening was not to a cavern but to a hangar which had been hollowed out of the living rock of the hill. As we got out of the car men pushed from the hangar a huge aeroplane, the wings of which were folded against the fuselage.

After that, events proceeded swiftly – too swiftly for me, I admit, and perhaps a trifle too swiftly for Holmes. After all, we had been born about a half century before the first areoplane had flown. We were not sure that the motor-car, a recent invention from our viewpoint, was altogether a beneficial device. And here we were being conducted by a commodore toward the monstrously large aircraft. Within a few minutes, according to him, we would be within its fuselage and leaving the good earth behind and beneath us.

Even as we walked toward it, its biplanes were unfolded and locked into place. By the time we reached it, its propellors had been spun by mechanics and the two motors had caught fire. Thunder rolled from its rotaries, and flames spat from its exhausts.

Whatever Holmes' true feelings, and his skin was rather grey, he could not suppress his driving curiosity, his need to know all that was relevant. However, he had to shout at the commodore to be heard above the roar of the warming-up rotors.

'The Admiralty ordered it to be outfitted for your use,' the commodore said. His expression told us that he thought that we must be very special people indeed if this areoplane was equipped just for us.

'It's the prototype model of the Handley Page 0/100,' he shouted. 'The first of the "bloody paralyser of an aeroplane" the Admiralty ordered for the bombing of Germany. It has two two-hundred-fifty-horsepower Rolls-Royce Eagle II motors, as you see. It has an enclosed crew cabin. The engine nacelles and the front part of the fuselage were armour-plated, but the armour has been removed to give the craft more speed.'

'What?' Holmes yelled. 'Removed?'

'Yes,' the commodore said. 'It shouldn't make any

difference to you. You'll be in the cabin, and it was never armour-plated.'

Holmes and I exchanged glances. The commodore continued, 'Extra petrol tanks have been installed to give the craft extended range. These will be just forward of the cabin . . .'

'And if we crash?' Holmes said.

'Poof!' the commodore said, smiling. 'No pain, my dear sir. If the smash doesn't kill you, the flaming petrol sears the lungs and causes instantaneous death. The only difficulty is in identifying the corpse. Charred, you know.'

We climbed up a short flight of wooden mobile steps and stepped into the cabin. The commodore closed the door, thus somewhat muting the roar. He pointed out the bunks that had been installed for our convenience and the W.C. This contained a small washbowl with a gravity-feed water tank and several thundermugs bolted to the deck.

'The prototype can carry a four-man crew,' the commodore said. 'There is, as you have observed, a cockpit for the nose gunner, with the pilot in a cockpit directly behind him. There is a cockpit near the rear for another machine gunner, and there is a trap-door through which a machine gun may be pointed to cover the rear area under the plane. You are standing on the trap-door.'

Holmes and I moved away, though not, I trust, with unseemly haste.

'We estimate that with its present load the craft can fly at approximately eight-five miles per hour. Under ideal conditions, of course. We have decided to eliminate the normal armament of machine guns in order to lighten the load. In fact, to this end, all of the crew except the pilot and co-pilot are eliminated. The pilot, I believe, is bringing his personal arms: a dagger, several pistols, a carbine, and his specially mounted Spandau machine gun, a trophy, by the way, taken from a Fokker E-1 which Captain Wentworth downed when he dropped an ash-tray on the pilot's head. Wentworth has also brought in several cases of hand grenades and a case of Scotch whisky.'

The door, or port, or whatever they call a door in the Royal Naval Air Service, opened, and a young man of medium height but with very broad shoulders and a narrow waist, entered. He wore the uniform of the R.N.A.S. He was a handsome young man with eyes as steely grey and as magnetic as Holmes'. There was also something strange about them. If I had known *how* strange, I would have stepped off that plane at that very second. Holmes would have preceded me.

He shook hands with us and spoke a few words. I was astonished to hear a flat midwestern American accent. When Wentworth had disappeared on some errand toward the stern, Holmes asked the commodore, 'Why wasn't a British pilot assigned to us? No doubt this Yank volunteer is quite capable, but really . . .'

'There is only one pilot who can match Wentworth's aerial genius. He is an American in the service of the Tsar. The Russians know him as Kentov, though that is not his real name. They refer to him with the honorific of *Chorniy Oryol*, the French call him *l'Aigle Noir* and the Germans are offering a hundred thousand marks for *Der Schwarz Adler*, dead or alive. The English translation is *The Black Eagle*.'

'Is he a Negro?' I said.

'No, the adjective refers to his sinister reputation,' replied the commodore. 'Kentov will take you on from Marseilles. Your mission is so important that we borrowed him from the Russians. Wentworth is being used only for the comparatively short haul since he is scheduled to carry out another mission soon. If you should crash, and survive, he would be able to guide you through enemy territory better than anyone we know of, excluding Kentov. Wentworth is an unparalleled master of disguise . . .'

'Really?' Holmes said, drawing himself up and frostily regarding the officer.

Aware that he had made a gaffe, the commodore changed the subject. He showed us how to don the bulky parachutes, which were to be kept stored under a bunk.

'What happened to young Drummond?' I asked him. 'Lord Greyminster's adopted son? Wasn't he supposed to be our pilot?'

'Oh, he's in hospital,' he said, smiling. 'Nothing serious. Several broken ribs and clavicle, a liver that may be ruptured, a concussion and possible fracture of the skull. The landing gear of his craft collapsed as he was making a deadstick landing, and he slid into a brick wall. He sends his regards.'

Captain Wentworth suddenly reappeared. Muttering to himself, he looked under our blankets and sheets and then under the bunks. Holmes said, 'What is it, captain?'

Wentworth straightened up and looked at us with those strange grey eyes. 'Thought I heard bats,' he said. 'Wings fluttering. Giant bats. But no sign of them.'

He left the cabin then, heading down a narrow tunnel which had been specially installed so that the pilot could get into the cockpit without having to go outside the craft. His co-pilot, a Lieutenant Nelson, had been warming the motors. The commodore left a minute later after wishing us luck. He looked as if he thought we'd need it.

Presently, Wentworth phoned in to us and told us to lie down in the bunks or grab hold of something solid. We were getting ready to take off. We got into the bunks, and I stared at the ceiling while the plane slowly taxied to the starting point, the motors were 'revved' up, and then it began to bump along the meadow. Within a short time its tail had lifted and we were suddenly aloft. Neither Holmes nor I could endure just lying there any more. We had to get up and look through the window in the door. The sight of the earth dropping away in the dusk, of houses, cows, and wagons, and brooks and then the Thames itself dwindling caused us to be both uneasy and exhilarated.

Holmes was still grey, but I am certain that it was not fear of altitude that affected him. It was being completely dependent upon someone else, being *not* in control of the situation. On the ground Holmes was his own master. Here his life and limb were in the hands of two strangers, one of whom had already impressed us as being very strange. It also become obvious only too soon that Holmes, no matter how steely his nerves and how calm his digestion on earth, was subject to airsickness.

The plane flew on and on, crossing the channel in the dark, crossing the westerly and then the south-western part of France. We landed on a strip lighted with flames. Holmes wanted to get out and stretch his legs but Wentworth forbade that.

'Who knows what's prowling around here, waiting to identify you and then to crouch and leap, destroying utterly?' he said.

After he had gone back to the cockpit, I said, 'Holmes, don't you think he puts the possibility of spies in somewhat strange language? And didn't you smell Scotch on his breath? Should a pilot drink while flying?'

'Frankly,' Holmes said, 'I'm too sick to care,' and he lay down outside the door to the W.C.

Midnight came with the great plane boring through the dark moonless atmosphere. Lieutenant Nelson crawled into his bunk with the cheery comment that we would be landing at a drome outside Marseilles by dawn. Holmes groaned. I bade the fellow, who seemed quite a decent sort, good-night. Presently I fell asleep, but I awoke some time later with a start. As an old veteran of Holmes' campaigns, however, I knew better than to reveal my awakened state. While I rolled over to one side as if I were doing it in my sleep, I watched through narrowed eyes.

A sound, or a vibration, or perhaps it was an old veteran's sixth sense, had awakened me. Across the aisle, illumined by the single bulb overhead, stood Lieutenant Nelson. His handsome youthful face bore an expression which the circumstances certainly did not seem to call for. He looked so malignant that my heart began thumping and perspiration poured out from me despite the cold outside the blankets. In his hand was a revolver, and when he lifted it my heart almost stopped. But he did not turn toward us. Instead he started toward the front end, toward the narrow tunnel leading to the pilot's cockpit.

Since his back was to me, I leaned over the edge of the bunk and reached down to get hold of Holmes. I had no need to warn him. Whatever his physical condition, he was still the same alert fox – an old fox, it is true, but still a fox. His head reached up and touched mine, and within a few seconds he was out of the bunk and on his feet. In his one hand he held his trusty Webley, which he raised to point at Nelson's back, crying out to halt at the same time.

I do not know if he heard Holmes above the roar of the motors. If he did, he did not have time to consider it. There was a report, almost inaudible in the din, and Nelson fell back and slid a few feet along the floor backward. Blood gushed from his shattered forehead.

The dim light fell on the face of Captain Wentworth, whose eyes seemed to blaze, though I am certain that was an optical illusion. The face was momentarily twisted, and then it smoothed out, and he stepped out into the light. I got down from the bunk and with Holmes approached him. I could smell the heavy, though fragrant, odour of excellent Scotch on his breath.

Wentworth looked at the revolver in Holmes' hand, smiled, and said, 'So – you are not overrated, Mr. Holmes! But I was waiting for him, I expected him to sneak in upon me while I should be concentrating on the instrument board. He thought he'd blow my a*s off!'

'He is, of course, a German spy,' Holmes said. 'But how did you determine that he was?'

'I suspect everybody,' Wentworth replied. 'I kept my eye on him, and when I saw him talking over the wireless, I listened in. It was too noisy to hear clearly, but he was talking in German. I caught several words, *schwanz* and *schweinhund*. Undoubtedly, he was informing the Imperial German Military Aviation Service of our location. If he didn't kill me, then we would be shot down. The Huns must be on their way to intercept us now.'

This was alarming enough, but both Holmes and I were struck at the same time with a far more disturbing thought. Holmes, as usual, was more quick in his reactions. He screamed, 'Who's flying the plane?'

Wentworth smiled lazily and said, 'Nobody. Don't worry. The controls are connected to a little device I invented last month. As long as the air is smooth, the plane will fly on an even keel all by itself.'

He stiffened suddenly, cocked his head to one side, and said, 'Do you hear it?'

'Great Scott, man!' I cried. 'How could we hear anything about the infernal racket of those motors?'

'Cockroaches!' Wentworth bellowed. 'Giant flying cockroaches! That evil scientist has released another horror upon the world!'

He whirled, and he was gone into the blackness of the tunnel.

Holmes and I stared at each other. Then Holmes said, 'We are at the mercy of a madman, Watson. And there is nothing we can do until we have landed.'

'We could parachute out,' I said.

'I would prefer not to,' Holmes said stiffly. 'Besides, it somehow doesn't seem cricket. The pilots have no parachutes, you know. These two were provided only because we are civilians.'

'I wasn't planning on asking Wentworth to ride down with me,' I mumbled, somewhat ashamed of myself for saying this.

Holmes didn't hear me; once again his stomach was trying to reject contents that did not exist.

III

Shortly after dawn, the German planes struck. These, as I was later told, were Fokker E-III's, single-seater monoplanes equipped with two Spandau machine guns. These were synchronized with the propellors to shoot bullets through the empty spaces between the whirling of the propellor blades.

Holmes was sitting on the floor, holding his head and groaning, and I was commiserating with him, though getting weary of his complaints, when the telephone bell rang. I removed the receiver from the box attached to the wall, or bulkhead, or whatever they call it. Wentworth's voice bellowed, 'Put on the parachutes and hang on to something tight! Twelve ****ing Fokkers, a whole *staffel*, coming in at eleven o'clock!'

I misunderstood him. I said, 'Yes, but what type of plane are they?'

'Fokkers!' he cried, adding, 'No, no! My eyes played tricks on me. They're giant flying cockroaches! Each one is being ridden by a Prussian officer, helmeted and goggled and armed with a boarding cutlass!'

'What did you say?' I screamed into the phone, but it had been disconnected.

I told Holmes what Wentworth had said, and he forgot about being airsick, though he looked no better than before. We staggered out to the door and looked through its window.

The night was now brighter than day, the result of flares thrown out from the attacking areoplanes. Their pilots intended to use the light to line up the sights of their machine guns on our helpless craft. Then, as if that were not bad enough, shells began exploding, some so near that our aeroplane shuddered and rocked under the impact of the blasts. Giant searchlights began playing about, some of them illuminating monoplanes with black crosses on their fuselages.

'Archy!' I exclaimed. 'The French anti-aircraft guns are firing at the Huns! The fools! They could hit us as well!'

Something flashed by. We lost sight of it, but a moment later we saw a fighter diving down toward us through the glare of the flares and the searchlights, ignoring the bursting shells around it. Two tiny red eyes flickered behind the propellor, but it was not until holes were suddenly punched in the fabric only a few feet from us that we realised that those were the muzzles of the machine guns. We dropped to the floor while the great plane rolled and dipped and rose and dropped and we were shot this way and that across the floor and against the bulkheads.

'We're doomed!' I cried to Holmes. 'Get the parachutes on! He can't shoot back at the planes, and our plane is too slow and clumsy to get away!'

101

How wrong I was. And what a demon that madman was. He did things with that big lumbering aeroplane that I wouldn't have believed possible. Several times we were upside down and we only kept from being smashed, like mice shaken in a tin, by hanging on desperately to the bunkposts.

Once, Holmes, whose sense of hearing was somewhat keener than mine, said, 'Watson, isn't that a******e shooting a machine gun? How can he fly this plane, put it through such manoeuvres, and still operate a weapon which he must hold in both hands to use effectively?'

'I don't know,' I confessed. At that moment both of us were dangling from the post, failing to fall only because of our tight grip. The plane was on its left side. Through the window beneath my feet I saw a German plane, smoke trailing from it, fall away. And then another followed it, becoming a ball of flame about a thousand feet or so from the ground.

The Handley Page righted itself, and I heard faint thumping noises overhead, followed by the chatter of a machine gun. Something exploded very near us and wreckage drifted by the window.

This shocked me, but even more shocking was the rapping on the window. This, to my astonishment, originated from a fist hammering on the door. I crawled over to it and stood up and looked through it. Upside down, staring at me through the isinglass, was Wentworth's face. His lips formed the words, 'Open the door! Let me in!'

Numbly, I obeyed. A moment later, with an acrobatic skill that I still find incredible, he swung through the door. In one hand he held a Spandau with a rifle stock. A moment later, while I held on to his waist, he had closed the door and shut out the cold shrilling blast of wind.

102

'There they are!' he yelled, and he pointed the machine gun at a point just past Holmes, lying on the floor, and sent three short bursts past Holmes' ear.

Holmes said, 'Really, old fellow . . .' Wentworth, raving, ran past him and a moment later we heard the chatter of the Spandau again.

'At least, he's back in the cockpit,' Holmes said weakly. However, this was one of the times when Holmes was wrong. A moment later the captain was back. He opened the trap-door, poked the barrel of his weapon through, let loose a single burst, said, 'Got you, you ****ing son of a *****!' closed the trap-door, and ran back toward the front.

Forty minutes later, the plane landed on a French military aerodrome outside of Marseilles. Its fuselage and wings were perforated with bullet holes in a hundred places, though fortunately no missiles had struck the petrol tanks. The French commander who inspected the plane pointed out that more of the holes were made by a fun firing from the inside than from guns firing from the outside.

'Damn right!' Wentworth said. 'The cockroaches and their allies, the flying leopards, were crawling all over inside the plane! They almost got these two old men!'

A few minutes later a British medical officer arrived. Wentworth, after fiercely fighting six men, was subdued and put into a straitjacket and carried off in an ambulance.

Wentworth was not the only one raving. Holmes, his pale face twisted, his fists clenched, was cursing his brother Mycroft, young Merrivale, and everyone else who could possibly be responsible, excepting, of course, His Majesty.

We were taken to an office occupied by several French and British officers of very high rank. The highest,

General Chatson-Dawes-Overleigh, said, 'Yes, my dear Mr. Holmes, we realise that he sometimes has these hallucinatory fits. Becomes quite mad, to be frank. But he is the best pilot and also the best espionage agent we have, even if he is a Colonial, and he has done heroic work for us. He never hallucinates negatively, that is, he never harms his fellows – though he did shoot an Italian once, but the fellow *was* only a private and he *was* an Italian and it *was* an accident – and so we feel that we must permit him to work for us. We can't permit a word of his condition to get back to the civilian populace, of course, so I must require you to swear silence about the whole affair. Which you would have to do as a matter of course, and, of course, of patriotism. He'll be given a little rest cure, a drying-out, too, and then returned to duty. Britain sorely needs him.'

Holmes raved some more, but he always was one to face realities and to govern himself accordingly. Even so, he could not resist making some sarcastic remarks about his life, which was also extremely valuable, being put into the care of a homicidal maniac. At least, cooling down, he said, 'And the pilot who will fly us to Egypt? Is he also an irresponsible madman? Will we be in more danger from him than from the enemy?'

'He is said to be every bit as good a pilot as Wentworth,' the general said. 'He is an American . . .'

'Great Scott!' Holmes said. He groaned, and he added, 'Why can't we have a pilot of good British stock, tried and true?'

'Both Wentworth and Kentov are of the best British stock,' Overleigh said stiffly. 'They're descended from some of the oldest and noblest stock of England. They have royal blood in them, as a matter of fact. But they happen to be Colonials. The man who will fly you from here has been working for His Majesty's cousin, the Tsar of all the Russias, as an espionage agent. The Tsar was kind enough to loan both him and one of the great Sikorski *Ilya Mourometz* Type V aeroplanes to us. Kentov flew here in it with a full crew, and it is ready to take off.'

Holmes' face became even paler, and I felt every minute of my sixty-four years of age. We were not to get a moment's rest, and yet we had gone through an experience which would have sent many a youth to bed for several days.

IV

General Overleigh himself conducted us to the colossal Russian aeroplane. As we approached it, he described certain features in answer to Holmes' questions.

'So far, the only four-engined heavier-than-air craft in the world has been built by the Russians,' he said. 'Much to the shame of the British. The first one was built, and flown, in 1913. This, as you can see, is a biplane, fitted with wheels and a ski undercarriage. It has four 150-horsepower Sunbeam water-cooled Vee-type engines. The Sunbeam, unfortunately, leaves much to be desired.'

'I would rather not have known that,' I murmured. The sudden ashen hue of Holmes' face indicated that his reactions were similar to mine.

'Its wing span is ninety-seven feet, nine and a half inches; the craft's length is fifty-six feet, one inch; its height is fifteen feet, five and seven-eighths inches. Its maximum speed is seventy-five miles per hour; its operational ceiling is 9,843 feet. And its endurance is five hours – under ideal conditions. It carries a crew of five, though it can carry more. The rear fuselage is fitted with compartments for sleeping and eating.'

Overleigh shook hands with us after he had handed us over to a Lieutenant Obrenov. The young officer led us to the steps into the fuselage and to the rear, where he showed us our compartment. Holmes chatted away with him in Russian, of which he had gained a certain mastery during his experience in Odessa with the Trepoff case. Holmes' insistence on speaking Russian seemed to annoy the officer somewhat, since, like all upper-class people of his country, he preferred to use French. But he was courteous, and after making sure we were comfortable, he bowed himself out. Certainly, we had little to complain about except possibly the size of the cabin. It had been prepared especially for us, had two swing-down beds, a thick rug which Holmes said was a genuine Persian, oil paintings on the walls which Holmes said were genuine Maleviches (I thought they were artistic nonsense), two comfortable chairs bolted to the deck, and a sideboard also bolted to the deck and holding alcoholic beverages. In one corner was a tiny cubicle containing all the furniture and necessities that one finds in a W.C.

Holmes and I lit up the fine Cuban cigars we found in a humidor and poured out some Scotch whisky, Duggan's Dew of Kirkintilloch, I believe. Suddenly, both of us leaped into the air, spilling our drinks over our cuffs. Seemingly from nowhere, a tall figure had silently appeared. How he had done it, I do not know, since the door had been closed and under observation at all times by one or both of us.

Holmes groaned and said, under his breath, 'Not another madman?'

The fellow certainly looked eccentric. He wore the uniform of a colonel of the Imperial Russian Air Service, but he also wore a long black opera cloak and a big black slouch hat. From under its floppy brim burned two of the most magnetic and fear-inspiring eyes I have ever seen. My attention, however, was somewhat diverted from these by the size and the aquilinity of the nose beneath them. It could have belonged to Cyrano de Bergerac.

I found that I had to sit down to catch my breath. The fellow introduced himself, in an Oxford accent, as Colonel Kentov. He had a surprisingly pleasant voice, deep, rich, and shot with authority. It was also heavily laced with bourbon.

'Are you all right?' he said.

'I think so,' I said. 'You gave me quite a start. A cloud seemed to pass over my mind. But I'm fine now, thank you.'

'I must go forward now,' he said, 'but I've assigned a crew member, a tail gunner now but once a butler, to serve you. Just ring that bell beside you if you need him.'

And he was gone, though this time he opened the door. At least, I think he did.

'I fear, my dear fellow, that we are in for another trying time,' Holmes said.

Actually, the voyage seemed quite pleasant once one got used to the roar of the four motors and the nerve-shaking jack-out-of-the-box appearances of Kentov. The trip was to take approximately twenty-eight hours, if all went well. About every four and a half hours we put down at a hastily constructed landing strip to which petrol and supplies had been rushed by ship, air, or camel some days before. With the Mediterranean Sea on our left and the shores of North Africa below us, we sped toward Cairo at an amazing average speed of seventy-point-three miles per hour, according to our commander. While we sipped various liquors or liqueurs and smoked Havanas, we read to pass the time. Holmes commented several times that he could use a little cocaine to relieve the tedium, but I believe that he said that just to needle me. Holmes had brought along a work of his own authorship, the privately printed *Practical Handbook of Bee Culture, with Some Observations Upon the Segregation of the Queen.* He had often urged me to read the results of his experience with his Sussex bees and so I now acceded to his urgings, mainly because all the other books available were in Russian.

I found it more interesting than I had expected, and I told Holmes so. This seemed to please him, though he had affected an air of indifference to my reaction before then.

'The techniques and tricks of apiculture are intriguing and complex enough,' he said. 'But I was called away from a project which goes far beyond anything any apiculturist – scientist or not – has attempted. It is my theory that bees have a language and they communicate such important information as the location of new clover, the approach of enemies, and so forth, my means of symbolic dancing. I was investigating this with a view to turning theory into fact when I got Mycroft's wire.'

I sat up so suddenly that the ash dropped off my cigar into my lap, and I was busy for a moment brushing off the coals before they burned a hole in my trousers. 'Really, Holmes,' I said, 'you are surely pulling my leg! Bees have a language? Next you'll be telling me they compose sonnets in honour of their queen's inauguration! Or perhaps when she gets married!'

'Epitases?' he said, regarding me scornfully. 'You mean epithalamiums, you blockhead! I suggest you use moderation while drinking the national beverage of Russia. Yes, Watson, bees do communicate, though not in the manner which *Homo sapiens* uses.'

'I understand that Lord Mowgli of the Seeonee claims that he can talk to beasts and reptiles . . .' I said, but I was interrupted by that sudden vagueness of mind which signalled the appearance of our commander. I always jumped and my heart beat hard when the cloud dissolved and I realized that Kentov was standing before me. My only consolation was that Holmes was just as startled.

'Confound it, man!' Holmes said, his face red. 'Couldn't you behave like a civilised being for once and knock before entering? Or don't Americans have such customs?'

This, of course, was sheer sarcasm, since Holmes had been to the States several times.

'We are only two hours from Cairo,' Kentov said, ignoring Holmes' remarks. 'But I have just learned from the wireless station in Cairo that a storm of severe proportions is approaching us from the north. We may be blown somewhat off our course. Also, our spies at Cos, in Turkey, report that a Zeppelin left there yesterday. They believe that it intends to pick up Von Bork. Somehow, he's slipped out past the cordon and is waiting in the desert for the airship.'

Holmes, gasping and sputtering, said, 'If this execrable voyage turns out to be for nothing . . . if I was forced to endure that madman's dangerous antics only to have . . . !'

Suddenly, the colonel was gone. Holmes regained his normal colour and composure, and he said, 'Do you know, Watson, I believe I know that man! Or, at least, his parents. I've been studying him at every opportunity, and though he is doubtless a master at dissimulation, that nose is false, he has a certain bone structure and a certain trait of walking, of turning his head, which leads me to believe . . .'

At that moment the telephone rang. Since I was closest to the instrument, I answered it. Our commander's voice said, 'Batten down all loose objects and tie yourself into your beds. We are in for a hell of a storm, the worst of this century, if the weather reports are accurate.'

For once, the meteorologists had not exaggerated. The next three hours were terrible. The giant aeroplane was tossed about as if it were a sheet of writing paper. The electric lamps on the walls flickered again and again and finally went out, leaving us in darkness. Holmes groaned and moaned and finally tried to crawl to the W.C. Unfortunately, the craft was bucking up and down like a wild horse and rolling and yawling like a rowboat caught in a rapids. Holmes managed to get back to his bed without breaking any bones but, I regret to say, proceeded to get rid of all the vodka and brandy (a combination itself not conducive to good digestion, I believe), beef stroganoff, cabbage soup, and black bread on which we had dined earlier. Even more regrettably, he leaned over the edge of the bed to perform this undeniable function, and though I did not get all of it, I did get too much. I did not have the heart to reprimand him. Besides, he would have killed me, or at least attempted to do so, if I had made any reproaches. His mood was not of the best.

Finally, I heard his voice, weak though it was, saying, 'Watson, promise me one thing.'

'What is that, Holmes?'

'Swear to me that once we've set foot on land you'll shoot me through the head if ever I show the slighest inclination to board a flying vehicle again. I don't think there's much danger of that, but even if His Majesty himself should plead with me to get into an aeroplane, or anything that flies, dirigible, balloon, anything, you will mercifully tender euthanasia of some sort. Promise me.'

I thought I was safe in promising. For one thing, I felt almost as strongly as he did about it.

At that moment, the door to our cabin opened, and our attendant, Ivan, appeared with a small electric lamp in his hand. He exchanged some excited words in Russian with Holmes and then left, leaving the lamp behind. Holmes crawled down from the bunk, saying, 'We've orders to abandon ship, Watson. We've been blown far south of Cairo and will be out of petrol in half an hour. We'll have to jump then, like it or not. Ivan says that the colonel has looked for a safe landing place, but he can't even see the ground. The air's filled with sand; visibility is nil; the sand is getting into the bearings of the engines and pitting the windshields. So, my dear old friend, we must don the parachutes.'

My heart warmed at being addressed so fondly, though my emotion was somewhat tempered in the next few minutes while we were assisting each other in strapping on the equipment. Holmes said, 'You have an abominable effluvia about you, Watson,' and I replied, testily, I must admit, 'You stink like the W.C. in an East End pub yourself, my dear Holmes. Besides, any odour emanating from me has originated from, or in, you. Surely you are aware of that.'

Holmes muttered something about the direction upwards, and I was about to ask him to clarify his comment when Ivan appeared again. This time he carried weapons which he distributed among the three of us. I was handed a cavalry sabre, a stiletto, a knout (which I discarded), and a revolver of some unknown make but of .50 calibre. Holmes was given a cutlass, a carbine, a belt full of ammunition, and a coil of rope at one end of which were grapping hooks. Ivan kept for himself another cutlass, two hand grenades dangling by their pins from his belt, and a dagger in his teeth.

We walked (rolled, rather) to the door, where three others stood, also fully, perhaps even over-, armed. There was a window further forward, and so Holmes and I went to it after a while to observe the storm. We could see little except clouds of dust for a few minutes and then the dust was suddenly gone. A heavy rain succeeded it, though the wind buffeted us as strongly as before. There was also much lightning, some of it exploding loudly close by.

A moment later Ivan joined us, pulling at Holmes' arm and shouting something in Russian. Holmes answered him and turning to me said, 'Kentov has sighted a Zeppelin!'

'Great Scott!' I cried. 'Surely it must be the one sent to pick up Von Bork! It, too, has been caught by the storm!'

'An elementary deduction,' Holmes said. But he seemed pleased about something. I surmised that he was happy because Von Bork had either missed the airship or, if he was in it, was in as perilous a plight as we. I failed to see any humour in the situation.

Holmes lost his grin several minutes later when we were informed that we were going to attack the Zeppelin.

'In this storm?' I said. 'Why, the colonel can't even keep us at the same altitude or attitude from one second to the next.'

'The man's a maniac!' Holmes shouted.

Just how mad, we were shortly to discover. Presently the great airship hove into view, painted silver above and black below to conceal it from search lights, the large designation on its side painted out, the control car in front, its pusher propellor spinning, the propellors on the front and rear of the two midships and one aft engine-gondolas spinning, the whole looking quite monstrous and sinister and yet beautiful.

The airship was bobbing and rolling and yawing like a toy boat afloat on a Scottish salmon stream. Its crew had to be airsick and they had to have their hands full just to keep from being pitched out of their vessel. This was heartening to some degree, since none of us on the aeroplane, except possibly Kentov, were in any state remotely resembling good health or aggression.

Ivan mumbled something, and Holmes said, 'He says that if the storm keeps up the airship will soon break up. Let us hope that it does and so spares us aerial combat.'

But the Zeppelin, though it did seem to be somewhat out of line, its frame slightly twisted, held together. Meanwhile, our four-engined colossus, so small compared to the airship, swept around to the vessel's stern. It was a ragged approach what with the constantly buffeting blasts, but the wonder was that it was accomplished at all.

'What's the fool doing?' Holmes said, and he spoke again to Ivan. Lightning rolled up the heavens then, and I saw that his face was a ghastly blue-grey.

'This yank is madder than the other!' he said. 'He's going to try to land on top of the Zeppelin!'

'How could he do that?' I gasped.

'How would I know what techniques he'll use, you dunce!' he shouted. 'Who cares? Whatver he does, the plane will fall off the ship, probably breaks its wings, and we'll fall to our deaths!'

'We can jump *now*!' I shouted.

'What? Desert?' he cried. 'Watson, we are British!'

'It was only a suggestion,' I said. 'Forgive me. Of course, we will stick it out. No Slav is going to say that we English lack courage.'

Ivan spoke again, and Holmes relayed his intelligence. 'He says that the colonel, who is probably the greatest flier in the world, even if he is a Yank, will come up over the stern of the Zeppelin and stall it just above the top machine-gun platform. As soon as the plane stops, we are to open the door and leap out. If we miss our footing or fall down, we can always use the parachutes. Kentov insisted on bringing them along over the protests of the Imperial

Russian General Staff – they should live so long. We will go down the ladder from the platform and board the ship. Kentov's final words, his last orders before we leave the plane are . . .'

He hesitated, and I said, 'Yes, Holmes?'

'Kill! Kill! Kill!'

'Good heavens!' I said. 'How barbaric!'

'Yes,' he answered. 'But one has to excuse him. He is obviously not sane.'

V

Following orders communicated through Obrenov, we lay down on the deck and grabbed whatever was solid and anchored in a world soon to become all too fluid and foundationless. The plane dived and we slid forward and then it rose sharply upward and we slid backward and then its nose suddenly lifted up, the roaring of the four engines becoming much more highly pitched, and suddenly we were pressed against the floor. And then the pressure was gone.

Slowly, but far too swiftly for me, the deck tilted to the left. This was in accordance with Kentov's plans. He has stalled the craft with its longitudinal axis, or centre-line, a little to the left of the airship's centre-line. Its weight would thus cause the airship on whose back it rode to roll to the left.

For a second, I did not realize what was happening. To be quite frank, I was scared out of my wits, numb with terror. I would never allow Holmes to see this, and so I overcame my frozen state, though not the stiffness and slowness due to my age and recent hardships. I got up and stumbled out through the door, the parachute banging the upper parts of the back of my thighs and feeling as if it

114

were made of lead, and sprawled out onto the small part of the platform left to me. I grabbed for the lowest end of an upright pipe forming the enclosure about the platform. The hatch had already been opened and Kentov was inside the airship. I could hear the booming of several guns. It was comparatively silent now, since Kentov had cut the engines just before the stalling. Nevertheless, one could hear the creaking of the girders of the ship's structure as it bent under the varying pressures. My ears hurt abominably because the airship was dropping swiftly under the weight of the giant aeroplane. The aeroplane was also making its own unmistakable noises, groaning, as its structure bent, tearing the fabric of the ship's covering as it slipped more and more to the left, then there was a loud ripping, and the ship beneath me rolled swiftly back, relieved of the enormous weight of the aeroplane. At the same time the Zeppelin soared aloft, and the two motions, the rolling and the levitation, almost tore me loose from my hold.

When the dirigible had ceased its major oscillations, the Russians rose and one by one disappeared into the well. Holmes and I worked our way across, passed the pedestals of the two quilt-swathed eight-millimetre Maxim machine guns, and descended the ladder. Just before I was all the way into the hatch, I looked across the back of the great beast that we were invading. I would have been shocked if I had not been so numb. The wheels and the ski undercarriage of the plane had ripped open a great wound along the thin skin of the vessel. Encountering the duralumin girders and rings of the framework, it had torn some apart and then its landing gear had itself been ripped off. The propellors, though no longer turning, had also done extensive damage. I wondered if the framework of the ship, the skeleton of the beast, as it were, might not have suffered so great a blow it would collapse and carry all of us down to our death.

I also had a second's admiration for the skull, no, the genius, of the pilot who had landed us.

And then I descended into the vast complex spiderweb of the ship's hull with its rings and girders and bulging hydrogen-filled gas cells and ballast sacks of water. I emerged at the keel of the ship, on the foot-wide catwalk that ran the length of the ship between triangular girders. It had been a nightmare before then; after that it became a nightmare having a nightmare. I remember dodging along, clinging to girders, swinging out and climbing around to avoid the fire of the German sailors in the bow. I remember Lieutenant Obrenov falling with fatal bullet wounds after sticking two Germans with his sabre (there was no room to swing it and so use the edge as regulations required).

I remember others falling, some managing to retain their grip and so avoiding the fall through the fabric of the cover and into the abyss below. I remember Holmes hiding behind a gas cell and firing away at the Germans who were afraid of firing back and perhaps setting the hydrogen aflame.

Most of all I remember the slouch-hatted cloaked form of Kentov leaping about, swinging from girders and brace wires, bouncing from a beam onto a great gas cell and back again, flitting like a phantom of the opera through the maze, firing two huge .45 automatic pistols (not at the same time, of course, otherwise he would have lost his grip). German after German cried out or fled while the maniac cackled with a blood-chilling laugh between the booming of the huge guns. But though he was worth a squadron in himself, his men died one by one. And so the inevitable hapened.

116

Perhaps it was a ricocheting bullet or perhaps he slipped. I do not know. All of a sudden he was falling off a girder, through a web cf wires, miraculously missing them, falling backward, now in each hand a thundering flame-spitting .45, killing two sailors as he fell, laughing loudly even as he broke through the thin fabric and disappeared into the dark rain over Africa.

Since he was wearing a parachute, he may have survived. I never heard of him again, though.

Presently the Germans approached cautiously, having heard Holmes and me call out that we surrendered. (We were out of ammunition and too nerveless even to lift a sabre.) We stood on the catwalk with our hands up, two tired beaten old men. Yet it was our finest hour. Nothing could ever rob us of the pleasure of seeing Von Bork's face when he recognised us. If the shock had been slightly more intense, he would have dropped dead from a heart attack.

VI

A few minutes later, we had climbed down the ladder from the hull to the control gondola under the fore part of the airship. Behind us, raving, restrained by a petty officer and the executive officer, Oberleutnant zur *See* Heinrich Tring, came Von Bork. He had ordered us thrown overboard then and there, but Tring, a decent fellow, had refused to obey his orders. We were introduced to the commander, Kapitänleutnant Victor Reich. He was also a decent fellow, openly admiring our feat of landing and boarding his ship even though it and his crew had suffered terribly. He rejected Von Bork's suggestion that we should be shot as spies since we were in civilian clothes and on a Russian warcraft. He knew of us, of course, and he would have nothing to do with a summary execution of the great Holmes and his colleague. ,After hearing our story, he made sure of our comfort. However, he refused to let Holmes smoke, cast his tobacco overboard then and there, in fact, and this made Holmes suffer. He had gone through so much that he desperately needed a pipeful of shag.

'It is fortunate that the storm is breaking up,' Reich said in excellent English. 'Otherwise, the ship would soon break up. Three of our motors are not operating. The clutch to the port motor has overheated, the water in the radiator of a motor in the starboard mid-car has boiled out, and something struck the propellor of the control car and shattered it. We are so far south that even if we could operate at one hundred percent efficiency, we would be out of petrol somewhere over Egypt on the return trip. Moreover, the controls to the elevators have been damaged. All we can do at present is drift with the wind and hope for the best.'

The days and nights that followed were full of suffering and anxiety. Seven of the crew had been killed during the fight, leaving only six to man the vessel. This alone was enough to make a voyage back to Turkey or Palestine impossible. Reich told us that he had received a radio message ordering him to get to the German forces in East Africa under Von Lettow-Vorbeck. There he was to burn the Zeppelin and join the forces. This, of course, was not all the message. Surely something must have been said about getting Von Bork to Germany, since he had the formula for mutating and culturing the 'sauerkraut bacilli.' I wondered then why the formula was not sent via radio to the German-Turkish base, but I found out later that no one aboard understood the formula well enough to transmit it.

When we were alone in the port mid-gondola, where we were kept during part of the voyage, Holmes commented on what he called the 'SB.'

'We must get possession of the formula, Watson,' he said. 'I did not tell you, but before you arrived at Mycroft's office I was informed that the SB is a two-edged weapon. It can be mutated to eat other foods. Imagine what would happen to our food supply, not to mention the blow to our morale, if the SB were changed to eat boiled meat? Or cabbage? Or potatoes?'

'Great Scott!' I said, and then, in a whisper, 'It could be worse, Holmes, far worse. What if the Germans dropped an SB over England which devoured stout and ale? Or think of how the spirits of our valiant Scots would sink if their whisky supply vanished before their eyes?'

Von Bork had been impressed into airship service but, being as untrained as we, was not of much use. Also, his injured left eye handicapped him as much as our age did us. It was very bloodshot and failed to coordinate with its partner. My professional opinion was that it was totally without sight. The other eye was healthy enough. It glared every time it lighted upon us. Its fires reflected the raging hatred in his heart, the lust to murder us.

However, the airship was in such straits that no one had much time or inclination to think about anything except survival. Some of the motors were still operating, thus enabling some kind of control. As long as we went south, with the wind behind us, we made headway. But due to the jammed elevators, the nose of the ship was downward and the tail was up. It flew at roughtly five degrees to the horizontal for some time. Reich put everybody to work, including us, since we had volunteered, at carrying indispensable equipment to the rear to help weigh it down. Anything that was dispensable, and there was not much, went overboard. In addition, much water ballast in the front was discharged.

Below us the sands of Sudan reeled by while the sun flamed in a cloudless blue. Its fiery breath heated the hydrogen in the cells, and great amounts hissed out from the automatic valves. The hot wind blew into the hull through the great hole made by the aeroplane when it had stalled into a landing on its top. The heat, of course, made the hydrogen expand, thus causing the ship to rise despite the loss of gas from the valves. At night, the air cooled very swiftly, and the ship dropped swiftly, too swiftly for the peace of mind of its passengers. During the day the updrafts of heat from the sands made the vessel buck and kick. All of us aboard got sick during these times.

By working like Herculeses despite all handicaps, the crew managed to get all the motors going again. On the fifth day, the elevator controls were fixed. Her hull was still twisted, and this, with the huge gap in the surface covering, made her aerodynamically unstable. At least, that was how Reich explained it to us. He, by the way, was not at all reticent in telling us about the vessel itself though he would not tell us our exact location. Perhaps this was because he wanted to make sure that we would not somehow get to the radio and send a message to the British in East Africa.

The flat desert gave way to rugged mountains. More ballast was dropped, and the vessel just barely avoided scraping some of the peaks. Night came with its cooling effects, and the ship dropped. The mountains were lower at this point, fortunately for us.

Two days later, as we lay sweltering on the catwalk that ran along the keel, Holmes said, 'I estimate that we are now somewhere over British East Africa, somewhere in the vicinity of Lake Victoria. It is evident that we will never get to Mahenge or indeed anywhere in German East Africa. The ship has lost too much hydrogen. I have overhead some guarded comments to this effect by Reich and Tring. They think we'll crash sometime tonight. Instead of seeking out the nearest British authorities and surrendering, as anyone with good sense would, they are determined to cross our territory to German territory. Do you know how many miles of veldt and jungle and swamp swarming with lions, rhinoceri, vipers, savages, malaria, dengue, and God knows what else we will have to walk? Attempt to walk, rather?'

'Perhaps we can slip away some night?'

'And then what will we do?' he said bitterly. 'Watson, you and I know the jungles of London well and are quite fitted to conduct our safaris through them. But here . . . no, Watson, any black child of eight is more competent, far more so, to survive in these wilds.'

'You don't paint a very good picture,' I said grimly.

'Though I am descended from the Vernets, the great French artists,' he said, 'I myself have little ability at painting pretty pictures.'

He chuckled then, and I was heartened by this example of pawky humour, feeble though it was. Holmes would never quit; his indomitable English spirit might be defeated, but it would go down fighting. And I would be at his side. And was it not after all better to die with one's boots on while one still had some vigour than when one was old and crippled and sick and perhaps an idiot drooling and doing all sorts of pitiful, sickening things?

That evening preparations were made to abandon the ship. Ballast water was put in every portable container, the food supply was stored in sacks made from the cotton fabric ripped off the hull, and we waited. Sometime after midnight, the end came. It was fortunately a cloudless

121

night with a moon bright enough for us to see, if not too sharply, the terrain beneath. This was a jungle up in the mountains, which were not at a great elevation. The ship was steered down a winding valley through which a stream ran silvery. Then, abruptly, we had to rise, and we could not do it.

We were in the control car when the hillside loomed before us. Reich gave the order and we threw our supplies out, thus lightening the load and giving us a few more seconds of grace. We two prisoners were allowed to drop out first. Reich did this because the ship would rise as the crew-members left, and he wanted us to be closest to the ground. We were old and not so agile, and he thought that we needed all the advantages we could get.

He was right. Even though Holmes and I fell into some bushes which eased our descent, we were still bruised and shaken up. We scrambled out, however, and made our way through the growth toward the supplies. The ship passed over us, sliding its great shadow like a cloak, and then it struck something. The whirring propellors were snapped off, the cars crumpled and came loose with a nerve-scraping sound, the ship lifted again with the weight of the cars gone, and it drifted out of sight. But its career was about over. A few minutes later, it exploded. Reich had left several time-bombs next to some gas cells.

The flames were very bright and very hot, outlining the dark skeleton of its framework. Birds flew up and around it. No doubt they and the beasts of the jungle were making a loud racket, but the roar of the flames drowned them out.

By their light we could see back down the hill, though not very far. We struggled through the heavy vegetation, hoping to get to the supplies before the others. We had agreed to take as much food and water as we could carry and set off by ourselves, if we got the chance. Surely, we reasoned, there must be some native village nearby, and once there we would ask for guidance to the nearest British post.

By pure luck, we came aross a pile of food and some bottles of water. Holmes said, 'Dame Fortune is with us, Watson!' but his chuckle died the next moment when Von Bork stepped out of the bushes. In his hand was a Luger automatic and in his one eye was the determination to use that before the others arrived. He could claim, of course, that we were fleeing or had attacked him and that he was forced to shoot us.

'Die, you pig-dogs!' he snarled, and he raised the gun. 'Before you do, though, know that I have the formula on me and that I will get it to the Fatherland and it will doom you English swine and the French swine and the Italian swine. The bacilli can be adapted to eat Yorkshire pudding and snails and spaghetti, anything that is edible! The beauty of it is that it's specific, and unless it's mutated to eat sauerkraut, it will starve rather than do so!'

We drew ourselves up, prepared to die as British men should. Holmes muttered out of the corner of his mouth, 'Jump to one side, Watson, and then we'll rush him! You take his blind side! Perhaps one of us can get to him!'

This was a noble plan, though I didn't know what I could do even if I got hold of Von Bork. After all, he was a young man and had a splendid physique.

At that moment there was a crashing in the bushes, Reich's loud voice commanding Von Bork not to shoot, and the commander, tears streaming from his face, stumbled into the clearing. Behind him came others. Von Bork said, 'I was merely holding them until you got here.'

Reich, I must add, was not weeping because of any danger to us. The fate of his airship had dealt him a terrible blow; he loved his vessel and to see it die was to him comparable to seeing his wife die. Perhaps it had even more impact, since, as I later found out, he was on the verge of a divorce.

Though he had saved us, he knew that we were ready to skip out at the first chance. He kept a close eye on us, though it was not as close as Von Bork's. Nevertheless, he allowed us to retreat behind bushes to attend to our comforts. And so, three days later, we strolled on away.

'Well, Watson,' Holmes said, as we sat panting under a tree several hours later, 'we have given them the slip. But we have no water and no food except these pieces of mouldy biscuit in our pockets. At this moment I would trade them for a handful of shag.'

We went to sleep finally and slept like the two old and exhausted men we were. I awoke several times, I think because of insects crawling over my face, but I always went back to sleep quickly. About eight in the morning, the light and the uproar of jungle life awoke us. I was the first to see the cobra slipping through the tall growths toward us. I got quickly, though unsteadily and painfully, to my feet. Holmes saw the reptile then and started to get up. The snake raised its upper part, its hood swelled, and it swayed as it turned its head this way and that.

'Steady, Watson!' Holmes said, though the advice would better have been given to himself. He was much closer to the cobra, within striking range, in fact, and he was shaking more violently than I. He could not be blamed for this, of course. He was in a more shakeable situation.

'I knew we should have brought along that flask of brandy,' I said. 'We have absolutely nothing for snake-bite.'

'No time for reproaches, you imbecile!' Holmes said.

'Besides, what kind of medical man are you? It's sheer superstitious nonsense that alcohol helps prevent the effects of venom.'

'Really, Holmes,' I said. He had been getting so irascible lately, so insulting. Part of this could be excused, since he became very nervous without the solace of tobacco. Even so, I thought . . .

The thought was never finished. The cobra struck, and Holmes and I jumped, yelling.

VII

For a moment both Holmes and I thought that he had been bitten. The blunt nose of the cobra, however, had only touched Holmes's leg. But he was in as perilous a situation as before, having jumped straight up instead of away and having come down in the same place, in his footprints in the mud, in fact. The cobra, meanwhile, had moved closer and now could not miss.

'Don't move, Holmes!' I cried. 'It may not strike again!'

'The cobra is like lightning; it always strikes the same place twice!' he said. 'For heaven's sake, Watson, divert it!'

I started to move around Holmes toward the creature, though not too closely, when I saw a bush ahead of me shake. Great Scott, I thought, is another venomous killer, perhaps its mate, coming to join it?

The bush ceased shaking, and from behind it stepped out a man such as I had never seen before. At least, I've never seen a totally naked man in a public place before, if the African jungle may be classed as such. I have viewed few with such a heavy bone structure and superb muscles, more like Apollo's than Hercules' though, more leopardish than lionish.

He stood perhaps six feet two inches and was very dark, definitely not an Englishman but not as dark as a Negro. His shoulder-length hair was straight and blue-black. Below the bulging atavistic supraorbital ridges were large long-lashed deep brown eyes. His face was indeed handsome, and he had the biggest [word blotted out by ink] I've ever seen, and as a medical man I've seen some startlers.

He was a magnificent specimen, unflawed except for an angry-red spot between and on the big toe and next toe of his left foot. This, I assumed, was caused by a birthmark or one of the fungi so rife in the jungle.

My statement that he was altogether unclothed is not quite accurate. He did wear a broad belt of crocodile hide, secured at the front by thongs tied in a knot, and the belt supported a crocodile-hide scabbard in which was a huge hunting knife.

The man advanced toward us, saying in English with an Oxford accent, 'Don't move a muscle, gentlemen.'

He looked at Holmes.

'Try to keep your teeth from chattering.'

He walked up quite close to the cobra and spoke to it in a language totally unfamiliar to me. Holmes, an accomplished linguist, later confessed to me that the language was also unknown to him.

The cobra twisted its body towards him and hissed a few times, its forked tongue shooting out. Then its hood collapsed, and it crawled off into the bush.

'White Hood is my brother,' the dark man said, 'and I explained to her that you were no danger to her and that she was under no obligation to the Law of the Jungle to attack you.'

Holmes surprised me by his reply, which I though under the circumstances was remarkably ungrateful.

'Really?' he said, sneering. 'Just how could she hear you, since cobras are totally deaf? And why do you call it brother, since it's a female?'

The man's dark eyes seemed to flame, and his hand went to the handle of the knife.

'Are you calling me a liar, sir?'

'My friend has been under a series of strains and stresses of high degree,' I hastily said. 'He is not quite himself. I assure you, sir, whoever you may be, that we are both very grateful to you for having rescued us from a possibly fatal situation. Nor do we doubt for a moment that you and the snake were carrying on a dialogue.

'Allow me to introduce us. That gentleman is Mr. Sherlock Holmes, of whom you may have heard, and I am his colleague, Doctor John H. Watson.'

'Another madman!' Holmes said, though softly. The ears of the stranger must have been singularly keen because he frowned and looked strangely at Holmes. However, he then grinned, but this did not ease my apprehension. His facial expression reminded me of Chaucer's line about 'the smiler with the knife.'

Holmes had by then somewhat regained his composure and was no doubt regretting his hasty and ill-considered words. He said, 'Yes, we owe you a great debt of gratitude.'

Then, his keen grey eyes narrowed, a slight smile – of triumph? – playing about his lips, he said, 'Sir Mowgli of the Seeonee, I presume?'

VIII

Our saviour was visibly startled. He said, 'We have met before? I don't remember your odor!'

'There is no reason to get personal,' Holmes said. 'No,

Sir Mowgli, we have not met elsewhere. But it is obvious to me that you must be that man who claims to have been reared from infancy by wolves, the man of whom Rudyard Kipling wrote so strikingly and beautifully. You are Mowgli – that is, translated from the universal jungle language, Frog. You are obviously of that branch of the dark Caucasian race which principally inhabits the chief jewel on the diadem of the British Empire, India. You are not of the light-skinned Caucasion branch to which several feral human beings of the African area belong. That is, to name a few, Tarzan the Ape-Man, Kaspa the Lion-Man, Kungai the Leopard-Man, Miota the Jackal-Girl, Ka-Zar the Lion-Man, Kalu the Baboon-Boy, Azan the Ape-Man, and several others whose names and titles I do not recall. All are said to be roaming the jungles and veldts of the Dark Continent, consorting with their various hairy companions, and breaking the necks or gashing the throats of evil men.

'You claim . . . I mean . . . you speak with a cobra and call it your brother, White Hood. So did Mowgli, according to your biographer, Kipling. You go naked, whereas the others I named, though not clad as if they were walking through Trafalgar Square, still are modest enough to wear loincloths of animal origin. Also, I happen to know that Sir Mowgli is in Africa, though I was informed that he was in Central, not East, Africa.'

'Yes, it is obvious, now that you explain it,' the baronet said.

Holmes' face twisted with anger as it does sometimes when I make the same remark.

The baronet said, 'I have heard of both of you, and I have read some of the chronicles of your adventures. I am as surprised at finding you here in this jungle, far away from the great but dingy and misery-ridden metropolis of

London, as you are at encountering me here. How did you happen to come here?'

Holmes told our story. When my companion had finished it, the baronet said, 'You are indeed fortunate to have survived such harrowing experiences.'

He turned and gestured at the bush behind which he had hidden and which again was shaking. He seemed to be indicating to someone to come out from hiding. Presently, that turned out to be so. The head of a white woman came from behind the bush and was followed after some hesitation by the body. She was, it was embarrassingly clear, clad only in a ragged and exceedingly dirty slip. I could not help observing that she had a magnificent figure – much like Irene Adler's, if I may reminisce – but the effect was spoiled by the mud, scratches, and rashes which seemed to cover most of the skin that was exposed, which was considerable.

Her long and curly auburn hair was a tangle of dirt and burrs. One big blue eye was quite beautiful, but the other was swollen shut by an insect bite. Or so I thought at the time.

Despite the scanty and torn attire, the lack of coiffure, and the various disfigurements, I recognized Liza Borden, the actress, whose true name was Mary Anne Liza Murdstone-Malcon, daughter of the Viscount of Utter Bickring, widow of the Earl of Murdstone-Malcon. Who would not recognize the face and body of this beauty who had played the lead female role in such movies as *The Divine Aspasia, Socrates' Wife, The Motor Maid, She Stooped to Holly, The Scarlet Mark,* and *The Witch of Endor?*

But the voice that accompanied that goddess-like beauty made me glad that the movies were silent. Its effect was that of a screech owl's shriek issuing from a nightingale's throat. It was high and whining and nasal and strident, what one might expect from a fishwife or a Siamese cat.

'Oh, gentlemen!' she cried as she ran toward us, purple and red furrowed arms outsretched. 'Save me! Save me!'

She fell sobbing into my arms, and her body shook with uncontrolled grief.

'There, there, you're all right. You are saved,' I said, patting her back.

'Save you from what, Madame?' Holmes said.

She tore herself from my embrace, whirled, and thrust an accusing finger at Sir Mowgli.

'From him the beast! He's an absolute savage, he doesn't know what decency or honor or kindness or consideration or civilization means! He has wronged me, wronged me, violated me many times over, night and day, day and night, despite all my pleas, my tearful protestations . . . !'

There was much more, but I would have felt more strongly about her accusations if I had not recognized that her words were exactly the same as those she had delivered in the film *Mrs. Milton's Revenge*. I will never forget those words, burning white in the subtitles.

'Now, now, my dear,' I said, 'just what do you mean, wronged you? When you say *violated* do you mean by that that . . . ?'

'Yes, I do!' she cried, her rasping voice not only scraping my nerves but driving birds for some distance around to soar screaming from the trees. 'He ravished me, took me against my will! It tears my heart out to utter such words, but I must!'

These words were not from *Mrs. Milton's Revenge* but from *The Divine Aspasia*.

'Sir, is this true?' I sputtered at the wild man. 'And have you no decency, standing naked before a white woman, a noble lady?'

'She's no lady,' he said, grinning, 'except in the titular sense. As for being ravished, it is the ravisher who accuses me, the ravishee-to-be, of being the ravisher. Though, actually, there was no foul deed, no carnal knowledge except for some brief unavoidable contact while I was fighting her off. I even had to blacken her eye and knock her down a few times before she understood that I am faithful to my marriage vows. The wolves take only one mate during their lifetime, and I am brother to the wolf.'

'You lie, you utter cad!' she screamed. She turned to me, and she said, 'Oh, sir, you look like a gentleman! Please defend me!'

'But . . . but . . .' I said, 'he's not attacking you!'

'Then please don't let him! Keep the beast away from me!'

'He will not touch you, I assure you, while I am alive to protect you,' I said.

'Don't worry,' Sir Mowgli said. 'The panther does not mate with the crocodile. Nor the eagle with the skunk. That is the Law of the Jungle, but she knows only the Law of Hollywood, the Law of the British Nobility, and both are decadent.'

'Sir!' I cried, 'a gentleman does not say anything about a lady's honor even if he is wronged!'

'*Ngaayah!*' he said. I supposed that it was an exclamation of disgust in the jungle language, and his spitting on the ground with vigor and his grimace confirmed my surmise.

'If you want to fill your bellies, follow me,' he said, and he walked around the bush out of our sight.

'Aren't you going to do anything?' the countess said.

I harrumphed several times and said, 'Under the, uh, circumstances, there seems little that I can do.'

'Or should,' Holmes said. 'We are not policemen to

131

arrest Sir Mowgli or judges to sentence him. I suggest, Your Ladyship, that you can bring suit against him when we return to civilisation. If we ever do.'

Holmes had winced every time she spoke. To him she was only a rather unpleasant creature who might or might not have just cause for her complaints. He never attended movies, and he had little regard for those who did and for those involved in their making.

He said, 'Your Ladyship, perhaps you would be kind enough to tell me how you came here?'

The countess, suddenly looking nervous, said, 'We'd best follow him. We might get lost.'

'From what you said,' I spoke, 'I'd suppose that you'd like to get rid of him.'

'I don't want to starve to death, you decrepit old simp!' she said. 'Or get eaten by a leopard.'

'Really?' I said coolly.

'Come, Watson,' Holmes said. 'Let's go after the baronet. He may be insane, but he seems to be adjusted to the jungle. He is at present our only hope for survival.'

We walked swiftly after the wild-man baronet; Lady Liza in the lead, and soon we saw his broad brown back, dappled by sunlight and the shadows of leaves. The countess told us her story while we continued to follow the baronet.

The movie, *Mowgli's Revenge*, was being filmed near a village about three hundred miles west of the place where we were. Only a few days had remained before its completion when a messenger had arrived. Though he had carried the letter on a forked stick, he was a British soldier, and the message was an order for Major Sir Mowgli to report to the East African Headquarters as soon as his part in the film was done. The baronet had received orders to that effect when the filming started, but the letter was a reminder. On the final day of shooting, however, trouble with the local natives had erupted. The tribe, led by its chief, had tried to abduct the countess.

'He wanted by fair white body,' she said.

'More likely, she had insulted him, and he wanted revenge,' Holmes muttered in my ear.

The baronet had played his final scene and had set out on foot for the east an hour before the tribe made its raid.

'If it was a raid,' Holmes said softly.

The countess had eluded the lustful chief and his henchmen and had fled eastward. Eventually, she had caught up with Sir Mowgli. To her indignation, he had refused to return and punish the chief and the other troublemakers.

'Probably with good reason,' Holmes said to me. 'He knew who was at fault.'

To her, he said, 'Your Ladyship, you claim that the chief was willing to incur the wrath of the white authorities, perhaps suffer execution, imprisonment certainly, because of his overriding lechery? What tribe, may I ask, did he belong to?'

'The Mbandwana,' she replied. 'What difference does that make?'

'Ah, the Mbandwana,' he said, his eyebrows shooting up. 'I am no anthropologist, My Lady, except among the denizens of London, but I happen to know something about that tribe.'

'Really?' she said coolly, if loudly. After a pause, she said, 'What of them?'

He said in a low voice to me, 'The Mbandwana have as their female ideal very fat women, the closer to a tub of lard, the better. They would regard the countess' body with indifference and even contempt.'

133

To her, he said, 'My Lady, were some of the tribesmen carrying a circular device of iron, a narrow band with a large square piece attached to the front?'

'Why, yes,' she screeched. 'So they were. I have no idea what they were for, but I supposed they were some form of torture instrument.'

'They were,' Holmes said. Aside, he said, 'Actually, they were instruments designed to prevent torture. The Mbandwana put them on the mouths of loud and nagging shrews to shut off their offending voices. Doubtless, the tribesmen intended to silence her. They must have been desperate indeed to attempt muzzling a wealthy, white, and well-known woman, but I can well understand and sympathize with them.'

'What are you saying?' the countess shrilled.

'Nothing of any importance, Your Ladyship,' Holmes said.

She glared at him but did not press her curiosity. A few minutes later, we came into a glade where the baronet was waiting for us. Near him, hanging head down, its hind legs tied by a grass rope to a tree-branch, was a freshly killed forest pig. The baronet had gutted it, and, despite the flies swarming over his face, was devouring a raw and bloody hunk of haunch.

'Lunch!' he said cheerfully, and he handed each of us a slice.

'Good God, are we supposed to eat this uncooked?' Holmes said.

'He's an utter filthy disgusting troglodytish cannibalistic Calibanian boorish savage lycanthropic freak,' the countess said. 'Utterly beyond the pale of humanity.'

'Thank you, Your Ladyship,' the baronet said gravely. 'You are too kind. However, though I'll eat just about anything if circumstances dictate it for survival, I would never eat you, My lady. And, despite the fact that we have been eating raw flesh, I really prefer my meat well cooked. A fire, however, attracts certain creatures whom I would prefer did not suspect our presence.

'For instance, just now I hear sounds in the jungle which indicate that a group of men are moving toward us. They may be Germans and their native askaris. Thus, no fire to draw their attention. Also, I request, and it's a strong request, that you lower your voice. In fact, why don't you just shut up?'

I tried to eat the piece of stinking pork, but I could not manage it despite my hunger. Holmes, however, munched on his as if it were a delicacy offered by one of the finer restaurants in London.

He caught my glance, and he said, 'It's superior to most examples of English cooking.'

I went to the edge of the glade where the loud noises of the countess devouring her pork would not interfere with my hearing. Though I strained my ears, I could detect only the usual sounds one heard in the jungle. After a while, driven by my conscienceless stomach, I returned to the flesh that I had cast down on the ground, wiped it off on my sleeve, and began chewing on it. Holmes was right; it was not so bad.

The wild man wiped some of the blood from his hands with leaves, licked the rest off, and said, 'Those men are getting closer. I'll go see who they are and what they're up to. You all stay here. And keep quiet. That means you, too, Your Ladyship, even if it kills you to do so. Which I hope it does.'

The countess had been squatting like one of those troglodytes she had referred to. Now she rose up and threw her piece of meat at the baronet, but he was disappearing into the green tangle surrounding us.

The missile missed him.

Minutes passed. We sat silently until the countess said, 'I'm going into the bushes.'

'Sir Mowgli said to wait here,' Holmes said sharply.

'To hell with that nigger baronet, that crazy sex-obsessed beast-man!' she said loudly, causing more birds to fly screaming from the trees. 'Anyway, I really have to go!'

'Go?' Holmes said, his eyebrows rising. 'Go where? And why?'

'Yes, go, you dunderhead!' she said. 'I have to take a [word blotted out and a marginal note by Watson to rephrase this scene]! Don't you know that even we aristocracy have to [word blotted out]!'

Holmes blushed, but he said, 'I am well aware that they do; they are no better than Hollywood film actresses or washerwomen and not as good as some.'

'[Word blotted out] you!' the countess cried, and she strode down the trail for about twenty feet and went around a bush.

'I hope a leopard gets her,' said Holmes. 'Or ants crawl up her [word blotted out].'

'Really, Holmes!' I gasped.

'The jungle brings out the worst in us,' he said. 'But it also demands the best – if we are to survive.'

'Your comment was uncharitable,' I said, 'but understandable.'

More silence ensued. Then Holmes burst out, 'How I miss my pipe, Watson! Nicotine is more than an aid to thought, it is a necessity! It's a wonder that anything was done in the sciences and the arts before the discovery of America!'

Absently, he reached out and picked up a stick off the ground. He put it in his mouth, no doubt intending to suck on it as a substitute, however unsatisfactory, for the desiderated pipe. The next moment he leaped up, with a yell that startled me. I cried, 'What have you found, Holmes? What is it?'

'That, curse it!' he shouted and pointed at the stick. It was travelling at a fast rate on a number of thin legs toward a refuge under a log.

'Great Scott!' I said. 'It's an insect, a mimetic!'

'How observant of you,' he said, snarling. But the next moment he was down on his knees and groping after the creature.

'What on earth are you doing?' I said.

'It does taste like tobacco,' he said. 'Expediency is the mark of a . . .'

I never heard the rest. An uproar broke out in the jungle nearby, the shouts of men mortally wounded.

'What is it?' I said. 'Could Mowgli have found the Germans?'

Then I fell silent and clutched him, as he clutched me, while a yell pierced the forest, a yell that froze our blood and hushed the jungle. It sounded to me like the victory cry of a wolf. There are no wild wolves in Africa, so I knew who had uttered that terrifying ululation.

IX

Holmes unfroze and started in the direction of the sound. I said, 'Wait, Holmes! Mowgli ordered us not to leave this place! He must have had his reasons for that!'

'He isn't going to order me around! Not now!' Holmes said. Nevertheless, he halted. It was not a change of mind about the command; it was the crashing of men thrusting through the jungle toward us. We turned and plunged into the bush in the opposite direction while a cry behind us told us that we had been seen. A moment later, heavy hands fell upon us and dragged us down. Someone gave an order in a language unknown to me, and we were jerked roughly to our feet.

Our captors were four tall men of a dark Caucasian race with features somewhat like those of the ancient Persians. They wore thick quilted helmets of some cloth, thin sleeveless shirts, short kilts, and knee-high leather boots. They were armed with small round steel shields, short heavy two-edged swords, heavy two-headed steel axes with long wooden shafts, and bows and arrows.

They said something to us. We looked blank. Then they turned as a weak cry came from the other side of the clearing. One of their own staggered out from the bush only to fall flat on his face and lie there unmoving. His own sword projected from his back.

Seeing this, the men became alarmed, though I suppose they had been alarmed all along. One ran out, examined the man, shook his head, and raced back. We were half-lifted, half-dragged along with them in a mad dash through vegetation that tore and ripped our clothes and us. Evidently they had run up against Mowgli, which was not a thing to be recommended at any time. I didn't know why they burdened themselves with two exhausted old men, but I surmised that it was for no beneficient purpose.

I will not recount in detail that terrible journey. Suffice it to say that we were four days and nights in the jungle, walking all day, trying to sleep at night. We were scratched, bitten, and torn, tormented with itches that wouldn't stop and sometimes sick from insect bites. We went through almost impenetrable jungle and waded waist-deep in swamps which held hordes of blood-sucking leeches. Half of the time, however, we progressed fairly swiftly along paths whose ease of access convinced me that they must be kept open by regular work parties.

The third day we started up a small mountain. The fourth day we went down it by being let down in a bamboo cage suspended by ropes from a bamboo boom. Below us lay the end of a lake that wound out of sight among the precipices that surrounded it. We were moved along at a fast pace toward a canyon into which the arm of the lake ran. Our captors pulled two dugouts out of concealment and we were paddled into the fjord. After rounding a corner, we saw before us a shore that sloped gently upward to a precipice several miles beyond it. A village of bamboo huts with thatched roofs spread along the shore and some distance inland.

The villagers came running when they saw us. A drum began beating some place, and to its beat we were marched up a narrow street and to a hut near the biggest hut. We were thrust into this, a gate of bamboo bars was lashed to the entrance, and we sat against its back wall while the villagers took turns looking in at us. As a whole, they were a good-looking people, the average of beauty being much higher than that seen in the East End of London, for instance. The women wore only long cloth skirts, though necklaces of shells hung around their necks and their long hair was decorated with flowers. The prepubescent children were stark naked.

Presently, food was brought to us. This consisted of delicious baked fish, roasted pgymy antelope, unleavened bread, and a brew that would under other circumstances have been too sweet for my taste. I am not ashamed to admit that Holmes and I gorged ourselves, devouring everything set before us.

I went to sleep shortly afterward, waking after dusk with a start. A torch flared in a stanchion just outside the entance, at which two guards stood. Holmes was sitting near it, reading his *Practical Handbook of Bee Culture, With Some Observations Upon the Segregation of the Queen.* 'Holmes,' I began, but he held up his hand for silence. His keen ears had detected a sound a few seconds before mine did. This swelled to a hubbub with the villagers swarming out while the drum beat again. A moment later we saw the cause of the uproar. Six warriors, with Reich and Von Bork among them, were marching toward us. And while we watched curiously the two Germans were shoved into our hut.

Though both were much younger than Holmes and I, they were in equally bad condition – probably, I suppose, because they had not practised the good old British custom of walking whenever possible. Von Bork refused to talk to us, but Reich, always a gentleman, told us what had happened to his party.

'We too heard the noises and that horrible cry,' he said, referring to the baronet's attack on our captors. 'We made our way cautiously toward it until we saw the carnage in a clearing. There were five dead men sprawled there, and six running in one direction and four in another. Standing with his foot on the chest of the largest corpse was a dark white man, utterly naked, a bloody knife in his hand. He was the one giving that awful cry, which I would swear no human throat could make.

'Three of the men had been pierced with arrows. The other two had obviously had their necks broken. The arrows were just like the dead men's, so I suppose that the killer stole a bow and arrows from them. Or perhaps he is a renegade seeking vengeance on his fellow tribesmen for some reason or other. I whispered to my men to fire at him. Before we could do so, he had leaped up and pulled himself by a branch into a tree, and he was gone. We searched for him for some time without success. Then we started out to the east, but at dusk one of my men fell with an arrow through his neck. The angle of the arrow showed that it had come from above. We looked upward but could see nothing. Then a voice, speaking in excellent German, but with an Oxford accent yet, ordered us to turn back. We were to march to the southwest. If we did not, one of us would die at dusk each day until no one was left. I asked him why we should do this, but there was no reply. Obviously, he had us entirely at his mercy – which, I suspected, from the looks of him, he utterly lacked.'

'He is Major Sir Mowgli of the Seeonee, a British officer and baronet of Indian origin,' Holmes said. 'He is the same Mowgli – or at least claims to be – the same Mowgli of whom Rudyard Kipling wrote in his *Jungle Book*.'

'*Ach, der Wolfmensch!*' Von Bork said. 'But I had thought that he was a myth, a creation of Herr Kipling's imagination!'

'Surely you must have read that the real Mowgli, or a man claiming to be the real one, appeared some time after Kipling's book was published. You must know that he was accepted as the genuine article and eventually inherited a vast fortune and was made a baronet by the queen. For what reason, I forget, though I'm sure that his monetary contributions to certain causes had something to do with it.'

'I read about him, yes,' Von Bork said. 'But . . . ?'

Holmes smiled and shrugged and also said, 'But . . . ?'

Reich continued his story:

'My first concern was the safety and well-being of my men. To have ignored the savage would have been to be brave but stupid. So I ordered the march to the southwest. After two days it became evident that the stalker intended for us to starve to death. All our food was stolen that night, and we dared not leave the line of march to hunt, even

141

though I doubt that we would have been able to shoot anything. The evening of the second day, I called out, begging that he let us at least hunt for food. He must have had some pangs of conscience, some mercy in him after all. That morning we woke to find a freshly killed wild pig, one of those orange-bristled swine, in the centre of the camp. From somewhere in the branches overhead his voice came mockingly. 'Pigs should eat pigs!'

'And so we struggled southwestward until today. We were attacked by these people. The stalker had not ordered us to lay down our arms, so we gave a good account of ourselves. But only Von Bork and I survived, and we were knocked unconscious by the flats of their axes. And marched here, the Lord only knows for what end.'

'I suspect that the Lord of the Jungle, one of Mowgli's unofficial titles, knows,' Holmes said. 'No doubt, he is lurking out there in the jungle somewhere. Oh, by the way, did you happen to see a white woman, an English-woman, while you were out there?'

'No, we did not,' Reich said.

'That's good,' Holmes said.

X

If the wild man did know, he did not appear to tell us what to expect. Several days passed while we slept and ate and talked to Reich. Von Bork continued to ignore us, even though Holmes several times addressed him. Holmes asked him about his health, which I though a strange concern for a man who had not killed us only because he lacked the opportunity.

Holmes seemed especially interested in his left eye, once coming up to within a few inches of it and staring at it. Von Bork became enraged at this close scrutiny.

'Get away from me, British swine!' he yelled. 'Or I will ruin both of your eyes!'

'Permit Dr. Watson to examine it,' Holmes said. 'He might be able to save it.'

'I want no incompetent English physician poking around it,' Von Bork said.

I became so indigant that I lectured him on the very high standards of British medicine, but he only turned his back on me. Holmes chuckled at this and winked at me.

At the end of the week, we were allowed to leave the hut during the day, unaccompanied by guards. Holmes and I were not restrained in any way, though the Germans were hobbled with shackles so that the could not walk very fast. Apparently, our captors decided that Holmes and I were too old to give them much of a run for their money.

We took advantage of our comparative freedom to stroll around the village, inspecting everything and also attempting to learn the language.

'I don't know what family it belongs to,' Holmes said. 'But it is related neither to Cornish nor Chaldean, of that I'm sure.'

Holmes was also interested in the white china of these people, which represented their highest art form. The black figures and designs they painted upon it reminded me somewhat of early Greek vase paintings. The vases and dishes were formed from kaolin deposits which existed to the north near the precipices. I mention this only because the white clay was to play an important part in our salvation in the near future.

At the end of the second week, Holmes, a superb linguist, had attained some fluency in the speech of our captors. 'It belongs to a completely unknown language family,' he said. 'But there are certain words which, degenerated though they are, obviously come from ancient

Persian. I would say at one time these people had contact with a wandering party of descendants of Darius. The party settled down here, and these people borrowed some words from their idiom.'

The village consisted of a hundred huts arranged in concentric circles. Each held a family ranging from two to eight members. Their fields lay north of the village on the slopes leading up to the precipices. The stock consisted of goats, pigs, and dwarf antelopes. Their alcoholic drink was a sort of mead made from the honey of wild bees. A few specimens of these ventured near the village, and Holmes secured some for study. They were about an inch long, striped black and white, and were armed with a long venom-ejecting barb. Holmes declared that they were of a new species, and he saw no reason not to classify them as *Apis holmesi*.

Once a week a party set out to the hills to collect honey. Its members were always clad in leather clothing and gloves and wore veils over their hats. Holmes asked permission to accompany them, explaining that he was wise in the ways of bees. To his disappointment, they refused him. A further inquiry by him resulted in the information that there was a negotiable, though difficult, pass through the precipices. It was used only for emergency purposes because of the vast number of bees that filled the narrow pass. Holmes obtained his data by questioning a child. Apparently, the adults had not thought to tell their young to keep silent about this means of exit.

'The bee-warding equipment is kept locked up in their temple,' Holmes said. 'And that makes it impossible to obtain it for an escape attempt.'

The temple was the great hut in the village's centre. We were not allowed to enter it or even to approach it within thirty feet. Through some discreet inquiries, and unashamed eavesdropping, Holmes discovered that the high priestess-and-queen lived within the temple. We had never seen her nor were we likely to do so. She had been born in the temple and was to reside there until she died. Just why she was so restricted Holmes could not determine. His theory was that she was a sort of hostage to the gods.

'Perhaps, Watson, she is confined because of a superstition that arose after the catastrophe which their myths say deluged this land and the great civilisation it haboured. The fishermen tell me they often see on the bottom of this lake the sunken ruins of the stone houses in which their ancestors lived. A curse was laid upon the land, they say, and they hint that only by keeping the high priestess-cum-queen inviolate, unseen by profane eyes, untouched by anyone after pubescence, can the wrath of the gods be averted. They are cagey in what they say, so I have had to surmise certain aspects of their religion.'

'That's terrible!' I said.

'The deluge?'

'No, that a woman should be denied freedom and love.'

'She has a name, but I have never overheard it. They refer to her as The Beautiful One.'

'Is there nothing we can do for her?' I said.

'I do not know that she wants to be helped. You must not allow your well-known gallantry to endanger us. But to satisfy a legitimate scientific interest, if anthropology is a science, we could perhaps attempt a look inside the temple. Its roof has a large circular hole in its centre. If we could get near the top of the high tree about twenty yards from it, we could look down into the building.'

'With the whole village watching us?' I said. 'No, Holmes, it is impossible to get up the tree unobserved during the day. And if we did so during the night, we could see nothing because of the darkness. In any event, it would probably mean instantaneous death even to make the attempt.'

'There are torches lit in the building at night,' he said. 'Come, Watson, if you have no taste for this arboreal adventure, I shall go it alone.'

And that was why, despite my deep misgivings, we climbed that towering tree on a cloudy night. After Von Bork and Reich had fallen asleep and our guards had dozed off and the village was silent except for a chanting in the temple, we crept out of our hut. Holmes had hidden a rope the day before, but even with this it was no easy task. We were not youths of twenty, agile as monkeys and as fearless aloft. Holmes threw the weighted end of the rope over the lowest branch, which was twenty feet up, and tied the two ends together. Then, grasping the rope with both hands, and bracing his feet against the trunk, he half-walked almost perpendicular to the trunk, up the tree. On reaching the branch, he rested for a long time while he gasped for breath so loudly that I feared he would wake up the nearest villagers. When he was quite recovered, he called down to me to make the ascent. Since I was heavier and several years older, and lacked his feline muscles, having more the physique of a bear, I experienced great difficulty in getting up. I wrapped my legs around the rope – no walking at a ninety-degree angle for me – and painfully and gaspingly hauled myself up. But I persisted – after all, I am British – and Holmes pulled me up at the final stage of what I was beginning to fear was my final journey.

After resting, we made a somewhat easier ascent via the branches to a position about ten feet below the top of the tree. From there we could look almost directly down through the hole in the middle of the roof. The torches within enabled us to see its interior quite clearly.

Both of us gasped when we saw the woman standing in the centre of the building by a stone altar. She was a beautiful woman, surely one of the daintiest things that ever graced this planet. She had long golden hair and eyes that looked dark from where we sat but which, we later found out, were a deep grey. She was wearing nothing except a necklace of some stones that sparkled as she moved. Though I was fascinated, I also felt something of shame, as if I were a peeping tom. I had to remind myself that the women wore nothing above the waist in their everyday attire and that when they swam in the lake they wore nothing at all. So we were doing nothing immoral by this spying. Despite this reasoning, my face (and other things) felt inflamed.

She stood there, doing nothing for a long time, which I expected would make Holmes impatient. He did not stir or make any comment, so I suppose that this time he did not mind a lack of action. The priestesses chanted and the priests walked around in a circle making signs with their hands and their fingers. Then a bound he-goat was brought in and placed on the altar, and, after some more mumbo-jumbo, the woman cut its throat. The blood was caught in a golden bowl and passed around in a sort of communion, the woman drinking first.

'A most unsanitary arrangement,' I murmured to Holmes.

'These people are, nevertheless, somewhat cleaner than your average Londoner,' Holmes replied. 'And much more cleanly than your Scots peasant.'

I was about to take umbrage at this, since I am of Scots descent on my mother's side. Holmes knew this and my sensitivity about it. He had been making too many

147

remarks of this nature recently, and though I attributed them to irritability arising from nicotine withdrawal, I was, to use an American phrase, getting fed up with them. I was about to remonstrate when my heart leaped into my throat and choked me.

A hand had come from above and clamped down upon my shoulder. I knew that it wasn't Holmes' because I could see both of his hands.

XI

Holmes almost fell off the branch but was saved by another hand, which grapsed him by the collar of his shirt. A familiar voice said, 'Silence!'

'Mowgli!' I gasped. And then, remembering that, after all, he was a baronet, I said, 'Your pardon. I mean, Sir Mowgli.'

'What are you doing up here, you baboon!' Holmes said.

I was shocked at this, though I knew that Holmes spoke thus only because he must have been thoroughly frightened. To address a baronet in this manner was not his custom.

'Tut, tut, Holmes,' I said.

'Tut, tut, yourself,' he replied. 'He's not paying me a fee! He's no client of mine. Besides, I doubt that he is entitled to his title!'

A growl that lifted the hairs on the back of my neck came from above. It was followed by the descent of the baronet's heavy body upon our branch, which bent alarmingly. But he squatted upon it, his hands free, with all the sense of balance of the baboon he had been accused of being.

'What does that last remark mean?' the baronet said.

At that moment the moon broke through the clouds. A ray fell upon Holmes' face, which had become as pale as when he was pretending to be sick in that case which I have titled 'The Adventure of the Dying Detective.'

Holmes said, 'This is neither the time nor the place for an investigation of your credentials. We are in a desperate plight, and . . .'

'You don't realize how desperate,' the baronet interrupted. 'I usually abide by human laws when I am in civilisation. But this is the jungle, and here I obey the Law of the Jungle as I learned it from Baloo, the Blind Brown Bear, the Law of the Seeonee Wolf-Pack, of Chil the Kite, Bagheera the Black Panther, and Kaa the Rock Python. And here, even though this is not my native land, India, in the central part of which I am king, not a mere baronet, I revert to my primal and happiest state, that of Mowgli, the Frog, brother to the Wolf and to Hathi, the Silent One, the Elephant . . .'

Good Lord! I thought. How this man does run on! I had supposed that feral men were reticent and laconic types who spoke seldom and then only in short declarative sentences. This man talked as if he were one of James Fenimore Cooper's noble savages.

' . . . then I obey my own laws, not those of humanity, for which I have the greatest contempt, barring a few specimens of such . . .'

(There was much more in this single statement, the length of which would have made any German philosopher proud. The gist of it was that if Holmes did not explain his remark now, he would have no chance to do so later. Nor was the baronet backward in stating that I would not be taking any news of Holmes' fate to the outside world.)

'He means it, Holmes!' I said.

'I am well aware of that, Watson. He is covered only

149

with a thin veneer of civilisation. Very well, Your Highness. It is not my custom to set forth a theory until I have enough evidence to make it a fact. But under the circumstances . . .'

I looked for Sir Mowgli to show some resentment at Holmes' sarcastic use of a title appropriate only to a monarch. He, however, only smiled. This, I believe, was a reaction of pleasure, of ignorance of Holmes' intent to cut him. He was sure that he deserved the title, and now that I have had time to reflect on it, I agree with him. He ruled a kingdom many times larger than our tight little isle. And he paid no taxes in it.

'The very fact that you threaten me,' Holmes said, 'tells me that I have some basis of validity in my reasoning.'

I thought that he spoke bravely but indiscreetly and it was discretion that was called for now. But I kept silent.

'I believe that the real Mowgli, if he exists or ever did exist, would be incapable of such a threat, Kipling's accounts of the Wolf-Boy's exploits lead me to believe that Mowgli would be of a high moral character. The genuine Mowgli, if he existed, would only have laughed at my hints of fraud.'

The baronet shifted his weight so that the branch under him creaked. The moon glittered on the sharp blade. He was scowling fiercely.

'What do you know of the true nature of the Wolf's Brother, Two-Legs?' he said harshly.

Holmes, seemingly unperturbed, replied, 'As I said, I know only what I've read about him. However, I have arrived at my conclusions through observation of you combined with my trifling powers of deduction. Which some, however, have been kind enough to state are those of a genius. Disregrading this, I still have some gifts worthy of consideration . . .'

Holmes, I thought, you are as wordy as the wild man.

'One of my dictums is that, when you have eliminated the impossible, whatever is left, however improbable, is the truth.'

'I have read that statement in Doctor Watson's narratives,' the baronet said. 'It's full of (word blotted out). What if you haven't included everything that could happen. What if you've overlooked something or are incapable of enough deductive powers to see all the patterns of certain clues? You may be a genius, Mr. Detective, but I have read some cases in which you made some serious, even stupid, errors.'

Even in the moonlight, I could see Holmes flush. But he did not reply sharply, perhaps because of the sharp edge so close to his jugular vein.

'Nevertheless,' he said determinedly, 'it is impossible for animals to talk. They may communicate by a rather limited system of signals. But they cannot use language. They are not sentient creatures like *Homo sapiens*.

'It is improbable, though barely possible, that a human infant could be raised by wolves. But it is impossible that wolves could have true speech. Therefore, Kipling's account is obviously fictitious. His *Jungle Book* is merely an extension of ancient myths, primitive folk-tales, and medieval fairy tales wherein animals do have speech.

'Thus, there was no Mowgli who talked to animals. It is highly improbable that there was a Mowgli of any kind.

'But, in 1899, a man claiming to be the genuine Wolf-Boy appeared in Bombay, having travelled all the way from the Seeonee Hills on foot. Or so he said. His claim was widely publicized, and he was the subject of much speculation, pro and con, by various notable personages and authorities. Not to mention some rather lunatic people.

'Investigation showed, or seemed to show, that the alleged Mowgli was indeed the son of a woodchopper and his wife and that they had been killed by a tiger and that the infant had disappeared.

'Further investigation revealed that the woodchopper was not a Hindu but a Parsee. Parsees are, as you know, the descendants of Persian fire-worshippers, Zoroastrians, who fled their native land when the Arab Moslems conquered it. They settled in India so that they could have freedom of worship.

'The woodchopper was a poor relative of Sir Jametsee Jejeebhoy, the Parsee baronet of Bombay. The woodchopper had at one time visited his wealthy second cousin to show him his son. The infant was flawless except for a red birthmark between the big toe and the next toe on the left foot. The man claiming to be Mowgli had such a birthmark.'

'As you see,' the baronet said, sticking out a singularly muscular leg and spreading his toes.

'That could be a fortunate coincidence and, in fact, the basis for action in a fraudulent claim,' Holmes said.

'*Ngaayah!*' the baronet snarled. 'You disgust me.'

'Sir Jametsee, son of the late baronet and himself childless, adopted Mowgli. When Sir Jametsee died, Mowgli inherited his vast fortune and, a few year later, was given a baronetcy by our queen.'

'I was investigated by Scotland Yard,' Sir Mowgli said. 'They found nothing wrong.'

'But they did not prove your claim,' Holmes said. 'They did not apply my deductive and investigative techniques. Their methods were, I regret to say, much like those of the inept and late Inspector Lestrade.'

Sir Mowgli shrugged his heavy shoulders.

'What do I care what you believe?'

'What I plan to do,' Holmes said, 'is to go to India when the war is over and investigate your claim. I will be a bloodhound, relentless, sniffing out every clue, true or false. I will pursue the trail to its end.'

'Why should you do that?' the baronet said.

'The truth is not only a means but the end. It is its own reward.'

I was trying to puzzle that out when the baronet said, 'I could kill you now and prevent all that trouble and publicity. I am heartily tired of such, I assure you. However . . .'

After a long pause, Holmes said, 'Yes?'

'It would be worth it to avoid such an investigation. Not because I am afraid of the truth, I'm not, but because I am weary of publicity.'

'Is that why you played yourself in a movie which will be shown everywhere on Earth?' Holmes said.

'Don't try me!' the baronet said huskily, and his knife flashed.

'Yes, my dear Holmes,' I said in, I fear, a trembling voice. 'There is no need to antagonize our only ally, our only hope for escape.'

'You are a sensible man, Doctor Watson,' the baronet said. 'Would that your colleague were. Very well. I have a proposition to make, Mr. Holmes. What if I hired you to investigate my claim, to ferret out the truth of my story?'

'What?' I said. His offer was so unexpected.

Holmes, however, was not startled. He seemed to have anticipated the suggestion.

'Such a project would require great expenses,' he said calmly.

'I believe it would. Tell me, what is the largest fee you ever received?'

'The highest was in the case of the Priory School.

153

Twelve thousand pounds.'

Quickly, he added, 'Of course, that sum was only *my* fee. Watson, as my colleague in the case, received the same amount.'

'Really Holmes,' I murmured.

'Twenty-four thousand pounds,' the baronet said, frowning.

'That fee was paid in 1901,' Holmes said. 'Inflation has sent prices sky-high since then, and the income tax rate is ascending as if it were a rocket.'

'For Heaven's sake, Holmes!' I cried. 'I do not see the necessity for this fishmarket bargaining! Surely . . .'

Holmes coldly interrupted. 'You will please leave the financial arrangements to me, the senior partner and the true professional in this matter.'

'You'll antagonize Sir Mowgli and . . .'

'Would sixty thousand pounds be adequate?' the baronet said.

'Well,' Holmes said, hesitating, 'God knows how wartime conditions will continue to cheapen the price of money in the next few years.'

The baronet turned the knife over as if he were considering using it.

'You are most generous,' Holmes said quickly. 'Sixty thousand pounds . . . quite satisfactory.'

I could not understand why the baronet would hire anyone to look into his claim unless he truly believed that it was valid. But Holmes, I was certain from his expression, did not have the same faith. I was wondering how I could find out just what Holmes was thinking when the baronet changed the subject.

'I travelled in this area before I agreed to make the movie. I went alone, unencumbered by a safari, and I discovered, rediscovered, I should say, this hidden land, I said nothing about it when I returned to civilization because I did not want these people invaded by hordes of Europeans bearing their usual gifts of gin, disease, and their thousand means of exploitation.'

He paused, then said, 'I also discovered that this is the land of Zu-Vendis.'

'What?' I said. 'You mean that the unknown civilization described by H. Rider Haggard in his novel, *Allan Quatermain*, is not fiction?'

Exactly,' the baronet said. Haggard presented the true adventures of the hunter and explorer. Allan Quatermain, as fiction because he, like me, did not want this country devastated.'

'Then we are the prisoners of the people of Zu-Vendis?' I said.

'Not for long, if I can help it,' said the baronet. 'However, either Quatermain or his agent and editor, Haggard, exaggerated the size of Zu-Vendis. It was supposed to be about the size of France but actually covered an area equal to that of Liechtenstein. In the main, however, except for the size of and location of Zu-Vendis, Quatermain's account is true. He was accompanied on his expedition by two Englishmen, a baronet, Sir Henry Curtis, and a naval captain, John Good. And that great Zulu warrior, Umslopogaas, a man whom I would have liked to have known. After the Zulu and Quatermain died, Curtis sent Quatermain's manuscript of the adventure to Haggard. Haggard apparently added some things of his own to give more verisimilitude to the chronicle. For one thing, he said that several British commissions were investigating Zu-Vendis with the intent of finding a more accessible means of travel to it. This was not so. Zu-Vendis was never found, except by me, and that is why most people concluded that the account was pure fiction.

Shortly after the manuscript was sent out by one of the natives who had accompanied the Quatermain party, the entire valley except for this high end was flooded.'

'Then poor Curtis and Good and their lovely Zu-Vendis wives were drowned?' I said.

'No,' the baronet said. 'They were among the dozen or so who reached safety. Apparently, they either could not get out of the valley then or decided to stay here. After all, Nylepthah, Curtis' wife, was the queen, and she would not want to abandon her people, few though they were. The two Englishmen settled down, taught the people the use of the bow, among other things, and died here. They were buried up in the hills.'

'What a sad story!' I said.

'All people must die,' Sir Mowgli replied, as if that told the whole story of the world. And perhaps it did.

He looked out at the temple, saying, 'That woman at whom you have been staring with a non-quite-scientific detachment . . .'

'Yes?' I said.

'Her name is also Nylepthah. She is the granddaughter of both Good and Curtis.'

'Will wonders never cease!' I said.

The baronet cleared his throat and said, 'Oh, yes, before I forget it . . .'

Holmes smiled as if he had been expecting that the baronet would recall something.

'I will pay you your fee as soon as possible. But you must not begin your investigation until I tell you that the time is ripe for it. I am a very busy man, I have much business to conduct, and it might be inconvenient for me to have to attend to you until I have certain matters cleared up. This might take a long time. Meanwhile, you will have the fee in your hands, and there will be no question asked about how you two handle the sums.

'Do you understand?'

'Perfectly, Holmes said, smiling even more broadly. 'We will await your consent to begin the investigation. No matter how much time passes.'

'Ah, then you do understand,' the baronet said quietly.

'Yes. The fee will enable me to live quite well in my retirement. I had enough when I first retired, but many of my investments went bad, and . . .'

'Can't you think about anything but money, Holmes!' I said. 'We must do something about that poor British woman parading around naked before those savages and held in close captivity!'

The baronet shrugged and said, 'It's their custom.'

'We must rescue her and get her back to the home of her ancestors!' I cried.

'Be quiet, Watson, or you'll have the whole pack howling for our blood,' Holmes growled. 'She seems quite contented with her lot. Or could it be,' he added, looking hard at me, 'that you have once agin fallen into love?'

He made it sound as if the grand passion were an open privy. Blushing, I said, 'I must admit that there is a certain feeling . . .'

'Well, the fair sex is your department,' he said. 'But really, Watson, at your age!'

('The Americans have a proverb,' I said. 'The older the buck, the stiffer the horn.')

'Be quiet, both of you,' the baronet said. 'I permitted the Zu-Vendis to capture you because I knew you'd be safe for a while. I drove the Germans this way because I expected that they would, like you, be picked up by the Zu-Vendis. Tomorrow night, all four of you prisoners are secheduled to be sacrificed on the temple altar. I got back an hour ago to get you two out.'

157

'That was cutting it close, wasn't it?' Holmes said.

'You mean to leave Von Bork and Reich here?' I said. 'To be slaughtered like sheep? And what about the woman, Nylepthah? What kind of life is that, being confined from birth to death in that house, being denied the love and companionship of a husband, forced to murder poor devils of captives?'

'Yes,' said Holmes. 'Reich is a very decent fellow and should be treated like a prisoner of war. I wouldn't mind at all if Von Bork were to die, but only he knows the location of the SP papers. The fate of Britain, of her allies, hangs on those papers. As for the woman, well, she is of good British stock and it seems a shame to leave her here in this squalidness.'

'So she can go to London and perhaps live in squalour there?' the baronet said.

'I'll see to it that that does not happen,' I said. 'You can have back my fee if you take that woman along.'

The baronet laughed softly and said, 'I couldn't refuse a man who loves love more than he loves money. And you can keep the fee.'

XII

At some time before dawn, the baronet entered our hut. The Germans were also waiting for him, since we had told them what to expect if they did not leave with us. He gestured for silence, unnecessarily, I thought, and we followed him outside. The two guards, gagged and trussed-up, lay by the door. Near them stood Nylepthah, also gagged, her hands bound before her and rope hobbling her. Her glorious body was concealed in a cloak. The baronet removed the hobble, gestured to us, took the woman by the arm, and we walked silently through the village. Out immediate goal was the beach, where we intended to steal two boats. We would paddle to the foot of the cliff on top of which was the bamboo boom and ascend the ropes. Then we would cut the rope so that we could not be followed. Sir Mowgli had come down on the rope after disposing of the guards at the boom. He would climb back up the rope and then pull us up.

Our plans died in the bud. As we approached the beach, we saw torches flaring on the water. Presently, as we watched from behind a hut, we saw fishermen paddling in with their catch of night-caught fish. Someone stirred in the hut beside which we crouched, and before we could get away, a woman, yawning and stretching came out. She must have been waiting for her fisherman husband. Whatever the case, she surprised us.

The baronet moved swiftly, but too late, toward her. She screamed loudly, and though she quit almost immediately, she had aroused the village.

There is no need to go into detail about the long and exhausting run we made through the village, while the people poured out, and up the slopes toward the faraway pass in the precipices. The baronet smote right and left and before him, and men and women went down like the Philistines before Samson. We were armed with the short swords he had stolen from the armory and so were of some aid to him. But by the time we had left the village and reached the fields, Holmes and I were breathing very hard.

'You two help the woman along between you,' Sir Mowgli commanded the Germans. Before we could protest, though what good it would have done if we had I don't know, we were picked up, one under each arm, and carried off. Burdened though he was, the baronet ran faster than the three behind him. The ground, only about a foot away from my face since I was dangling like a rag doll in his arm, reeled by. After about a mile. Sir Mowgli stopped and released us. He did this my simply dropping us. My face hit the dirt at the same time my knees did. I was somewhat pained, but I thought it indiscreet to complain. Holmes, however, displayed a knowledge of swear words which would have delighted a dock worker. The baronet ignored him, urging us to push on. Far behind us we could see the torches of our pursuers and hear their clamour.

By dawn the Zu-Vendis had gotten closer. All of us, except for the indefatigable Wolf-Man, were tiring swiftly. The pass was only a half mile away, and once we were through that, he said, we would be safe. The savages behind us, though, were beginning to shoot their arrows at us.

'We can't get through the pass anyway!' I said between gasps to Holmes. 'We have no equipment to keep the bees of us! If the arrows don't kill us, the bee-stings will!'

Ahead of us, where the hills suddenly moved in and formed the entrance to the path, a vast buzzing filled the air. Fifty thousand tiny, but deadly, insects swirled in a thick cloud as they prepared to voyage to the sea of flowers which held the precious nectar.

We stopped to catch our breath and consider the situation.

'We can't go back and we can't go ahead!' I said. 'What shall we do?'

The baronet pointed at the nearby hill, at the base of which was the white clay used by the Zu-Vendis to make their fine pots and dishes.

'Coat yourselves with that!' he said. 'It should be somewhat of a shield!' And he hastened to take his own advice.

160

I hesitated. The baronet had stripped off his loin-cloth and had jumped into the stream which ran nearby. Then he had scooped out with his hands a quantity of clay, had mixed it with water, and was smearing it over him everywhere. Holmes was removing his clothing before going into the stream. The Germans were getting ready to do likewise, while the beautiful Nylepthah stood abandoned. I did the only thing a gentleman could do. I went to her and removed her cloak, under which she wore nothing. I told her in my halting Zu-Vendis that I was ready to sacrifice myself for her. Though the bees, alarmed, were now moving in a great cloud toward us, I would make sure that I smeared the clay all over her before I took care of myself.

Nylepthah said, 'I know an easier way to escape the bees. Let me run back to the village.'

'Poor deluded girl!' I said. 'You do not know what is best for you! Trust me, and I will see you safely to England, the home of your ancestors. And then . . .'

I did not get a chance to promise to marry her. Holmes and the Germans cried out, causing me to look up just in time to see Sir Mowgli falling unconscious to the ground. An arrow had hit him in the head, and though it had struck a glancing blow, it had knocked him out and made a large nasty wound.

I thought we were indeed lost. Behind us was the howling hordes of savages, their arrows and spears and axes flying through the air at us. Ahead was a swarm of giant bees, a cloud so dense that I could barely see the hills behind them. The buzzing was deafening. The one man who was strong enough and jungle wise enough to pull us through was out of action for the time being. And if the bees attacked soon, which they would do, he would be in that state permanently. So would all of us.

161

Holmes shouted at me. 'Never mind taking advantage of that woman, Watson! Come here, quickly, and help me!'

'This is no time to indulge in jealousy, Holmes,' I muttered, but nevertheless I obeyed him. 'No, Watson,' Holmes said. 'I'll put on the clay! You daub on me that excellent black dirt there along the banks of the stream! Put it on in stripes, thus, white and black alternating!'

'Have you gone mad, Holmes?'

'There's no time to talk,' said Holmes. 'The bees are almost upon us! Oh, they are deadly, deadly, Watson! Quick, the mud!'

Within a minute, striped like a zebra, Holmes stood before me. He ran to the pile of clothes and took from the pocket of his jacket the large magnifying glass that had been his faithful companion all these years. And then he did something that caused me to cry out in utter despair. He ran directly toward the deadly buzzing cloud.

I shouted after him as I ran to drag him away from his futile and senseless act. It was too late to get him away from the swiftly advancing insects. I knew that, just as I knew that I would die horribly with him. Nevertheless, I would be with him. We had been comrades too many years for me to even contemplate for a second abandoning him.

He turned when he heard my voice and shouted, 'Go back, Watson! Go back! Get the others to one side! Drag the baronet out of their path! I know what I'm doing! Get away! I command you, Watson!'

The conditioning of our many years of association turned me and sent me back to the group. I'd obeyed his orders too long to refuse them now. But I was weeping, convinced that he was out of his mind, or, if he did have a plan, it would fail. I got Reich to help me drag the senseless and heavily bleeding baronet half into the stream, and I ordered Von Bork and Nylepthah to lie

162

down in the stream. The clay coating, I was convinced, was not an adequate protection. We could submerge ourselves when the bees passed over us. The stream was only inches deep, but perhaps the water flowing over our bodies would discourage the insects.

Lying in the stream, holding Sir Mowgli's head up to keep him from drowning, I watched Holmes.

He had indeed gone crazy. He was dancing around and around, stopping now and then to bend over and wiggle his buttocks in a most undignified manner. Then he would hold up the magnifying glass so that the sunlight flashed through it at the Zu-Vendis. These, by the way, had halted to stare open-mouthed at Holmes.

'Whatever are you doing?' I shouted.

He shook his head angrily at me to indicate that I should keep quiet. At that moment I became aware that he was himself making a loud buzzing sound. It was almost submerged in the louder noise of the swarm, but I was near enough to hear it faintly.

Again and again Holmes whirled, danced, stopped, pointing his wriggling buttocks at the Zu-Vendis savages and letting the sun pass through the magnifying glass at a certain angle. His actions seemed to puzzle not only the humans but the bees. The swarm had stopped its forward movement and it was hanging in the air, seemingly pointed at Holmes.

Suddenly, as Holmes completed his obscene dance for the seventh time, the swarm flew forward. I cried out, expecting to see him covered with the huge black-and-white striped horrors. But the mass split in two, leaving him an island in their midst. And then they were all gone, and the Zu-Vendis were running away screaming, their bodies black and fuzzy with a covering of bees. Some of them dropped in their flight, rolling back and forth,

163

screaming, batting at the insects, and then becoming still and silent.

I ran to Holmes, crying, 'How did you do it?'

'Do you remember your scepticism when I told you that I had made an astounding discovery? One that will enshrine my name among the greats in the hall of science?'

'You don't mean . . .?'

He nodded. 'Yes, bees do have a language, even African bees. It is actually a system of signals, not a true language. Bees who have discovered a new source of honey return to the hive and there perform a dance which indicates clearly the direction of and the distance at which the honey lies. I have also discovered that the bee communicates the advent of an enemy to the swarm. It was this dance which I performed, and the swarm attacked the indicated enemy, The Zu-Vendis. The dance movements are intricate, and certain polarisations of light play a necessary part in the message. These I simulated with my magnifying glass. But come, Watson, let us get our clothes on and be off before the swarm returns! I do not think I can pull that trick again. We do not want to be the game afoot.'

We got the baronet to his feet and half-carried him to the pass. Though he recovered consciousness, he seemed to have reverted to a totally savage state. He did not attack us but he regarded us suspiciously and made threatening growls if we got too close. We were at a loss to explain this frightening change in him. The frightening part came not so much from any danger he represented as from the dangers he was supposed to save us from. We had depended upon him to guide us and to feed us and protect us on the way back. Without him even the incomparable Holmes was lost.

Fortunately, the baronet recovered the next day and provided the explanation himself.

'For some reason I seem to be prone to receiving blows on the head,' he said. 'I have a thick skull, but every once in a while I get such a blow that even its walls cannot withstand the force. Sometimes, say about one out of three times, a complete amnesia results. I then revert to the state in which I was before I encountered white people. I am once again the uncivilised Wolf-Man. I have no memory of anything that occurred before I was fourteen years old. This state may last for only a day, as you have seen, or it may persist for months.'

'I would venture to say,' Holmes said, 'that this readiness to forget your contact with civilised peoples indicates an unconscious desire to avoid them. You are happiest when in the jungle and with no obligations. Hence your unconscious seizes upon every opportunity, such as a blow on the head, to go back to the happy primal time.'

'Perhaps you are right,' the baronet said. 'I would like to forget civilisation even exists.'

Later, when Holmes and I were alone, Holmes said, 'The man is a fraud but a magnificent fraud, I'm convinced of that. However, he is in a sense not a liar. He truly belives that he is Mowgli, brother to the Wolves, the Black Panther, and the Brown Bear. In the beginning, he was a hoaxer, for profit, I'm certain. But he cast himself so thoroughly into the role that he became insane, descended into a madness reflecting Kipling's world of *The Jungle Book*. It is, however a rather harmless insanity and one profitable for us.'

'Holmes,' I said, 'I've been meaning to speak to you about this. Don't you think that there's extortion involved in this, a form of blackmail . . .'

He drew himself up and cut me off sharply.

'Not at all! I am ready to begin the investigation, a sincere one to which I shall apply a lifetime of experience, the moment he gives the word.'

'Which he is not going to do,' I said.

'We don't know that,' he said. 'Besides, that's his business.'

It took more than a month for us to get to Nairobi. During the journey, I had ample time to teach Nylepthah the English language and to get well acquainted with her. Before we reached the Lake Victoria railhead, I had proposed to her and been accepted. I will never forget that night. The moon was bright, and a hyena was laughing nearby.

The day before we reached the railhead, the baronet went up a tree to check out the territory. A branch broke under his feet, and he landed on his head. When he regained consciousness, he was again the Wolf-Man. We could not come near him without his baring his teeth and growling menacingly. And that night he disappeared.

Holmes was very downcast by this. 'What if he never gets over his amnesia, Watson? Then we will be cheated out of our fees.'

'My dear Holmes,' I said, somewhat coolly, 'we never earned the fee in the first place. Actually, we were allowing ourselves to be bribed by the baronet to keep silent.'

'You never did understand the subtle interplay of economics and ethics,' Holmes replied.

'There goes Von Bork,' I said, glad to change the subject. I pointed to the fellow, who was sprinting across the veldt as if a lion were after him.

'He is mad if he thinks he can make his way alone to German East Africa,' Holmes said. 'But we must go after him! He has on him the formula for the SB.'

'Where?' I asked for the hundredth time. 'We have stripped him a dozen times and gone over every inch of his clothes and his skin. We have looked into his mouth and up . . .'

At that moment I observed Von Bork turn his head to the right to look at a rhinoceros which had come around a tall termite hill. The next moment, he had run the left side of his head and body into an acacia tree with such force that he bounced back several feet. He did not get up, which was just as well. The rhinoceros was looking for him and would have detected any movement by Von Bork. After prancing around and sniffing the air in several directions, the weak-eyed beast trotted off. Holmes and I hastened to Von Bork before he got his senses back and ran off once more.

'I believe I know where the formula is,' Holmes said.

'And how could you know that?' I said, for the thousandth time since I had first met him.

'I will bet my fee against yours that I can show you the formula within the next two minutes,' he said, but I did not reply.

He kneeled down beside the German, who was lying on his back, his mouth and eyes open. His pulse, however, beat strongly.

Holmes spaced the tips of his thumb under Von Bork's left eye. I stared aghast as the eye popped out.

'It's glass, Watson,' Holmes said. 'I had suspected that for some time, but I saw no reason to verify my suspicions until he was in a British prison. I was certain that his vision was limited to his right side when I saw him run into that tree. Even with his head turned away he would have seen it if his left eye had been effective.'

He rotated the glass eye between thumb and finger while examining it through the magnifying glass. 'Aha!' he exclaimed and then, handing the eye and glass to me, said, 'See for yourself, Watson.'

'Why,' I said, 'what I had thought were massive haemorrhages due to eye injury are tiny red lines of chemical formulae on the surface of the glass – if it *is* glass, and not some special material prepared to receive inscriptions.'

'Very good, Watson,' Holmes said. 'Undoubtedly, Von Bork did not merely receive an injury to the eye in that motor-car crash of which I heard rumours. He lost it, but the wily fellow had it replaced with an artificial eye which had more uses than – ahem – met the eye.

'After stealing the SB formula, he inscribed the surface of this false organ with the symbols. These, except through a magnifier, look like the results of dissipation or of an accident. He must have been laughing at us when we examined him so thoroughly, but he will laugh no more.'

He took the eye back and pocketed it. 'Well, Watson, let us rouse him from whatever dreams he is indulging in and get him into the proper hands. This time he shall pay the penalty for espionage.'

Two months later were were back in England. We travelled by water, despite the danger of U-boats, since Holmes had sworn never again to get into an aircraft of any type. He was in a bad humour throughout the voyage. He was certain that the baronet, even if he recovered his memory, would not send the promised cheques.

He turned the glass eye over to Mycroft, who sent it on to his superiors. That was the last we ever heard of it, and since the SB was never used, I surmise that the War Office decided that it would be too horrible a weapon. I was happy about this, since it just did not seem British to wage germ warfare. I have often wondered, though, what would have happened if Von Bork's mission had been successful. Would the Kaiser have countenanced SB as a weapon against his English cousins?

There were still two years of war to get through. I found

lodgings for my wife and myself, and, despite the terrible conditions, the air raids, the food and material shortages, the dismaying reports from the front, we managed to be happy. In 1917 Nylepthah did what none of my previous wives had ever done. She presented me with a son. I was delirious with joy, even though I had to endure much joshing from my colleagues about fatherhood at my age. I did not inform Holmes of the baby. I dreaded his sarcastic remarks.

On November 11, 1919, however, a year after the news that turned the entire Allied world into a carnival of happiness, though a brief one, I received a wire.

'Bringing a bottle and cigars to celebrate the good tidings. Holmes.'

I naturally assumed that he referred to the anniversary of the Armistice. My surprise was indeed great when he showed up not only with the bottle of Scotch and a box of Havanas but a bundle of new clothes and toys for the baby and a box of chocolates for Nylepthah. The latter was a rarity at this time and must have cost Holmes some time and money to obtain.

'Tut, tut, my dear fellow,' he said when I tried to express my thanks. 'I've known for some time that you were the proud father. I have always intended to show up and tender my respects to the aged, but still energetic, father and to the beautiful Mrs. Watson. Never mind waking the infant up to show him to me, Watson. All babies look alike, and I will take your word for it that he is beautiful.'

'You are certainly jovial,' I said. 'I do not ever remember seeing you more so.'

'With good reason, Watson, with good reason!'

He dipped his hand into his pocket and brought out a cheque.

I looked at it and almost staggered. It was made out to me for the sum of thirty thousand pounds.

'I had given up on Sir Mowgli,' he said. 'I heard that he was missing, lost somewhere in deepest Africa, probably dead. Then I heard that that utter bitch, Countess Murdstone-Malcon, had managed to get to safety and civilisation. It seemed to me to be one of the ironies of fate, or of the vast indifference of nature, that she should survive and he die. But, Watson, he did surface eventually, he was in good health, and, most fortunate for us, he had recovered his memory!

'And so, my dear fellow, one of the first things he did on getting to Nairobi was to send the cheques! Both in my care, of course!'

'I can certainly use it,' I said. 'This will enable me to retire instead of working until I am eighty.'

I poured two drinks for us and we toasted our good fortune. Holmes sat back in the chair, puffing upon the excellent Havana and watching Mrs. Watson bustle about her housework.

'She won't allow me to hire a maid,' I said. 'She insists on doing all the work, including the cooking, herself. Except for the baby and myself, she does not like to touch anyone or be touched by anyone. Sometimes I think . . .'

'Then she has shut herself off from all but you and the baby,' he said.

'You might say that,' I replied. 'She is happy, though, and that is what matters.'

Holmes took out a small notebook and began making notes in it. He would look up at Nylepthah, watch her for a minute, and record something.

'What are you doing, Holmes?' I said.

His answer showed me that he, too, could indulge in a pawky humour when his spirits were high.

'I am making some observations upon the segregation of the queen.'

Mr Montalba, Obsequist

H. F. HEARD

I nervously took a pinch at the bell-chain. From inside the house there answered a deep musical clang. 'If you take a pinch then give you a knell,' I tittered to myself. I always fall into puns when I'm nervous. I also always notice a number of irrelevant things – I noticed that the house was really in too good taste. The door was mahogany polished till it was like tortoise shell. Its rich tawnyness was framed in a beautiful mellow freestone, Naples yellow in tone, obviously too perfect in grain ever to have come from a quarry: the façade rose in perfect proportions right up to a balustraded cornice where, against a powder-blue sky, stood at decent intervals elegant high-shouldered urns. 'A gentleman who is really well dressed,' I quoted to myself, 'always has on one thing that is old.' The house was a brand-new piece of traditional art.

A sound made my eye come to earth. The door had opened. In it stood a man illustrating, better than the house, my remark. He was dressed in a morning suit made of the finest dove-grey worsted, a silver grey cravat at his neck, grey kid gloves on his hands. He had already remarked, 'Please enter.' I had done so and a coloured servant in a maroon livery had 'relieved me' of my hat and cane before I had my wits sufficiently about me to begin:

'I've come . . '

'Only too pleased to show you,' sheared off the body of my explanation and I found myself being ushered slowly

down a long passage while, in contrast to our processional
pace, a flood of the quickest and strangest 'patter' I'd ever
heard poured voluminously into my ears.

'This way to the Obsequarium.'

'The *what*?'

'Ah, you don't know? *Le mot juste*, I think you must
allow. It came to me in a moment, and with it I knew I
could give *le coup de grâce* to all competition. It's patented,
of course – as is, naturally, the process. But what's a
process without a name? Indeed, I believe that had I to
choose to make my way with either the process or the
name, I'd choose the name. Of course the process *is*
fascinating to a technician and naturally one *has* the
specialist's interest. But how could the public? They want
a word and what is more they demand a *non*-descriptive
word. Our profession is a key profession just because of
that. We undertake' – the word was just a little raised – 'to
make possible for people to mention the unmentionable.
There's where I saw my opportunity. The others were
content to follow public taste or, if you will, *dis*-taste. I
was the first to show that fashions could be made. If in
finery, why not in funerals? The profession was clinging to
the past. The black mourning tradition? What was all that
but a confession of defeat – cover up everything, have the
event at night, keep everything in the shadow. I was the
first to say, 'We solicit the closest inspection. We take the
public fully into our confidence.' Indeed, the time was
overdue for a break with tradition. Morticians! Funeral
Homes!! I know they meant well. But you know to what
place the way is paved with good intentions. They wanted
people to face up to death and be soberly bright about it.
But these good fellows were more than a little out of date. I
saw that. There's now no need for the public to face up to
death – at least, not to anyone else's. Aeternitas settled

that! You didn't know about Aeternitas? Of course this *is* an age of specialization. Still Aeternitas did rather step over frontiers. It was a German invention. They used it, with considerable commercial success, at the big Berlin Zoo. How? "Take an inmate home. Have a permanentized pet." There they lay, curled up in solid sleep – cats, dogs, lion pups, rare apes. The Zoo casualty list had been capitalized – a loss turned into a profit. The dead paid for the living. More, there wasn't a limit to size – a beetle to an elephant, it was all the same. There wasn't any taxidermy trickery about it. No, what you got was a *real animal* – so real that if you chose to cut it right through, you'd find cross-sectioned every bit of it, every organ. That, I own, was what set my mind on it. You know all that romance about hearts kept in gold cases and vases. Well, of course, you could have a piece – excuse my anatomical expertism – a piece of gristle, but a heart – No. But with Aeternitas – why, I saw at once there was the real thing, shapely, the plump curves, and hard – well, not as stone but as a good plastic – stand up to any amount of handling and quite a moderate amount of not too bitter tears without even losing its gloss. But why stop at hearts – why not go straight for wholes? Who'd carry a heart about in a vase when they could have the departed entire, sitting at home! Grim? No grimmer than a photograph! Grimness, grue- someness? All that, I do assure you, is *vieux jeu* – the *frisson* of an age which had to be *macabre faute de mieux.* Aeternitas is the triumph of sanity and sanitation over false and musty romance. That was my first stroke. "Meet your dear one again at my reception parlour, *and take him back home!*" "Why leave him in the tomb when you may have him at the table?" From that it was only a step to parties.'

Mr. Montalba threw open the door at the end of the long passage along which he had discharged his soliloquy.

The chamber was large. Through high windows on the left a flood of golden light – far more mellow than our common-or-garden sun ever emits – poured, in slanting rays, onto a fine Persian carpet. It was possible to see through the window. The ground outside it sparkled smoothly snow-white.

'Cosiness set in purity,' whispered Mr. Montalba in my ear, 'that's what we want when we are' – he paused, not so much to get the word as to see that I did – '*adjusting* to the new relationship.'

On the side from the window was a cheerful fireplace where logs which had reached a perfect glow of incandescence continued indefinitely to candesce. The appositeness was so obvious that he only waved a kid-glove hand towards it. Two fine Sheraton armchairs were drawn up each side of the hearth. Each was occupied, the occupants gazing meditatively at the glow.

'Perfect lighting for a restful impression – the gentle flickering light gives a sense of peace without any solemn rigidity. You see, the smiles seem almost to play. We flatter ourselves on our smiles and feel they deserve the best of lighting to bring them out. Anything set would be worse than a droop. We aim at a quiet playfulness and I am sure you will agree that we have hit it. When the loved one returns home, permamently' – the word was stressed – 'we always arrange the home-coming. We have planned a series of "settings" to suit every purse, from the simplest "cosy-corner" just for one inmate to the family wing to be built on to mansions. We have just completed quite an ambitious design – the old family butler is seated in a small back room looking contentedly at some perfect rustless-steel replicas of the family silver, with his polishing cloth still in his hand. In the front room are the grandparents each side of the fire, with a few spare chairs for relations

174

who drop in for a few moments – or come for good. Upstairs, at the piano, is their daughter, the charming consumptive, and turning her music, the young man who when she became permanent, for a while went quite to pieces, but now is perfectly recollected, composed. Keats would have found his Grecian Urn surpassed – "For ever will he love and she be fair." In the room above is the nursery, presided over, as it should be, by the dear old family nurse brooding over the little angel in his crib and the two-year-old gazing with childish solemnity at the fire.'

'I'm not the Press,' I got out at last.

'Oh, I'm so sorry.' Mr. Montalba's style changed in a twinkling. 'Forgive me. We've only opened lately in this new mansion and of course we have roused much intelligent curiosity. I thought you were from a woman's magazine. But,' and he already had my fingers between two grey gloved hands, 'you had come for an appointment? You have a dear one ready or nearly ready to be permanented? Oh, please, don't start – yes, we like a little notice. Sometimes I drop around and make just a study or two from life – get the pose, you know. Many people make all arrangements with me – in advance. Then I can – how may I put it – avoid any awkward little hiatus.'

At last I broke through this millrace of commercialized Lethe.

'Mr. Montalba,' I said, 'I have called to ask if you have received the – the remains of a Mr. Sibon?'

'Remains!' He breathed out the word as a smoker resists at the first whiff a base tobacco. 'Please, please, quite the unhappiest of words. "Relics" even have about them a quite unnecessary flavour of abandonement. "Form" is the word. Everything we say and do is in good form, indeed the best. We receive the Form – an obsequious

175

touch or two and "Not marble's self nor the gilded monuments of princes can compare for lasting quality." '

I stuck my ground.

'Have you the Form of Mr. Sibon?'

'A relation?' He cooed.

'No, no, only an acquaintance.'

'Well,' he became confidential, 'of course it's really very unprofessional, Mr . . . Mr.?'

'Mr. Silchester.'

'Mr. Silchester, we have to have our rules. I'm sure you'll understand. Next of kin have their rights, though I'm glad to say we so win confidence that they nearly always waive them. For all others – yes, even for blood relations – nothing till the opening day. Still, I will make an exception on your behalf. I don't mind telling you that from the moment I saw you, I saw you might have – I like the ecclesiastical word; our professions so neatly parallel – a vocation. Yes, Mr. Sibon is here, resting.'

'He's alive then?' I'm afraid I blurted.

Mr. Montalba became arch. '"Resting," I said,' he corrected me. 'Life is such a rush now. Always keeping up and keeping up appearances. And now he will be kept up. The upkeep is practically nominal. We include a ten-year guarantee and inspection service with the initial costs.'

'When did he die?' I shot in.

'Again I'm being so very unprofessional. My heart over my head, you know. But why shouldn't I? You're not the Press. And, I can't help it, I love a fellow enthusiast, as I see you are. Mr. Sibon was among the first of my clients to avail himself of our "advance service"; when he felt that he was, as we put it, losing form, he sent for me. So I was able to be at his apartment when he – again a phrase we have put into circulation – handed over. So advisable for the transformation to have, as I have said, no hiatus. No, he hadn't been indisposed long. Just a little palpitation. It makes the calm all the more appreciated, by everyone, when the heart has been altogether a little too febrile.'

He paused and then put his fat grey glove on my shoulder. It settled there like a heavy hot pigeon and then gave me a gentle push. His other hand pressed the panel of the big apartment's third wall. It swung back and he pushed me through. In my ear he whispered, 'You are privileged. You shall see a newcomer before he has been actually fitted with his setting.' The door closed behind us. We were in a dim passage with faint pink lights in the ceiling. Out of it another door opened. A light switched on. The room, its apricot glow lit up, was small but painted a cheerful rose. It contained only one article of furniture – a chair. But that was a comfortable one. And so the occupant seemed to find it. Dozing easily in it was – I knew at once from my previous visit to him – Sibon. I stepped up quickly and touched him on the shoulder.

'Oh, you shouldn't, you shouldn't!' Without looking round I could sense the smile in Mr. Montalba's whisper. 'But you couldn't resist, could you? And I couldn't resist either, just letting you. We're fellow enthusiasts. I knew it.'

For I had started back more quickly than I'd sprung forward. The shoulder I had touched was as hard and stiff as wood.

'Didn't you understand? Of course I can't help being pleased. It's His Master's Voice, isn't it, all over again. But this time it's the eye that's completely taken in, not the ear. Still I do hope you haven't been shocked. I did try, you will own, to save you *any* shock.'

My mind was in an unpleasant whirl. I must sort out my impressions. First, this beastly taxidermist was, I could have no doubt, an enthusiast. He didn't care a straw for

177

the living. It was corpses he loved. A modern 'resurrection man,' a civilized – not head-hunter but whole-body snatcher. Secondly, Sibon was dead – not a doubt of it. That horribly firm contact spoke volumes on the ultimate silence. The disgusting preservative had already turned him into a solid block. I remembered that in the short interview we had had before his death, he still had found time to complain of his heart and indeed seemed in some trouble with it.

Well, all that remained was to thank Mr. Montalba, Obsequist, and to report back. I turned. He was regarding me with an easy complacency.

'Are Mr. Sibon's relations coming to fetch him?' I asked.

'I'm afraid he had none.'

'Then . . .?' I paused.

'Well, again in confidence, I can tell you he bought himself a seat.'

'A seat?'

'Yes, just before you go, please one more glance at our range of services.' He ushered me out of the room and switched off the light. We went down the rose-lit passage. At the end was a large door. Mr. Montalba threw it open. That movement evidently set an organ playing. We were looking down quite a large choir. Stalls rose on either hand. Some were vacant but many were occupied by a congregation, some kneeling, others sitting.

'A number of clients, especially when the home atmosphere hasn't been completely cooperative, prefer to take to a more specifically ecclesiastical air. Home is surely sacred but here we have an alternative sanctity.'

It certainly was. Incense for the nose. Electric candles and stained glass for the eyes. Subdued Gregorian chanting for the ear.

178

I retreated. Here was complete closure. Across the ultimate mystery Mr. Montalba had drawn the thickest tapestry of sham man had ever woven. And here Sibon – or all that the Law could look for – the body of Sibon, would stay secure ('Immaculate' would have been Mr. Montalba's word) in the heaviest odour of sanctity. What a getaway for the cleverest of international crooks, just as a convict's garb, if not a hempen cravat, was being got ready for him!

Mr. Montalba waved to me from the door. 'Come again, and of course whenever you feel need of service you will remember ours is – I don't boast, I know – incomparable.'

I hailed a taxi and drove back to our hotel. In his usual way, Mr. Mycroft showed no surprise as I gave him my surely unusual story. As he made no comment, and that's always a little galling, I added as a colophon, 'Well, the mission you sent me on has closed the case.'

'Why?' he asked with a sort of irritating innocence.

'Well, I've seen Sibon and, unpleasant but convincing fact, actually touched him.'

'Does that prove he's got away?'

'Well, when you took me along to see him, I was as close to him as I'm to you now; and I was as close as this, this afternoon, to what's left of him now.'

'Yes, yes, but he knew why we had come. If the game wasn't closing I wouldn't have taken you. It gave a second witness and prevented him – he's Gascon and so impulsive – from giving way to any melodramatic action which, while of course fatal to his chances, might have been even more fatal to my expectations.'

'But he *was* ill.'

'Possibly, possibly: though you recall, after his valet had gone to tell him we'd called, though he kept us waiting a little while, he then came to the door himself.'

179

'But I don't see . . .'

'Did I say I expected that of *you*?'

'But I have seen the corpse and you haven't!'

'If I allow your conclusion, perhaps I may be permitted to doubt your initial premise.'

When Mr. Mycroft is like that I've learned to leave him alone. I venture to believe that being right as often as he has – and so often when people thought him wrong – has slightly affected his judgment. So I simply asked, 'Why did you send me to see, then, and not go yourself?' But of course that was a mistake – I saw that the moment I'd said it. And Mr. Mycroft's quiet checkmate, 'Because I thought Mr. Montalba and you would get on better than he and I,' left me no opening but to leave the room. As I was leaving, however, as usual, the old master relented:

'Please remember that you did something I couldn't have done. I am not going to say you weren't *taken* in. I really don't know. But I am going to allow that you *got* in so far as to bring back much more than I had hoped. Now, Mr. Silchester, if you will use your other great gift by ordering one of your excellently planned dinners to be sent up to this small sitting-room of ours – while you plan that strategy, I'll go over this other game and see whether it is as closed as it seems. *Au revoir* for an hour.'

I left the old bird quite gay. After all, as he'd more than once remarked, we were complementary – quite a compliment from him.

Certainly whatever Mr. Mycroft thought of me as a messenger, he left me in no unpleasant doubts as to his opinion of my gift as a *maître d'hôtel*. The hotel in which we stayed during this affair was one of bungalows served from a central and excellent kitchen. There, with a fine chief-of-staff, I planned something that even during the

180

planning took the taste of preservative out of my mouth. When the attack was deployed, Mr. Mycroft executed dignified justice on some decapitated prawns which had absorbed into their systems a white wine sauce and awaited sentence on anchovy toast. He stirred the cream into his bortsch, watching the white and crimson maze with a professional eye. With a neat surgical touch he disclosed the truffles and chestnuts which the roast pheasant was concealing on her person. The structure of the *bombe glacé* he demonstrated with technical ease. The angels-on-horseback that brought up the rear he dismounted with a chivalrous lance.

As we sat over our coffee he said: 'I wonder whether I can answer this little mortician mystery anything like as well as you have today solved the perennial problem of the menu! We must remember precisely where we are. If you see precisely where you are, you can generally see considerably further than you think.'

Yes, that was a typical prologue and promised well. I made a sound which I'd discovered was the perfect antiphon – a kind of *Humph* – half 'hear, hear' and half 'Howdymean?'

'First, there's Sibon himself – getting on in years. Real crooks never carry their years well. Sibon is of course the "grand manner" crook, seldom stooping to anything under the 50,000 figure and of course in his heyday he would never have been under so *outré* as to go armed. His name will always have its niche in the annals of crime because we may say that he really opened up that large neglected mine, the Indian Rajahs' palaces. Till his date crooks took such tropical fish as swarm into their northern nets, as an occasional purloining of a really fine stone, a bit of none too pretty blackmail about some all too pretty white female. But Sibon had the pioneer's pluck to go out

181

and open up that rich field. He is said to have had some equally odd adventures. If you're caught in those preserves you are not so much held as parted. The Rajah usually holds a piece of your anatomy as a pledge against your return. Sibon us evidently still fairly intact – if you leave out that problematical heart. But he has extradition proceedings closing round him. He's old, yes, and may be ill, and he is certainly ready, very ready to be forgotten. But that is not quite the same as saying that he is prepared to go to where all things are forgotten. Sibon's wish – we want his wish to know his possible whereabouts – is to disappear.

'Secondly, there's myself. I want Sibon because his range of past activities awakes my professional curiosity. I'm ready to catch him now. I went with you to see him a couple of days ago because I wanted him to stand his ground and I judged he would if he knew I was nearly ready to pounce. All went well, you recall. He kept his head when he saw us. And when he keeps his head I'd gladly exchange mine for his. He saw at once I wouldn't go to see him if I had *all* my clues ready, but I would go when I was nearly ready, just to see how the land lay. He was no doubt ill. But his illness was also charmingly apposite. I repeat, really bad heart cases don't dismiss their valet and come themselves to welcome uninvited guests. This morning we learn that he'd had a fatal attack in the night and, in accord with modern hygiene, the most fashionable mortician – I beg Mr. Montalba's pardon, obsequist – took over the Form. Yes, I like that word. Mr. Sibon may have been out of condition but he was certainly in form.

'So, thirdly, you come in. You call on Mr. Montalba and ask if Mr. Sibon has settled in. Straight questions are always best especially when asked,' he paused a moment and I thought he was going to say, 'by simple people,' but he repeated the happier adjective 'straight.'

'But then the story runs too straight. True crime like true love never does. Mr. Montalba's reception of you' – he looked up at me with that long twisted smile of his. 'Mr. Silchester, we have hunted together until we both appreciate each other's gifted oddities. I know, I allow, that whereas I might have made a competent surgeon or pharmacist, you might have made more than a moderate success as a *maître d'hôtel* – but a mortician, even if called an obsequist, never! Why did Mr. Montalba welcome you with the high title of confrère?'

'He mistook me for the Press.'

'That was only at the start. Besides the Press aren't confrères of such confectioners as Mr. Montalba. They are blood brothers of the police. They both prefer their quarry fresh and sanguinary, not a waxen preservative. No, you were such a *succès fou* with this modist of the morgue that my curiosity is aroused. Let sleeping Sibon lie. Maybe he is sleeping as heavily as you thought. Even wanted crooks have died conveniently, for themselves. There's nothing too coincidental about that. Being hunted at over fifty is certainly not good for the heart. But your description of the present possessor of his Form does, I own, intrigue me. I must see for myself. After all, until I have, as coroners say, viewed the body, I can't officially enter the case as closed.'

The next morning our cab drew up under the *porte cochère* of the Montalba building. As we alit I glanced up at the front. There was nothing secretive about even the side façade. Windows stood open with flowers in them. Then my eye caught sight of someone glancing down at us, beside a large vase of wall flowers and forget-me-not. I expected the observer, seeing himself observed, would withdraw his head, but he retained his casually curious glance too long. Of course, I should have known at once: it was a Form taking the air, so as to show clients what a charming summer, semi-out-of-door effect could be composed, when the hot weather made dreaming by the fireside a seasonal anachronism.

When I looked down, the door was already open and Mr. Mycroft was enquiring, for Mr. Montalba himself had not answered the door. Instead a junior Obsequist was bowing us in – an understudy of the master modelled in the same uniform of pearl grey morning suit.

'Mr. Montalba will be with you in a moment.'

And we were left in a cheerful small study looking out into a little court where an almond tree was in almost too full bloom.

'The master knows his Ecclesiastes, I see,' said Mr. Mycroft, glancing at it, but I had bent to stroke a particularly fine grey Persian which was dozing in a seat by the window. I nearly collided with Mr. Mycroft in my recoil. Of course the beautiful creature was cold and hard as a block.

'You didn't,' remarked Mr. Mycroft, 'expect to find anything but Forms here? The animal funeral business has grown with modern sentimentality until it's too profitable a sideline not to be combined with the human traffic.'

The door opened.

'You've come again and brought another interested party. An advance visit! How wise. We do learn with the advancing years to take Time by the forelock and make every rightful provision. And, as I said yesterday, as an artist – and now not speaking in my other role as family adviser – I, too, deeply appreciate the opportunity for preliminary study, to get an impression from the life, the fleeting life, which afterwards I may be permitted, privileged, to make enduring and place above, safely

184

above, the eroding tides of Time. And, if I may say so, what a noble presence we shall here preserve unchanging for the future. So often – I confess it – I have to extemporize just a little. Look at the Form as I will, with whatever generosity of appreciation, still it remains stubbornly jejune. Even death cannot ennoble those who lived commonplace.'

I wondered what mischief Mr. Mycroft would make of this attack. He didn't: he simply ignored it. Apparently it struck him as neither funny nor significant. I'd noticed that in him before. If he felt that the man he was with was acting he was far too interested in watching the act and wondering why it was being put on, to be amused, far less disconcerted. And in his queer way Mr. Montalba was all actor, all a series of stock parts, artist, family friend, business manager – evidently he, too, didn't care a straw if one of the parts didn't get over. As quickly as a sportsman who has missed reloads and shoots again, he shot off another little speech.

'But you wanted to tell me something, just a little confidential.' The family friend was of course all discretion, tact and oblique deference.

'You were good enough to let my friend Mr. Silchester see your latest masterpiece. I had the privilege of studying Mr. Sibon in the life. I would value the opportunity to see him in Aeternitas.'

I felt sure that Mr. Montalba must resist such a frontal attack. After all he had the 'blood-relation' formula to hand. I experienced a fresh, and I must an unpleasant, surprise, when Mr. Mycroft's challenge was welcomed with a fresh burst of synthetic pleasure.

'Delighted, delighted! I've told Mr. Silchester that it *is* a privilege to have the private view before the masterpiece – as you so kindly phrase it – is framed. But rules should never be rigid – indeed, my motto might well be that of Life itself, "Good Form is never rigid." I welcome the opportunity to compare notes with another student of the Sibon form.'

We had been swept along to the accompaniment of this rear-action smoke-screen – through the parlour of post-humous preserves with its synthetic sunlight, firelight and flesh – into that passage leading to the final sanctuary. The small door on the left was swung open: and there was Sibon as still as the Statues of Memnon and more silent.

The only change was that the light seemed even kinder, more rosy. But when I brought myself to scan the too too solid Form of Sibon, I viewed it with repugnance. Mr. Mycroft's interest was as great, though without repugnance. He was peering down at it with little grunts of admiring recognition. I glanced up and saw Mr. Montalba's own glassy good form relax for a moment with a gleam of triumph.

'A pretty piece of work, you allow, Mr. Mycroft?'

'Remarkable, indeed.'

And with that Mr. Mycroft whipped out of his pocket a large pair of horned-rimmed spectacles and popped them onto his nose. I would have been far less startled had he whipped out a pair of handcuffs and clapped them onto Mr. Montalba's wrists. For I knew my old dominie's eyes were sharper than anyone's. He used to say, 'Picking up clues exercises the eye muscles.' I could only think that the rosy glow threw out his vision temporarily. But it was clear that the glasses didn't help. More it was clear that he couldn't have been used to wearing them. For he had no sooner leaned forward to study the exhibit, than the spectacles slid down his long nose so swiftly that before he could catch them, they fell plump on the plump Sibon hand which lay relaxed in its lap.

'Oh, forgive me. I'm new to glasses. My admiration made me anxious not to miss the really wonderful detail.'

He retrieved the glasses deftly and popped them closed into his pocket.

'Too kind, too kind,' he murmured turning to Mr. Montalba, who was already bowing us through the door. 'Quite wonderful. Who can deny progress when at last here we see Time arrested?'

'Truly glad that you appreciate our effort to round out and complete the modern programme of social endeavour.'

The two masked fencers kept up their rally until the front door closed between them. I was at a loss to know which had scored most points. Neither seemed to have made an actual 'touch.'

And in the automobile Mr. Mycroft, perhaps I need hardly say, did not enlighten me. When we were back in our apartment he still preserved his silence. I took up a book. But he didn't do anything but sit. Then after a few minutes I saw him move. He put his hand into his breast pocket and pulled out those glasses. He looked at them; not through them. He was examining the right-hand hinge. He began to work at the hinge and then drew towards him a small piece of notepaper. On working the hinge again, he seemed content and put the glasses aside on the table and picked up the small sheet. Then he took that rather melodramatic lens out of his waistcoat pocket and began to study the paper.

Bored with watching this routine – as routine as a cat washing its whiskers when the mouse had temporarily given it the slip – I idly picked up the spectacles Mr. Mycroft had abandoned. I tried one lens and then the other. Finally I slipped them on.

'But these . . .' I began. And then the silly things slid

off my nose just as, in the obsequarium, they had skidded down from Mr. Mycroft's beak. The small clatter and my unfinished sentence made Mr. Mycroft look up.

'You're surprised at the simplicity of those lenses?' he questioned. 'The spectacles are made – as you've demonstrated – rather to give the slip than to detect it. But if you will look you'll see they're sharp enough in their way. That's blood on your finger.'

I saw I'd made a small but clean little cut on my knuckles as I'd tried to save the silly stage-property spectacles from falling.

'I don't see why you should fool about with sham spectacles that won't even stay on, and are so badly made as to scratch one's fingers.'

I was a little tart. But Mr. Mycroft had gone back to considering his scrap of paper. After dabbing my finger with iodine, I saw Mr. Mycroft rise, fetch his microscope, and put his precious scrap on its specimen rack. That, though, didn't satisfy him and he fetched an electric torch to add to the illumination. After all, I thought, maybe his eyes are going. But the torch didn't seem to help either. Instead, he now began poking at his precious object with a small glass rod which he took out of a phial. Suddenly the whole thing seemed to bore him. He put the microscope aside, not troubling even to remove the small piece of paper which he had been studying, and remarking over his shoulder, 'I've a call to make,' left the room. He was back, though, in a couple of minutes saying, 'It's not to late to make a call.'

'I thought you'd made one,' I began. But he didn't seem to hear and did assume that I was going along with him. 'Hotel Magnifique,' which he said to the taximan as we got into the cab, made me assume that he was going again to try and pump its bland but ultra-discreet management about its late guest. The reception clerk's 'M. Sibon is away' was certainly a parry. Mr. Mycroft's 'But his valet's in: I'll leave a message with him' swept it aside and in a couple of minutes we found ourselves standing outside the door of the late Sibon's luxurious suite. Nor did we experience a check there. The door was opened by the dapper, very French-looking man-servant who had admitted us on our original visit. As before, he bowed so low that his black pointed beard must have stuck into his cravat while he presented to us a mass of black polished hair smooth as silk. I thought he started for an instant when Mr. Mycroft shot out: 'Is M. Sibon at home? Then bending still lower and with a catch in his voice:

'Haven't you heard, sir? Called away, called away.'

I was just wondering whether this was a euphemism for falling into Mr. Montalba's very asserting hands, when the valet added, 'He left a note for you, sir. I didn't know you'd call this evening. I have it in the pantry,' and he stepped back into a small side door which evidently led to the servant's quarters. The door swung to behind him. But Mr. Mycroft was just in time to prevent it latching. He flung it back, I followed, and we hurried into the small pantry, just as the door at its other end snapped to.

'Through the dining-room!' called Mr. Mycroft, wheeling round on me. We doubled back, raced through the dining-room into the kitchen. As we reached it we heard the sound of the service elevator on the back staircase begin to whir. We were out on those stairs in five seconds but only to catch sight of the floor of the elevator ascending.

'Up the stairs!' Mr. Mycroft was already up half a dozen of the steps. What he was up to, chasing a dead man's valet, I couldn't imagine, but I felt I couldn't leave the old fellow now. Fortunately Sibon had liked penthouse privacy, so we had only one fight to scramble. As we tumbled out on the roof I saw the valet looking back at us, his strained face clear in the light from the well shaft. To my huge relief he made no stand, and as even the smallest dog will chase a bull if it turns tail, I rushed after Mr. Mycroft. The roof area of the Magnifique is not only extensive, it is also rich in what golf players call hazards. I tripped over pipes, doubled round flues and chimneys in the wake of Mr. Mycroft's comet-like coat, and stumbled in rain gutters. It was after one of these that I lost the hunt and only after peering round half a dozen smokestacks, at last came upon Mr. Mycroft kneeling. Beside him, seated rather carelessly against a cased-in pipe, was the valet. He was certainly very much out of breath – far more than either of us, though he had had a lift-start. Then, through the panting, I could hear him saying to Mr. Mycroft, 'In my left upper waistcoat pocket. Quick. It's Amyl Nitrate.' Without a word Mr. Mycroft did as he was told and put something to the valet's nose; then he remarked slowly, 'You shouldn't practise such exercises.'

The other said faintly, 'I ran because I was frightened and my heart gave out.'

'No, no,' came the reply. 'You speak English as well as I do. I said exercises not exercise. Your heart hasn't given out just because of this evening's amble over the eaves.'

The valet's 'How do you know?' left me more lost than ever. And Mr. Mycroft's 'Because I'm as fit as I am,' completed my bewilderment. But neither had a moment's care for my unenlightened condition. They were quite taken up with each other. Evidently Mr. Mycroft could remember me as soon as I could be of any use. He had hold of the valet, how or why it was too dark to see, and without turning said, 'Go down and get the hotel doctor at once.'

In five minutes I was back with the very capable medico which the Magnifique retained for its guests. We brought a couple of torches with us. As soon as we picked up Mr. Mycroft I saw that the valet was gone. In his place, looking far less life-like than Mr. Montalba's creation, lay Sibon.

'Dr. Armstrong,' Mr. Mycroft had turned on us. 'Please examine this body. I believe he is now dead.' The doctor knelt beside Mr. Mycroft. After a moment I heard him say, 'Yes, yes, not a doubt about it. He's limp enough now . . . But I don't undertstand . . . how . . .?'

'Oh, you were quite justified considering your premises,' replied Mr. Mycroft. 'I must keep the actual Hows and Whys for the Police. A plain-clothes man has at my request been stationed at the main entrance the last hour. If you would be so good as to stay with the body, I'll drop down and have a word with him. Come, Mr. Silchester.'

The word was quite brief. They seemed to understand each other. The quietly dressed man who looked as though he might be an insurance agent slipped across the big lounge and disappeared towards the back premises.

'We shan't be wanted till tomorrow and then you needn't come. I expect you've had enough of even the most modern of morgues and where Aristide Sibon's Form will rest tonight – and be interviewed tomorrow – is not a very obsequious obsequarium. And now for dinner.'

In spite of our hunt having ended in a *morte*, I must say we both did justice to our evening meal. My curiosity revived. And evidently Mr. Mycroft was also relaxed and ready to feed my mind as well as I had fed his form.

I began naturally at the end: 'I thought that Dr. Armstrong signed Sibon's death certificate a couple of days ago?'

'He certainly did. Without that, not even Mr. Montalba's patter could have won him "the fair desired form."'

191

'But I don't understand –'

'Don't you think we might omit the obvious?' asked Mr. Mycroft, smiling. 'The story has points, I own, which only out-of-the-way knowledge would catch. I shall enjoy running over them. First, we are agreed Dr. Armstrong is capable. Dr. Armstrong sees Sibon, sees him alive, and sees him, he is equally sure, dead. The certificate is Syncope. But you remember the doctor's remark, "He's limp enough now"?'

'Yes, that's a natural enough remark– simply meant he was dead.'

'That bulb is quite hot,' said Mr. Mycroft's voice in my ear. 'But, you see, the scrap of mastic does not soften. So it isn't paraffin wax, the basis for the Aeternitas treatment. But this essential oil, on the glass rod tip, does begin to melt it.'

True enough, as the rod touched the lump it began to 'lose form.' Mr. Mycroft pushed the microscope away.

'That scrap is not from a body treated by the Aeternitas method. It's from a gutta-percha model. I knew in that sunset-glowing room, I'd have to touch that Form to make sure. Pink light's the devil's delight: you can't see anything in it clearly and you think you can. That's why mediums love a rosy illumination. More, I should really get an actual specimen. So I had these glasses made with the facet of one of the hinges as sharp as a razor – like a small scoop. And I took care, of course, that the spectacles themselves *didn't* fit, and so would be sure to fall off my nose onto the Form's hand as soon as I peered admiringly at it. As I retrieved my clumsy blunder, it was easy to make the little blade dredge a specimen of the skin.'

'So *I* saw Sibon – the real Sibon!'

'You had that honour. Mr. Montalba probably thought he'd better show you that Sibon was there and as the

192

model wasn't ready, and he feared such a call, he kept Sibon in trance. Had he felt safe and had time, no doubt he'd have taken the crook out of his catalepsy sooner. But he wasn't going to take the risk of being found without the body and, should a search be called for, the discovery of a half-made model. That would have been too awkward. So he took the risk with his sleeping partner instead, who for once had to stay as he was put and not even speak when spoken to.'

'Risk?'

'Oh, yes, very considerable. He kept him longer in catalepsy than is safe. Of course, men who are amazingly fit can stay "out" for many days. But not Sibon. The exercise is not to be recommended for the heart and Sibon had a heart, either from that kind of effort at lying low or the opposite effort of keeping on the run – perhaps both combined. Well, after you leave, Mr. Montalba *does* bring him to and substitutes the model. Sibon can then go back to the Magnifique. The safest place, when you're wanted, is home – if you're disguised; and he was – as his valet.'

'But where was his valet?'

'*He* was. That was rather neat preparation, don't you think? Remember when we called – there was a pause after the valet went to call him and then the great man graciously came out himself and welcomed us. The pause, of course, was because, in theatre language, he was "doubling the parts" and so he had to make a "quick change." As soon as I was quite sure that was a gutta-percha model, I knew that Sibon was back at his hotel. The phone call I then made was to the police – to tell them to watch the downstairs exits and arrest Mr. Sibon's valet, if he tried to leave. I knew then he'd bolt for the roof. He'd soon find that the police were on below. Those men are always inspecting their exists, as a bird turns round between every pull at a worm – second nature. He'd feel safe, though, in his disguise, with an alibi body amply viewed elsewhere. He'd bolt only when we turned up. I guessed we'd have an easy run, for I was pretty sure with all those cataleptic tricks he'd have a bad heart. Still I thought we'd have a catch, not a kill. Both those fellows, Sibon and Montalba, are by nature largely mountebanks. But one played possum once too often. If you play at death, that grim player may take you in earnest.'

'Poor Sibon! He should have been a psychologist. Fancy going to India and learning so much about the mind-body just to get away safely with a few gewgaws and trinkets – most of them in execrable taste.'

'But I understand he stole some of the finest jewels in Asia!'

'Still I repeat,' said Mr. Mycroft, getting up and moving towards his bedroom door, 'Sibon brought back only the pearl case, not the pearl, or the synthetic instead of the real pearl in the lotus, if you like that better.'

'I don't understand,' hopped out from my lips like the frog instead of the pearl in the fairy story.

He smiled as he opened the door and passed through. 'Well, sleep wisely but not too well and don't dream to much about good form.'

A Trifling Affair

H. R. F. KEATING

Trifles, Sherlock Holmes was wont to remark, may bear an importance altogether contrary to their apparent worth, and I venture to think that there cannot have been a case more trifling in all Holmes's adventures than that of the affair of the poet of childhood and the ink-blotted verse volume. Yet, unimportant though it was, it nevertheless had in it for me a lesson which I hope I shall not forget.

It was a day in the spring of 1898 when from among the early post Holmes selected a particular letter, still in its envelope, and tossed it to me across the breakfast table.

'Well, Watson,' he said, 'tell me what you make of that. A somewhat unusual missive for a consulting detective to receive, I think.'

I took the envelope and turned it over once or twice in my hands. It appeared to be of no particular distinction. The paper was neither cheap nor very expensive. The postmark, I saw, was that of Brighton and Hove for the previous afternoon. The writing of the address, 'Sherlock Holmes Esq., 221B Baker Street, London W.', was plainly that of a gentleman, though the letters were not perhaps as confidently formed as they might have been. The sole peculiarity that I could observe was that the writer's name had been put upon the reverse of the envelope, 'Phillip Hughes Esq.'.

'Possibly an American who writes,' I ventured at last,

when from the tapping of Holmes's lean fingers on the tablecloth I became aware of his impatience. 'I believe that the custom of putting the writer's name on the outside of a letter is more practised on the far side of the Atalantic than here. And certainly the handwriting is not that of any contintental.'

'Good, Watson. Excellent. Clearly my correspondent does not come from the Continent of Europe. But is there no more you can tell from the plentiful signs that any person addressing an envelope is bound to leave behind?'

I looked at the letter once more, a little mortified that Holmes had added his disparaging rider to the praise for my first deduction.

'Perhaps the writer was in a state of some perturbation,' I suggested. 'The formation of some of the letters is certainly rather ragged, although the hand in itself is by no means uneducated. It is just the sort I learnt painfully at school myself.'

Holmes clapped his hands in delight.

'Yes, indeed, Watson. You have gone to the heart of it with all your usual perspicacity.'

I busied myself in taking some marmalade. The truth of the matter was that I could not for the life of me see in what I had been so perspicacious, though I was not sorry to have earned Holmes's unstinted praise.

A silence fell. Darting a glance at my companion from my perhaps over-busy buttering of my hot toast, I found that he was leaning back in his chair, half-empty coffee cup neglected, regarding me with unremitting steadiness.

I was constrained to look back at him.

'You have no further comment to make?' he asked me at last.

I picked up the envelope once again.

'No, no, my dear fellow, not the envelope. I must

suppose that you have long ago extracted all the information you are likely to get from that. I meant have you no comment to make upon my remarking on your perspicacity in pointing to the style of my correspondent's hand.'

'Why, no, Holmes. No, I think not. No, there is nothing more to be said about that. I think.'

'Not even that undoubtedly the writer of the letter is a schoolboy?'

'A schoolboy? But how . . .'

'That educated hand, yet with many of the letters curiously unformed. Why, you have only to compare the capital H of Holmes with that of Hughes to observe the significant differences. No, undoubtedly my correspondent is still at school, and indeed not yet at any of our great public schools but a mere boy of no more than twelve. And, as you must know, the South Coast is greatly favoured by private scholastic establishments. Open the letter, Watson, and let us hear why a schoolboy wishes to consult Sherlock Holmes.'

Obediently I took up a paperknife and slit open the envelope, hoping the while, I must confess, that just once Holmes's confident deductions might prove false. But a single glance at the address on the letter within confirmed him exactly in his surmise. 'St George's School, Hove,' it was headed.

'Read it, Watson. Read it.'

'Dear Mr Holmes,' I read. 'All of us boys at St George's are jolly interested in your cases, except that Dr Smyllie, our headmaster, forbids us to read about you. But, Mr Holmes, a fearful injustice has been done. He has said that our holiday for St George's Day, which has been our right ever since the beginning of the world, will be cancelled unless someone owns up. But, Mr Holmes, nobody did it. Every chap in the school is certain of that. No one did it at all, and still he says our holiday will be cancelled. Your obedient servant, Phillip Hughes. P.S. It was spilling ink on his precious book, and why should any fellow do that?'

I laid down Master Hughes's letter with tears of laughter in my eyes.

'Upon my soul, Holmes,' I said. 'Here's a case that will try your methods to the utmost.'

'Yes, indeed, Watson. There are features in it, are there not, of considerable interest. I think a trip to the Sussex coast might prove distinctly stimulating.'

My laughter was quenched.

'Surely,' I said, 'you cannot be serious?'

Yet already I knew from the look of deep preoccupation on my friend's countenance that he did indeed fully intend to go down to Hove and investigate our young correspondent's indignant complaint.

'My dear Watson,' he answered with some asperity. 'If a council of schoolboys declares upon oath in a purely private communication that a certain event did not occur among them, you can take it as pretty much of a fact that that event did not happen. They know altogether too much about each other. There is only one circumstance I can think of that might prove an exception.'

'And that is?'

He gave me a quick frown.

'Why, if the deed in question should have been perpetrated by the writer of the letter himself, of course. And we can make certain of that only by speaking to the young man face to face.'

'Yes, I suppose so,' I answered. 'But all the same, a visit to Hove will take us most of a day if not more, and you have the business of the Bank of England oyster dinner still in hand.'

'My dear Watson, an injustice has been done. Or almost

certainly so. I hope I am not the man to allow any mere pecuniary considerations to stand in my way under such circumstances. St George's Day is but two days hence. Have the goodness to look up a train to Brighton. We will go down this morning.'

I went at once to Bradshaw in its familiar place upon our shelves.

But I was not yet to tell Holmes how soon we could be off on this extraordinary errand. Before I had had time to run my finger down the Brighton departures column there entered our page, Billy, with upon the salver that he carried a single large visiting card.

Holmes picked it up and read it aloud.

'Dr A. Smyllie, M.A., Ph.D., St George's School for the Preliminary Education of Young Gentlemen, Hove, near Brighton, Sussex. Why, Watson, here is the very dominie under whose stern edict our young friend is suffering. Bring him up, Billy. Bring him up.'

In a few moments Master Hughes's headmaster stood before us. He was not the sort of man I would have imagined a headmaster to be, even the headmaster of an establishment for twelve-year-olds. Far from being an imposing figure able to exert authority with a glance, he was reedy and undulating to a degree. Correctly enough dressed in frock-coat and striped trousers, he yet wore a loosely knotted cravat at his throat. His face was very pale, and he seemed more than a little agitated.

'Mr Sherlock Holmes?' he asked in a high-pitched, almost sqeaky, voice, turning not to Holmes but to myself.

I corrected his mistake, which seemed unduly to disconcert him, and introduced my friend.

Dr Smyllie extended a somewhat limp hand at the end of an extraordinarily long arm, and winced a little when Holmes took it in his firm grasp.

'And what can I have the honour of doing for the poet of childhood?' Holmes asked.

Upon Dr Smyllie's pallid countenance there appeared a faint flush of pleasure.

'You know my work, Mr Holmes? I had hardly dared to hope that a person of your – of your – of your direction in life would be aware of my few, humble efforts.'

'You do yourself an injustice, Dr Smyllie,' Holmes replied. 'Who does not know those lines of yours that conclude so touchingly "Take up the spangled web of words –"'

'"Then lay it gently on my grave,"' I completed the poem, surprised only that Holmes, so contemptous of the softer things of life, should be able to quote those verses 'For My Infant Son', often though they have been reprinted.

Now I understood why Holmes had addressed Dr Smyllie as 'the poet of childhood'. For such Algernon Smyllie had been dubbed some thirty years earlier when his very successful volume of verse had first appeared, poems concerned with every tender aspect of a child's life, of which the verses 'To My Infant Son' were the crown.

But now, it seemed, the young poet had become the mature schoolmaster. Algernon Smyllie had become Dr A. Smyllie, M.A., Ph. D. Yet he still looked, I thought to myself, more the sensitive poet than the awe-inspiring headmaster.

Indeed, faced with telling Holmes the reason for his visit, he positively hung his head and scraped at our Turkey carpet with the inside of his right foot, upon which, I saw, the boot buttons were mismatched at the top.

'Now, sir,' Holmes said encouragingly.

Dr Smyllie blushed again.

'It is a trifling matter, Mr Holmes,' he said.

Holmes's lips flickered in the merest hint of a smile.

'But trifling matters, as I have more than once explained to my friend, Dr Watson, can on occasion be of the utmost significance,' he said.

Dr Smyllie stepped back a pace, and even glanced at the door as if he were contemplating immediate flight. But he succeeded in standing his ground at last.

'No, no, Mr Holmes,' he said, the words tumbling out of him. 'No, indeed. I assure you, my dear sir, quite the contrary. Altogether the other way about. I would not have disturbed you at all, my dear sir, only that I happened to be passing this way and I thought – I thought . . .'

Holmes stayed silent, sucking at an empty pipe which he had picked up from the mantelpiece.

Dr Smyllie gave an immense swallow, the Adam's apple in his long throat above that loosely tied cravat rising and falling.

'No, my dear sir,' he resumed, 'I would have dismissed the matter by writing a mere note, perhaps not even by that, only it so happened that my business takes me past – er – your door and it – er – occurred to me to call and settle it with a few words.'

'And the matter is?' Holmes asked, with a certain sharpness.

'Oh, nothing, sir. A mere trif – Nothing, sir, of any importance.'

'But, nevertheless, since you have called upon us, it would be as well to unburden yourself of its substance.'

The willowy poet-headmaster blushed again at Holmes's rebuke. But he did now contrive to bring out what it was that had brought him to call.

'Mr Holmes,' he said, 'I have reason to believe that one

201

of my pupils – I assure you, sir, that they are not generally so disgracefully behaved – that one of my pupils may have had the temerity to address a letter to your good self. A letter concerning a trifling – that is, the merest matter of necessary discipline. And happening, as I say, to be passing, I – er – thought I would merely call in to – to assure you, sir, that you need do nothing in the matter. Nothing at all, sir. I merely wished to offer you an apology, as it were. An apology on behalf of – er – St George's School.'

Holmes replaced his pipe upon the mantelpiece and gave our visitor a cool nod.

'If you will excuse me one moment, Dr Smyllie,' he said. 'I have a small domestic matter to attend to. A word with our landlady about my arrangements for the day. She needs to know in good time in order to do her marketing.'

He left the room, quietly closing the door behind him, and Dr Smyllie and I stood facing each other in a somewhat awkward silence. I felt myself a little annoyed with my friend. He did not usually leave me with a client in this manner, and nor was it often his custom to consult so much Mrs Hudson's convenience. However, he returned before I had had time to do more than offer our visitor some few comments on the prevailing weather, and he at once resumed the consultation.

'I take it then, sir,' he said to Dr Smyllie, 'that this extempore visit was with the intention simply of reassuring me that I need take no particular notice of any communication I might receive from any of your pupils?'

'Exactly so, sir. Exactly so.'

Holmes regarded the schoolmaster-poet with an expression of the utmost seriousness.

'Then, sir, you may take it that the object of your visit has been thoroughly achieved,' he said.

Dr Smyllie bowed and thanked Holmes with, I thought, perhaps more effusiveness than was necessary, and in a few minutes he had left us.

'Well, Watson,' Holmes said, as our visitor's tread could be heard descending the stairs, 'have you any observations to make?'

I pondered.

'I hardly think so,' I replied. 'Except perhaps that Dr Smyllie need hardly have put himself out even to the extent of halting his cab outside our door to tell us that young Hughes's letter is, after all, a very trifling – that is, not a matter of great importance.'

'You think so? But, tell me, did you notice anything more about our poet of childhood?'

'Why, no. No. Unless perhaps that his right boot was mis-buttoned.'

'Good, Watson. I knew I could rely upon you to seize on the significant detail.'

'Significant, Holmes?'

'Why, surely so. When a peron comes to our rooms here all the way from the Sussex coast while we are at breakfast, and, though correctly dressed, appears with a mis-buttoned boot and with a small shaving cut upon his right cheek, something which I fear you failed to notice, then there is only one conclusion to be drawn.'

'And that is?'

'That he left home in a very great hurry precisely in order to see myself as soon as he possibly could.'

'But, no, Holmes,' I could not help expostulating. 'He told us that he had an appointment in town elsewhere. No doubt it was for an early hour and he is already on his way there again.'

'You think so? Well, perhaps we shall soon see.'

At that moment Billy came back into the room, a look of

sharp triumph on his always eager face.

'Victoria Station, Mr Holmes, sir,' he announced without preliminary.

'There you are, Watson.'

'But I don't quite understand. What about Victoria Station?'

'That it was to there that Dr Smyllie directed his cab,' Holmes replied. 'I made an opportunity to leave the room and instruct Billy to wait out on the steps and overhear any directions our visitor might give. You surely did not think I was so concerned about our dinner tonight that I went out for that purpose?'

'No, no. Of course not. So Dr Smyllie is returning directly to Hove. What do you see as the significance of that?'

'Simply that he is unduly concerned that I should take no action as the result of that letter. Now, if what might seem to be a mere trifle caused him to go to so much trouble, I think we should make all haste to follow in his footsteps. You were consulting Bradshaw, I believe.'

Although Sherlock Holmes is a master of disguise, and I have frequently seen him so transformed that it has taken me no little time to recognize him even at close quarters, it has been seldom in the course of our adventures that he has called upon me to assume an appearance other than my own. At Hove, however, once we had found St George's School and examined the neighbourhood round about, he did require me to adopt a disguise. So it was that I found myself on the afternoon of that day waiting in the road where the school stood, clad in a not altogether sweet-smelling coat belonging to the owner of a four-wheeler whom Holmes had persuaded for a consideration to lend us both vehicle and garment. From where I sat high up on the driving seat I could see in the garden of the house next to St George's, a residence that had luckily chanced to be unoccupied, the stooping figure of a gardener methodically digging in a flower-bed close to the fence dividing the two premises. Had I not known for a fact that this man was Holmes himself I would not, even at the comparatively short distance that separated us, have recognized him.

I had not been in position long before I heard the clangour of a bell from within the school and saw a few moments later some score of youngsters come pouring out into the grounds to play. None of them, I think, paid any heed to the old gardener at work on the other side of the fence. But when, after a little, one of the boys happened to go near, Holmes called out something in a quiet voice, and before long I was able to see another of the happy youngsters running and playing there, a handsome red-headed lad, go over and lean against the fence just where the gardener was at work. But no one who was not within a yard or two of the boy could have seen that he was engaged in converse with the man on the far side. It was a conversation that lasted a full quarter of an hour, and at its end the gardener carefully scraped clean his spade and made his way off, trudging along as if well tired after a good day's labour.

I jerked the reins in my lap and the four-wheeler's old horse set off at a sedate walk. Round the next corner I saw waiting for me a tall, upright and sprightly figure resembling not at all the ancient gardener in the empty garden, for all that his clothes were not unlike.

In a moment Holmes was seated in the cab behind me and telling me the result of his unconventional consultation with master Phillip Hughes.

'It is much as I thought, Watson. It seems that in the

entrance hall of the school there is kept in a place of honour, in a locked glass case, a copy of Algernon Smyllie's book *Poems of Childhood*, together with a letter to the poet from Her Majesty herself. It is the custom for the chief boy of the school, the Dux as they call him, to turn one page of the book each day. Now, just a week ago our friend, young Hughes, who had omitted to learn the evening before a prescribed passage from Horace, came downstairs very early to, as he said, "mug up the beastly stuff". Glancing at the display case to see which in particular of (again I use his own words) "the vicious verses" was on show, since if he failed to present his passage of Horace correctly it would be his punishment by tradition to learn that poem, he saw, not entirely to his dismay, that someone had poured ink with conspicuous liberality all over the page, which happened indeed to be that on which appear the quatrains you yourself so much admire, the ones entitled "For My Infant Son".'

'Ah, yes. "Take up the spangled web of words, Then lay it gently on my grave."'

'Exactly. Though I fear young Hughes does not share your enthusiasm. However, that is not the end of his account. Scarcely had he, he told me, absorbed the fact of the desecration than he heard behind him the voice of his headmaster which a moment later, when he too had perceived what had happened, was raised in the most terrible ire. An anger that persisted, when no culprit would come forward, and soon resulted in the cancellation of the long-honoured St George's Day holiday.'

'And are you satisfied, Holmes, that young Hughes did not himself commit the very act he summonued you to investigate?'

'Yes, I flatter myself that no young man of twelve years of age could long deceive me. And, besides, there is no possible advantage to him in committing the crime.'

'I suppose not. Yet, pray, consider. Youngsters are notoriously mettlesome. They revel in all sorts of pranks. Why, I remember from my own schooldays –'

'I dare say, Watson. And I am very aware of the nature of schoolboys. It would not have been inconceivable that one of these youngsters had crept down in the middle of the night and played this trick were it not for two circumstances.'

'Yes?'

'First, as I explained to you at the outset of the affair, the act would be certain to have become known to at least one of his fellow pupils, aware of each other's habits and inclinations as schoolboys invariably are. And, secondly, the case in which the book is kept is always locked, and there are only two keys to it, one held by Dr Smyllie himself and the other by his son, Arthur, a young man of twenty-two or twenty-three who assists in the running of the establishment.'

'Then it seems to me that we must find some way of speaking to young Arthur Smyllie, if you are indeed satisfied that the cabinet can be opened in no other way than by its keys.'

'Watson, I could not yet be satisfied of that myself. But Phillip Hughes and his fellow pupils most certainly are so, and I am well disposed to take their word for it, as interested parties.'

Holmes had ascertained from young Hughes that Mr Arthur Smyllie was in the habit of taking an evening stroll. 'The young shaver intimated, Watson, that the Lion Hotel might be his destination, a suggestion that I felt bound to scout.' But it was outside the Lion Hotel that we waited that evening in the expectation of accosting the son of the

207

headmaster of St George's School. I was myself a little apprehensive over what reception we might be given when we disclosed the reason for our seeking his company. But I need not have worried. The moment Holmes greeted the young fellow, a fine upstanding ruddy-faced specimen of British manhood, and pronounced his own name, his face lip up in an expression of profound delight.

'Mr Sherlock Holmes,' he exclaimed. 'Why, I could not have wished more dearly to meet any other soul upon earth. And is this Dr Watson? Sir, I have read your accounts of Mr Holmes's cases with the keenest interest. I must tell you, Mr Holmes, that I am of a scientific turn myself. Indeed, I hope to be leaving for London at the start of the next university year to read for a degree in the physical sciences.'

'A most commendable ambition,' Holmes said. 'But won't you miss the rewards of schoolmastering?'

The young man grinned.

'Keeping all those cheeky young devils in order for my father? Well, I shan't altogether miss that, I promise you. And yet you're right, Mr Holmes, of course. There are rewards for a schoolmaster, and I dare say I shall miss the little blighters in the end after all.'

Holmes offered the young man some hospitality and we all three repaired to the hotel to discuss a bottle of wine. It was some time before Holmes was able to bring the conversation round to the affair of St George's School so keen was Arthur Smyllie to learn all he could of scientific methods of detection. But at last Holmes contrived an adroitly phrased question about our guest's present life among his father's 'little blighters'.

'Well, yes, Mr Holmes, they can be nothing but pests at times, I admit, for all that at other times they are delightfully willing to learn every blessed thing I can teach them.'

'Up to all sorts of tricks, however, I make no doubt,' Holmes said.

Arthur Smyllie laughed.

'Oh, yes, indeed. Can you guess what their latest escapade has been?'

'I am sure I cannot.'

'Well, one of the little beasts has poured ink all over a precious copy of my father's book *Poems of Childhood*. You know that I am the only heir of the man who wote "For My Infant Son"?'

'Are you, indeed, Mr Smyllie? And you say that one of your father's pupils poured ink on a copy of that book?'

'A copy sir, sir?' More than just a copy, I assure you. A very precious one, signed by Her Majesty, no less, and enclosed in a glass case together with a letter from the Queen to my father. It really was too bad of the little beast who spoiled it. And yet . . . Well, to tell you the truth, that poem has hung round my neck like a milestone all my life, and I'm not altogether sorry that it was that particular page that received the inky deluge.'

'I'm surprised that the display case was left open when there are schoolboys about, always apt to carelessness and pranks.'

'Oh, no, Mr Holmes, the case was never left open. Once a day, true, it is unlocked by the Dux of the school and a page is turned. But he always had to obtain a key from either my father or myself and to return it immediately.'

'But perhaps the case can be opened without benefit of key?'

'No, again, Mr Holmes. It's stoutly locked, I can assure you.'

Holmes smiled.

'Why then,' he said, 'it seems you have produced for me

a mystery worthy of my best powers. Who committed the crime within the locked cabinet? And how was the deed done?'

Arthur Smyllie laughed aloud in delight.

'Yet, you know,' Holmes interjected with some acerbity, 'if there were a problem of more importance but with the identical set of circumstances, it would not take me long to put my finger on the crux of it. If it were possible for a room or a cabinet to be opened except with its keys, then I should look pretty sharply to the holders of the keys, whoever they were, for my criminal.'

Young Smyllie lost his cheerful look in an instant.

'Mr Holmes,' he said, 'you are not suggesting that I defaced that book of my father's?'

'My dear sir, I am asking only if it has to be the holders of the keys and no one else who could gain access to the volume.'

Arthur Smyllie's face, formerly so ruddily cheerful, was white now as a sheet.

'Mr Holmes,' he said, rising abruptly from the table, 'I will bid you good night.'

He had left before either of us had had time to remonstrate.

'Holmes,' I asked, 'is there some way to get into that display case without using either of its keys?'

'My dear Watson, you heard yourself Arthur Smyllie tell us that there was not.'

'Is there no other key then? A key that one of the boys could have obtained by some means?'

'If there were such a thing,' Holmes answered me, 'we should have heard about it from Hughes. Nothing could keep its existence a secret within a school, believe me.'

'But then Arthur Smyllie must have defaced the book himself, as indeed his conduct just now can only lead us to believe. But why should he do such a thing? It escapes me.'

'Oh, come,' Holmes replied. 'Did you not hear Arthur tell us that he is going to London University to read for a degree in science? Did you not hear how that poem of his father's, with its public plea to him to "take up the spangled web of words", to become a poet in his turn, weighs like a millstone on him?'

I sighed. Holmes's words were only too convincing.

'Then I suppose that tomorrow we must go to Dr Smyllie and tell him that no boy in his school committed the outrage,' I said.

'Yes, that certainly we must do.'

Our adventures in Hove were not, however, yet ended. We took the only room which the Lion had vacant for the night, and I know that I lay long restless thinking of the message that we had to deliver next day, although it seemed to me that Holmes in the other bed slept soundly enough. So it was I who heard at an hour well after midnight an insistent creaking sound just outside our window. At first I took it for the action of the wind on the branches of the tree that grew close to the building at just that point. But before long I realized that the night was, in fact, singularly calm, and yet the creaking persisted.

Without waking Holmes, I slipped from my bed, put on slippers and a dressing-gown and looked about the darkened room for some weapon. At last I recalled that there was a good set of fire-irons in the chimney place. I crept across and secured the poker.

Armed with this, I advanced to the window, paused for a moment, heard the creaking continue and flung wide the casement. There was a swift movement among the branches of the tree just outside. I leapt forward,

211

snatching with my free hand at a pale form I could vaguely discern. There came a loud yelp. The form wriggled, abominably in my grasp. I raised the poker to deliver a sound blow.

'Oh, come, Watson, spare the rod,' said the voice of Sherlock Holmes from behind me.

'Spare the rod?' I said refraining from bringing the poker down but keeping a firm grip on my opponent's clothing. 'Holmes, we have a burglar here. Pray assist me.'

'A burglar, yes,' Holmes answered. 'But only a small one, I venture to think.'

I heard the sound of him striking a match behind me. The rays from the candle he lit shone out into the night. By then I saw that I was detaining none other than the young red-haired Phillip Hughes.

I hauled him out of the tree and inside.

'Now, young sir,' I said, 'what is the meaning of this new jape of yours?'

But Sherlock Holmes answered for him.

'No new jape, Watson, I think, since I believe I told you that in my opinion the lad committed no old jape.'

'But, Holmes, he has this instant proved himself a night prowler, and a determined one at that. There can no longer be any doubt about who blotted that book.'

'No, Watson, there never has been any doubt about that. But let us hear what brought our determined little ally prowling all the way over to us here.'

The boy looked up at Holmes, his eyes alight with admiration.

'You knew then that I had come to tell you, sir?' he asked.

Holmes's lips curved in a faint smile.

'I hardly think you would have risked so perilous a journey for any other purpose,' he said. 'I take it that you found out from Mr Arthur Smyllie where we lodged?'

'Yes, sir.'

'Then tell us what you have to tell us.'

'Sir, I think I know how that book got to be covered in ink, sir.'

Holmes's eyes gleamed momentarily.

'I wonder if you do,' he said. 'Let us hear.'

'Well, sir, it's not easy to believe.'

'The truth very often isn't. Your human being is a very tricky piece of machinery, my lad.'

'Yes, sir. Well, sir, I was lying awake tonight, thinking about you coming all the way down from London and everything, and wondering whether you would solve the mystery, sir. Well, not really that. I knew you would solve it, sir, but I wondered what the answer could possibly be. And then, sir, I remembered Thompson Minor. He left last year, sir.'

'Thompson Minor,' I exclaimed. 'Did a boy come back to the school and –'

'Watson, let young Hughes tell us in his own way.'

'Of course, of course. Speak up, young fellow me lad.'

'Yes, sir. Well, I thought about Thompson Minor and the way he used to get into great bates. And then, Mr Holmes, well, he would do things that only hurt him himself. Once when he was in a specially bad temper he threw his champion pocket-knife into the fire, sir. He did really.'

Holmes's eyes were glowing sombrely now.

'So, young Hughes,' he said, 'draw your conclusions. Bring your account to a proper end, and my friend Watson here shall record it for you.'

The boy looked back at him, white-faced and intent in the candlelight.

'Sir, Dr Smyllie did it himself, didn't he, sir? It must

213

have been him. Mr Arthur's too decent ever to do a thing like that, and the only other key was Dr Smyllie's. Sir, he did it to spite himself because Mr Arthur won't be a poet but a scientist, sir. Isn't that it? Isn't it?'

'Yes,' said Sherlock Holmes. 'That is it, my boy.'

He turned to me.

'And, as you suggested, Watson,' he said, 'in the morning we shall have to go to Dr Smyllie and tell him what his son guessed this evening, that no boy committed our crime. And it's "Hurrah for St George" and a whole day of holiday.'

The Great Detective

STEPHEN LEACOCK

The Great Detective sat in his office. He wore a long green gown and half a dozen secret badges pinned to the outside of it.

Three or four pairs of false whiskers hung on a whisker-stand beside him.

Goggles, blue spectacles, and motor glasses lay within easy reach.

He could completely disguise himself at a second's notice.

Half a bucket of cocaine and a dipper stood on a chair at his elbow.

His face was absolutely impenetrable.

A pile of cryptograms lay on the desk. The Great Detective hastily tore them open one after the other, solved them, and threw them down the cryptogram-shute at his side.

There was a rap at the door.

The Great Detective hurriedly wrapped himself in a pink domino, adjusted a pair of false black whiskers and cried:

'Come in.'

His secretary entered. 'Ha,' said the detective, 'it is you!'

He laid aside his disguise.

'Sir,' said the young man in intense excitement, 'a

mystery has been committed!'

'Ha!' said the Great Detective, his eye kindling, 'is it such as to completely baffle the police of the entire continent?'

'They are so completely baffled with it,' said the secretary, 'that they are lying collapsed in heaps; many of them have committed suicide.'

'So,' said the detective, 'and is the mystery one that is absolutely unparalleled in the whole recorded annals of the London police?'

'It is.'

'And I suppose,' said the detective, 'that it involves names which you would scarcely dare to breathe, at least without first using some kind of atomizer or throat-gargle.'

'Exactly.'

'And it is connected, I presume, with the highest diplomatic consequences, so that if we fail to solve it England will be at war with the whole world in sixteen minutes?'

His secretary, still quivering with excitement, again answered yes.

'And finally,' said the Great Detective, 'I presume that it was committed in broad daylight, in some such place as the entrance of the Bank of England, or in the cloak-room of the House of Commons, and under the very eyes of the police?'

'Those,' said the secretary, 'are the very conditions of the mystery.'

'Good,' said the Great Detective, 'now wrap yourself in this disguise, put on these brown whiskers and tell me what it is.'

The secretary wrapped himself in a blue domino with lace insertions, then, bending over, he whispered in the ear of the Great Detective:

'The Prince of Wurttemberg has been kidnapped.'

The Great Detective bounded from his chair as if he had been kicked from below.

A prince stolen! Evidently a Bourbon! The scion of one of the oldest families in Europe kidnapped. Here was a mystery indeed worthy of his analytical brain.

His mind began to move like lightning.

'Stop!' he said, 'how do you know this?'

The secretary handed him a telegram. It was from the Prefect of Police of Paris. It read: 'The Prince of Wurttemberg stolen. Probably forwarded to London. Must have him here for the opening day of Exhibition. £1000 reward.'

So! The Prince had been kidnapped out of Paris at the very time when his appearance at the International Exposition would have been a political event of the first magnitude.

With the Great Detective to think was to act, and to act was to think. Frequently he could do both together.

'Wire to Paris for a description of the Prince.'

The secretary bowed and left.

At the same moment there was a slight scratching at the door.

A visitor entered. He crawled stealthily on his hands and knees. A hearthrug thrown over his head and shoulders disguised his identity.

He crawled to the middle of the room.

Then he rose.

Great Heaven!

It was the Prime Minister of England.

'You!' said the detective.

'Me,' said the Prime Minister.

'You have come in regard to the kidnapping of the Prince of Wurttemberg?'

'How do you know?' he said.

The Great Detective smiled his inscrutable smile.

'Yes,' said the Prime Minister. 'I will use no conceal-ment. I am interested, deeply interested. Find the Prince of Wurttemberg, get him safe back to Paris and I will add £500 to the reward already offered. But listen,' he said impressively as he left the room, 'see to it that no attempt is made to alter the marking of the prince, or to clip his tail.'

So! To clip the Prince's tail! The brain of the Great Detective reeled. So! a gang of miscreants had conspired to – but no! the thing was not possible.

There was another rap at the door.

A second visitor was seen. He wormed his way in, lying almost prone upon his stomach, and wriggling across the floor. He was enveloped in a long purple cloak. He stood up and peeped over the top of it.

Great Heaven!

It was the Archbishop of Canterbury!

'Your Grace!' exclaimed the detective in amazement – 'pray do not stand, I beg you. Sit down, lie down, anything rather than stand.'

The Archbishop took off his mitre and laid it wearily on the whisker-stand.

'You are here in regard to the Prince of Wurttemberg.'

The Archbishop started and crossed himself. Was the man a magician?

'Yes,' he said, 'much depends on getting him back. But I have only come to say this: my sister is desirous of seeing you. She is coming here. She has been extremely indiscreet and her fortune hangs upon the Prince. Get him back to Paris or I fear she will be ruined.'

The Archbishop regained his mitre, uncrossed himself, wrapped his cloak about him, and crawled stealthily out on his hands and knees, purring like a cat.

The face of the Great Detective showed the most profound sympathy. It ran up and down in furrows. 'So,' he muttered, 'the sister of the Archbishop, the Countess of Dashleigh!' Accustomed as he was to the life of the aristocracy, even the Great Detective felt that there was here intrigue of more than customary complexity.

There was a loud rapping at the door.

There entered the Countess of Dashleigh. She was all in furs.

She was the most beautiful woman in England. She strode imperiously into the room. She seized a chair imperiously and seated herself on it, imperial side up.

She took off her tiara of diamonds and put it on the tiara-holder beside her and uncoiled her boa of pearls and put it on the pearl-stand.

'You have come,' said the Great Detective, 'about the Prince of Wurttemberg.'

'Wretched little pup!' said the Countess of Dashleigh in disgust.

So! A further complication! Far from being in love with the Prince, the Countess denounced the young Bourbon as a pup!

'You are interested in him, I believe.'

'Interested!' said the Countess. 'I should rather say so. Why, I bred him!'

'You which?' gasped the Great Detective, his usually impassive features suffused with a carmine blush.

'I bred him,' said the Countess, 'and I've got £10,000 upon his chances, so no wonder I want him back in Paris. Only listen,' she said, 'if they've got hold of the Prince and cut his tail or spoiled the markings of his stomach it would be far better to have him quietly put out of the way here.'

The Great Detective reeled and leaned up against the

side of the room. So! The cold-blooded admission of the beautiful woman for the moment took away his breath! Herself the mother of the young Bourbon, misallied with one of the greatest families of Europe, staking her fortune on a Royalist plot, and yet with so instinctive a knowledge of European politics as to know that any removal of the hereditary birth-marks of the Prince would forfeit for him the sympathy of the French populace.

The Countess resumed her tiara.

She left.

The secretary re-entered.

'I have three telegrams from Paris,' he said, 'they are completely baffling.'

He handed over the first telegram.

It read:

'The Prince of Wurttemberg has a long, wet snout, broad ears, very long body, and short hind legs.'

The Great Detective looked puzzled.

He read the second telegram.

'The Prince of Wurttemberg is easily recognized by his deep bark.'

And then the third.

'The Prince of Wurttemberg can be recognized by the patch of white hair across the centre of his back.'

The two men looked at one another. The mystery was maddening, impenetrable.

The Great Detective spoke.

'Give me my domino,' he said. 'These clues must be followed up,' then pausing, while his quick brain analysed and summed up the evidence before him – 'a young man,' he muttered, 'evidently young since described as a "pup," with a long, wet snout (ha! addicted obviously to drinking), a streak of white hair across his back (a first sign of the results of his abandoned life) – yes, yes,' he continued, 'with this clue I shall find him easily.'

The Great Detective rose.

He wrapped himself in a long black cloak with white whiskers and blue spectacles attached.

Completely disguised, he issued forth.

He began to search.

For four days he visited every corner of London.

He entered every saloon in the city. In each of them he drank a glass of rum. In some of them he assumed the disguise of a sailor. In others he entered as a soldier. Into others he penetrated as a clergyman. His disguise was perfect. Nobody paid any attention to him as long as he had the price of a drink.

The search proved fruitless.

Two young men were arrested under suspicion of being the Prince, only to be released.

The identification was imcomplete in each case.

One had a long wet snout but no hair on his back.

The other had hair on his back but couldn't bark.

Neither of them was the young Bourbon.

The Great Detective continued his search.

He stopped at nothing.

Secretly, after nightfall, he visited the home of the Prime Minister. He examined it from top to bottom. He measured all the doors and windows. He took up the flooring. He inspected the plumbing. He examined the furniture. He found nothing.

With equal secrecy he penetrated into the palace of the Archbishop. He examined it from top to bottom. Disguised as a choir-boy he took part in the offices of the church. He found nothing.

Still undismayed, the Great Detective made his way into the home of the Countess of Dashleigh. Diguised as a housemaid, he entered the service of the Countess.

Then at last the clue came which gave him a solution of the mystery.

On the wall of the Countess' boudoir was a large framed engraving.

It was a portrait.

Under it was a printed legend:

THE PRINCE OF WURTTEMBERG

The portrait was that of a dachshund.

The long body, the broad ears, the unclipped tail, the short hind legs – all was there.

In the fraction of a second the lightning mind of the Great Detective had penetrated the whole mystery.

THE PRINCE WAS A DOG!!!!

Hastily throwing a domino over his housemaid's dress, he rushed to the street. He summoned a passing hansom, and in a few minutes was at his house.

'I have it,' he gasped to his secretary, 'the mystery is solved. I have pieced it together. By sheer analysis I have reasoned it out. Listen – hind legs, hair on back, wet snout, pup – eh, what? Does that suggest nothing to you?'

'Nothing,' said the secreatry; 'it seems perfecly hopeless.'

The Great Detective, now recovered from his excitement, smiled faintly.

'It means simply this, my dear fellow. The Prince of Wurttemberg is a dog, a prize dachshund. The Countess of Dashleigh bred him, and he is worth some £25,000 in addition to the prize of £10,000 offered at the Paris dog show. Can you wonder that –'

At that moment the Great Detective was interrupted by the scream of a woman.

'Great Heaven!'

The Countess of Dashleigh dashed into the room.

Her face was wild.

Her tiara was in disorder.

Her pearls were dripping all over the place.

She wrung her hand and moaned.

'They have cut his tail,' she gasped, 'and taken all the hair off his back. What can I do? I am undone!'

'Madame,' said the Great Detective, calm as bronze, 'do yourself up. I can save you yet.'

'You!'

'Me!'

'How?'

'Listen. This is how. The Prince was to have been shown at Paris.'

The Countess nodded.

'Your fortune was staked on him?'

The Countess nodded again.

'The dog was stolen, carried to London, his tail cut and his marks disfigured.'

Amazed at the quiet penetration of the Great Detective, the Countess kept on nodding and nodding.

'And you are ruined?'

'I am,' she gasped, and sank down on the floor in a heap of pearls.

'Madame,' said the Great Detective, 'all is not lost.'

He straightened himself up to his full height. A look of inflinchable unflexibility flickered over his features.

The honour of England, the fortune of the most beautiful woman in England was at stake.

'I will do it,' he murmured.

'Rise, dear lady,' he continued. 'Fear nothing. I WILL IMPERSONATE THE DOG!!!'

That night the Great Detective might have been seen on the deck of the Calais packet-boat with his secretary. He was on his hands and knees in a long black cloak, and his secretary had him on a short chain.

He barked at the waves exultingly and licked the secretary's hand.

'What a beautiful dog,' said the passengers.

The disguise was absolutely complete.

The Great Detective had been coated over with mucilage to which dogs hairs had been applied. The markings on his back were perfect. His tail, adjusted with an automatic coupler, moved up and down responsive to every thought. His deep eyes were full of intelligence.

Next day he was exhibited in the dachshund class at the International show.

He won all hearts.

'*Quel beau chien!*' cried the French people.

'*Ach! was ein Dog!*' cried the Spanish.

The Great Detective took the first prize!

The fortune of the Countess was saved.

Unfortunately as the Great Detective had neglected to pay the dog tax, he was caught and destroyed by the dog-catchers. But that is, of course, quite outside of the present narrative, and is only mentioned as an odd fact in conclusion.

The Singularge Experiece of Miss Anne Duffield

JOHN LENNON

I find it recornered in my nosebook that it was a dokey and winnie dave towart the end of Marge in the ear of our Loaf 1892 in Much Bladder, a city off the North Wold. Shamrock Womlbs had receeded a telephart whilst we sat at our lunch eating. He made no remark but the matter ran down his head, for he stud in front of the fire with a thoughtfowl face, smirking his pile, and casting an occasional gland at the massage. Quite sydney without warping he turd upod me with a miscarriage twinkle in his isle.

'Ellifitzgerrald my dear Whopper,' he grimmond then sharply 'Guess whom has broken out of jail Whopper?' My mind immediately recoughed all the caramels that had recently escaped or escaped from Wormy Scabs.

'Eric Morley?' I ventured. He shook his bed. 'Oxo Whitney?' I queered, he knotted in the infirmary. 'Rygo Hargraves?' I winston agreably.

'No, my dear Whopper, it's OXO WHITNEY' he bellowed as if I was in another room, and I wasn't.

'How d'you know Womlbs?' I whispered excretely.

'Harrybellafonte, my dear Whopper.' At that precise morman a tall rather angularce tall thin man knocked on the door. 'By all accounts that must be he, Whopper.' I marvelled at his acute osbert lancaster.

'How on urge do you know Womlbs' I asped, revealing my bad armchair.

'Eliphantitus my deaf Whopper' he baggage knocking out his pip on his large leather leg. In warped the favourite Oxo Whitney none the worse for worms.

'I'm an escaped primrose Mr Womlbs' he grate darting franetically about the room.

'Calm down Mr Whitney!' I interpolled 'or you'll have a nervous breadvan.'

'You must be Doctored Whopper' he pharted. My friend was starving at Whitney with a strange hook on his eager face, that tightening of the lips, that quiver of the nostriches and constapation of the heavy tufted brows which I knew so well.

'Gorra ciggie Oxo' said Womlbs quickly. I looked at my colledge, hoping for some clue as to the reason for this sodden outboard, he gave me no sign except a slight movement of his good leg as he kicked Oxo Whitney to the floor. 'Gorra ciggie Oxo' he reapeted almouth hysterically.

'What on urn are you doing my dear Womlbs' I imply; 'nay I besiege you, stop lest you do this poor wretch an injury!'

'Shut yer face yer blubbering owld get' screamed Womlbs like a man fermented, and laid into Mr Whitney something powerful nat. This wasn't not the Shamrock Womlbs I used to nose, I thought puzzled and hearn at this suddy change in my old friend.

Mary Atkins pruned herselves in the mirrage, running her hand wantanly through her large blond hair. Her tight dress was cut low revealingly three or four blackheads, carefully scrubbed on her chess. She addled the final touches to her makeup and fixed her teeth firmly in her head. 'He's going to want me tonight' she thought and pictured his hamsome black curly face and jaundice. She

226

looked at her clocks impatiently and went to the window, then leapt into her favorite armchurch, picking up the paper she glassed at the headlines. 'MORE NEGOES IN THE CONGO' it read, and there was, but it was the Stop Press which corked her eye. 'JACK THE NIPPLE STRIKE AGAIN.' She went cold all over, it was Sydnees and he'd left the door open.

'Hello lover' he said slapping her on the butter.

'Oh you did give me a start Sydnees' she shrieked laughing arf arfily.

'I always do my love' he replied jumping on all fours. She joined him and they galloffed quickly downstairs into a harrased cab. 'Follow that calf' yelped Sydnees pointing a rude fingure.

'White hole mate!' said the scabbie.

'Why are we bellowing that card Sydnees?' inquried Mary fashionably.

'He might know where the party' explained Sydnees.

'Oh I see' said Mary looking up at him as if to say.

The journey parssed pleasantly enough with Sydnees and Mary pointing out places of interest to the scab driver; such as Buckinghell Parcel, the Horses of Parliamint, the Chasing of the Guards. One place of particularge interest was the Statue of Eric in Picanniny Surplass.

'They say that if you stand there long enough you'll meet a friend' said Sydnees knowingly, 'that's if your not run over.'

'God Save the Queens' shouted the scabbie as they passed the Parcel for maybe the fourth time.

'Jack the Nipple' said Womlbs puffing deeply on his wife, 'is not only a vicious murderer but a sex meany of the lowest orgy.' Then my steamed collic relit his pig and walkered to the windy of his famous flat in Bugger St in London where it all happened. I pondled on his state-

mouth for a mormon then turding sharply I said. 'But how do you know Womlbs?'

'Alibabba my dead Whopper, I have seen the film' I knew him toby right for I had only read the comic.

That evenig we had an unexpeckled visitor, Inspectre Basil, I knew him by his tell-tale unicorn.

'Ah Inspectre Basil mon cher amie' said Womlbs spotting him at once. 'What brings you to our humble rich establisment?'

'I come on behave of thousands' the Inspectre said sitting quietly on his operation.

'I feel I know why you are here Basil' said Womlbs eyeing he leg. 'It's about Jock the Cripple is it not?' The Inspectre smiled smiling.

'How did you guess?' I inquired all puzzle.

'Alecguiness my deep Whopper, the mud on the Inspectre's left, and also the buttock on his waistbox is misting.'

The Inspectre looked astoundagast and fidgeted nervously from one fat to the other. 'You neville sieze to amass me Mr Womlbs.'

'A drink genitalmen' I ventured, 'before we get down to the businose in hand in hand?' They both knotted in egremont and I went to the cocky cabinet. 'What would you prepare Basil, Bordom '83 or?'

'I'd rather have rather have rather' said the Inspectre who was a gourmless. After a drink and a few sam leeches Womlbs got up and paced the floor up and down up and down pacing.

'Why are you pacing the floor up and down up and down pacing dear Womlbs' I inquiet.

'I'm thinking alowed my deaf Whopper.' I looked over at the Inspectre and knew that he couldn't hear him either.

'Guess who's out of jail Mr Womlbs' the Inspectre said

228

subbenly. Womlbs looked at me knowingly.

'Eric Morley?' I asked, they shook their heaths. 'Oxo Whitney?' I quart, again they shoot their heaps. 'Rygo Hargraves?' I wimpied.

'No my dear Whopper, OXO WHITNEY!' shouted Womlbs leaping to his foot. I looked at him admiring this great man all the morphia.

Meanwire in a ghasly lit street in Chelthea, a darkly clocked man with a fearful weapon, creeped about serging for revenge on the women of the streets for giving him the dreadfoot V.D. (Valentine Dyall). 'I'll kill them all womb by womb' he muffled between scenes. He was like a black shadow or negro on that dumb foggy night as he furtively looked for his neck victim. His minds wandered back to his childhook, remembering a vague thing or two like his mother and farmer and how they had beaten him for eating his sister. 'I'm demented' he said checking his dictionary. 'I should bean at home on a knife like these.' He turned into a dim darky and spotted a light.

Mary Atkins pruned herselves in the mirrage running her hand wantanly through her large blond hair. Her tight dress was cut low revealing three or four *more* blackheads carefully scrubbed on her chess. Business had been bad lately and what with the cost of limping. She hurriedly tucked in her gooseberries and opened the door. 'No wonder business is bad' she remarked as she caught size of her hump in the hall mirror. 'My warts are showing.' With a carefree yodel she slept into the street and caught a cab to her happy humping grounds. 'That Sydnees's nothing but a pimple living on me thus' she thought 'lazing about day in day off, and here's me plowing my train up and down like Soft Arthur and you know how soft Arthur.' She got off as uterus at Nats Café and took up her position. 'They'll never even see me in this fog' she muttered switching on her lamps. Just then a blasted Policemat walked by. 'Blasted Policemat' she shouted, but luckily he was deaf. 'Blasted deaf Policemat' she shouted. 'Why don't yer gerra job!'

Little did she gnome that the infamous Jack the Nipple was only a few street away. 'I hope that blasted Jack the Nipple isn't only a few streets away,' she said, 'he's not right in the heads.'

'How much lady' a voice shocked her from the doorways of Nats. Lucky for him there was a sale on so they soon retched an agreamant. A very high class genderman she thought as they walked quickly together down the now famous Carringto Average.

'I tell yer she whore a good woman Mr Womlbs sir' said Sydnees Aspinall.

'I quite believe you Mr Asterpoll, after all you knew her better than me and dear old buddy friend Whopper, but we are not here to discuss her merits good or otherwives, we are here, Mr Astronaute, to discover as much information as we can about the unfortunate and untidy death of Mary Atkins.' Womlbs looked the man in the face effortlessly.

'The name's Aspinall guvnor' said the wretched man.

'I'm deleware of your name Mr Astracan.' Womlbs said looking as if he was going to smash him.

'Well as long as you know,' said Aspinall wishing he'd gone to Safely Safely Sunday Trip. Womlbs took down the entrails from Aspinall as quickly as he could, I could see that they weren't on the same waveleg.

'The thing that puddles me Womlbs,' I said when we were alone, 'is what happened to Oxo Whitney?' Womlbs looged at me intently, I could see that great mind was thinking as his tufted eyepencil kit toboggen, his strong

230

jew jutted out, his nosepack flared, and the limes on his fourheads wrinkled.

'That's a question Whopper,' he said and I marveled at his grammer. Next day Womlbs was up at the crack of dorchester, he didn't evening look at the moaning papers. As yewtrew I fixed his breakfat of bogard, a gottle of geer, a slice of jewish bread, three eggs with little liars on, two rashes of bacon, a bowel of Rice Krustchovs, a fresh grapeful, mushrudes, some freed tomorrows, a basket of fruits, and a cup of teens.

'Breakfeet are ready' I showbody 'It's on the table.' But to my supplies he'd already gone. 'Blast the wicker basket yer grannie sleeps in.' I thought 'Only kidding Shamrock' I said remembering his habit of hiding in the cupboard.

That day was an anxious one for me as I waited for news of my dear friend, I became fretful and couldn't finish my Kennomeat, it wasn't like Shamrock to leave me here all by my own, lonely; without him I was at large. I rang up a few close itamate friends but they didn't know either, even Inspectre Basil didn't know, and if anybody should know, Inspectre Basil should 'cause he's a Police. I was a week lately when I saw him again and I was shocked by his apeerless, he was a dishovelled rock. 'My God Womlbs' I cried 'My God, what on earth have you been?'

'All in good time Whopper' he trousered. 'Wait till I get my breast back.'

I poked the fire and warmed his kippers, when he had mini-coopered he told me a story which to this day I can't remember.

The Affair of the Midnight Midget

ARDATH MAYHAR

221A Baker Street
3 November

Dear Doctor Watson,

It is with some trepidation that I take pen in hand to interrupt your convalescence (I hope that you are now able to walk with more ease and comfort). My apologies to your good lady for the intrusion of my affairs into her regimen, and I hope that she will forgive me for it.

However, after observing Mr. Holmes's behavior for some time, I have determined that something very strange is taking place. As you know all too well, this is nothing new with Mr. Holmes, but so bizarre is this new matter that I feel you will agree that it needs some attention from one who understands and makes allowances for his eccentricities.

He has, for the past fortnight, been arriving home very late. Indeed, I might even say that on several occasions he has not come in at all. This would give me no occasion for uneasiness, except for the fact that he has suffered from a bronchial infection, and the weather has been notably chilly and damp. Remaining out at night seems rash, when one considers the risk.

In addition, the array of small boys has stopped coming altogether. For many years, I have been used to having street urchins cluttering my doorstep, and I must admit that I rather miss their shrill voices, if not their grimy feet on my hall carpet. But this, if nothing else, has alarmed me. If Mr. Holmes no longer needs the services of his Irregulars, either he is far more ill than he has shown or admitted to me, or he has some venture on hand that is too desperate for risking the persons of his young colleagues.

Having kept a cool head over the years of his tenancy, under, I believe that you will agree, some extremely alarming circumstances, I feel that I am not showing undue concern, at this point. And in order to prove to you that this is true, I will list the oddities I have noticed lately in order of their seeming importance:

1. A well-dressed midget arriv?d four days ago, while Mr. Holmes was out. Knowing my lodger's habits, I scrutinized the man closely and decided that under no circumstances could Mr. Holmes have compressed his lanky height into such a minuscule form, and so I denied him entrance. He turned upon me a scurrilous attack, and that proved past question that it was not our friend, for he is invariably civil in his treatment of me. However, the midget left behind a packet, which I placed on the hall table.

2. Mr. Holmes must have come in without my hearing him, though I hardly see how that could be. However, I was awakened at three o'clock yesterday morning by a muffled explosion. Donning my dressing gown at once, I hurried downstairs, to find Mr. Holmes standing in the hallway, holding what seemed to be the remnant of wrapping from that same packet.

'Do not be alarmed, Mrs. Hudson,' he said, as I approached, in some dismay. 'Nothing is seriously damaged – not even the intended victim.' Here he laughed in a rather bitter manner and turned back into his rooms, still holding the wrapping. Shortly afterward, I heard his violin

233

start up, and it was a dreadfully dismal air that he played.

Now you know quite well that this is not the first violent occurrence in the chambers at 221B. I have never objected to such matters, for it seems clear that a detective's life is subject to this sort of happening, and the rental paid is more than enough to cover incidental damage. However, when I entered the chambers the next morning to lay out his breakfast, I found that the room, though tidier than usual, still reeked of something like gunpowder. There was, in addition, a bloodstain on the carpet, although it had been scrubbed almost clean.

I observed no wound upon Mr. Holmes's person, nor any blood, the night before, and it occurs to me that if the blood is not his, there is someone else hiding in his rooms. Would you have any notion as to who that might be?

3. This morning, when I tapped on the door before entering with the tray, I received no reply, though there was indubitably the sound of movement inside the room. I called out several times, asking if he might be ill, but, while I heard footsteps crossing the uncarpeted area of the floor, I still received no reply. The steps were brisk and did not drag, as one would expect those of a sick or injured man to do.

As you might suspect, I am extremely worried and upset. It is obvious that someone is posing a danger to my tenant. It seems obvious, also, that he is hiding someone (perhaps sheltering them from harm?) in his chambers.

Yet he is exhibiting none of his usual methods of dealing with such problems. Not one person has approached in weeks, with the single exception of that objectionable midget. He is, I believe, more often in than out, though I can no longer be certain of anything concerning his movements.

And, early this morning, his brother Mycroft sent

around a note by the hand of one of the ushers at his club. I have not been able to receive an answer to my knocks, and I hesitate to slip it under the door, in the event that the person inside is one who should not know whatever message that note contains.

Dr. Watson, I badly need advice. If I should call at your home tomorrow, would you be so kind as to see and to advise your respectful

Martha Hudson

221A Baker Street
5 November

Dear Doctor Watson,

It was most gracious of you and your lady to receive me, as well as to advise me concerning the current problem. Indeed, I will gladly keep you abreast of the situation, as events come to my attention.

I have taken your advice and hired an extra cleaning-woman, who is charged with scouring every staircase in the house from top to bottom, taking her time and doing the thing properly. As this involves mops and pails, brooms and scrubbing brushes, which seem to be scattered along every length of steps in the house, it is quite probable that I will know if anyone tries to creep upstairs.

Mr. Holmes is definitely out, at the moment. I saw him go, myself, not an hour past. He looked very drawn, with his throat muffled closely. I do worry about that bronchitis. He seems thinner than before, and he did not walk with his usual decisive tread. Something is worrying him.

Immediately after watching him from view, I climbed the steps, being careful to avoid every obstacle that Tilly left there, and listened at the door of the rooms. Someone was pacing back and forth, and I thought that I caught the hint of a whistled tune, though that was quickly discontinued.

And here come Mr. Holmes, back already. I must put away my writing things and prepare his tea – he has taken none for several afternoons.

* * *

Later

Dear Doctor Watson,

My plans were disrupted by the arrival of Inspector Lestrade of the London Police. Would you credit it? He arrived with a warrant and proceeded to search Mr. Holmes's chambers from top to bottom. He was searching, if you can believe this, for my tenant's *nephew*!

This was a great surprise to me. I have known that there was a brother, a recluse, I believe, and I would have thought *him* a misogynist, as well. However, it seems that in his early youth, our Mr. Holmes's relation contracted a marriage with a young woman who died after producing an infant. This child was reared by a distant cousin and is now in his early twenties. He has been accused of murdering the father of a young person who, he claims, is his fiancée.

No trace of anyone other than my lawful tenant was found on the premises, which puzzled me a great deal, for a time. And then I recalled the false ceiling that Mr. Holmes asked to have installed in his study. I suspect that the young man is, even as I write, cramped and dusty in the darkness of that narrow space between the new and the old.

This explains the person hiding in the rooms, true, but it leaves almost more questions unanswered. Who was that midget, and why was a bomb left for Mr. Holmes? Why is he keeping his usual contacts at a distance? And why is he hiding a person who is wanted by the law, when, if the boy is innocent, he might promptly prove that to be true?

As you may suppose, I am bewildered, but I will continue to report. I hope that your relapse is a short one, and that you will soon feel up to getting about.

With sincere regards,
Martha Hudson

★ ★ ★

November 10

Dear Doctor Watson,

Although you may think me neglectful, I have not written simply because there has been nothing to report. Mr. Holmes seems content to remain indoors, after receiving his brother's note, and has kept to his chambers for several days. The young man, his nephew, I am certain is still in the house, though there has been no further instance by means of which I could prove that.

However, this morning found matters altered. Mr. Holmes rang for breakfast a full two hours earlier than usual, and when I took up the tray, he was pale, and his cough shook him painfully. He was so ill that he asked me to remain while he drank a bit of tea and crumbled a piece of toast. When I insisted that he allow me to call a physician, he sighed and nodded.

'A pity that Watson is under the weather, but that seems advisable. Yes, Mrs. Hudson, call in your doctor. I believe that I am too ill to go on.'

This astonished me, as you may well imagine. Never before have I heard him admit that he was not well, no matter how obvious that might be to the unaided eye. However, I called Tilly and sent her after Dr. Jermyn, whom you may recall as living two streets over and one down.

237

When that gentleman arrived, he insisted that Mr. Holmes be taken at once to hospital, as his bronchitis had become pneumonia. This left my tenant in a quandary, as you might think, for I was not supposed to know of the presence of the nephew. However, he took the opportunity, while the doctor sent for a carriage, to speak with me.

'Mrs. Hudson,' he said, staring into my eyes as if to read my thoughts, 'I need a favor. You have never failed me, and I trust that you will aid me now. My brother's son, Andrew, is staying with me. He is, as you probably gathered from the visit of our brilliant Lestrade, in a bit of trouble, at the moment, and only this damnable illness has prevented my finding the true culprit and freeing him from this dangerous situation.'

'I knew he was here,' I assured him. 'And I suspect that he hid in the overhead, while the police searched.'

He looked surprised, though why that should be true I cannot think. But I went on, 'I handed in that note from your brother, as well, and that told me something, though I have no idea what was written there.'

'Mycroft has learned something vital. His own life may be in danger, for the father of that young woman was Lord Tinningsly, the Chancellor of the Exchequer. A plot has been afoot to discredit the British currency, and the Chancellor was murdered in order to conceal its existence. My unfortunate nephew was inadvertently caught in a web of international monetary manipulation, and if he is apprehended it will mean that the true culprits will never be brought to book.'

Dr. Jermyn's steps approached along the hallway. Mr. Holmes laid a small envelope in my hand. 'Care for him as you would for me. I will return, and those who intend to kill him, claiming that they acted in self defense, must not find him before that time comes.'

Naturally, I trusted his words implicitly, for although he sometimes takes a devious route, I have never known Mr. Holmes to arrive at anything other than the truth. I tucked the envelope into my apron pocket and assisted the men as they carried the sick man down the stairs. I removed the brooms and mops as they passed, but before they were out of sight I had them all replaced. Now, more than ever, we needed a functioning alarm system.

When Tilly left, that evening, I went upstairs and tapped on the door of 221B. 'Mr. Holmes! Mr. Andrew Holmes! Your uncle has entrusted you to my care, and I need to talk with you. Will you open the door?'

After a long interval, during which I thought more than once that the young man was not going to risk unlocking the door, the key turned in the lock. A pale face, long in the bone like his uncle's, stared out at me. Along his cheek was a partially healed cut, which would, I was certain, have been caused by that bomb.

'You are Mrs. Hudson?' he asked. Even his voice was like, and when I entered the room and saw him in full I could see that the Holmes bone structure was there. His hands were long and thin, and they twitched, as Mr. Holmes's do sometimes when he wants to play his violin but is prevented by other affairs.

'It is a pity the illness came on him so quickly,' I said. 'He knows who killed your young lady's father, and he would prove it like a shot, if he were able.'

He sighed. 'I know, too. Danvers, the secretary, was the key to the entire plot, and Lord Tinningsly caught him out. He told me, before he was killed, but little good will that do me. Everyone thinks that I killed him because he objected when I courted Millicent. And he didn't even object. Not really. He simply wants – wanted – us to wait until she is eighteen before we announce our engagement.'

I believed him. I think that I would have, even had Mr. Holmes not told me the facts in the case.

I smiled at the boy. 'Keep the blinds drawn closely,' I said. 'We want no light to show in the street, for the rooms are supposed to be empty. I will bring up your breakfast early, before the servants arrive, and your dinner will be served at about nine o'clock. I hope you will not become too hungry, in the time between. Keep the door locked and the chain up. And remain in the back rooms, if you can manage to. Even if you pace, no one will hear you, there.'

He nodded. I felt it a pity that so likely a youngster must have so harsh an initiation into the world, but that comes when it comes, and nobody can alter that.

I was abed before midnight, and I slept deeply, after the excitements of the day. Yet when the first pail clanged down the steps and the array of mops and brooms began their clattering falls, I was up in a moment, wide awake. Lighting a lamp, I hurried down the stairs toward the landing at 221B. The disturbance came from farther down, however, and I continued on my way.

The door opened as I passed, and Andrew Holmes looked out. 'Trouble?' he asked.

I nodded without speaking, for I was wondering how I could cope with those who seemed determined to climb my stair, no matter what clamor they set up. I seized a mop that leaned against the railing and charged downward into the darkness.

Behind me, I could hear Master Holmes's slippers flapping on the carpet. 'Are you armed?' I asked, over my shoulder yet keeping my gaze fixed on the motion below.

'Now I am,' he said, his voice grim. 'You are not alone!'

Even armed only with mop handles, I found that

comforting. I had given my word, and anyone coming up the steps to harm this young man was going to answer to Martha Hudson!

I stumbled over the midget. He rolled beneath my feet, and I saved myself by grabbing the railing. Another shape, much larger than the first, loomed against the dim light from the foyer lamp, and I aimed my mop handle and rammed it into his waistcoat. He grunted and folded over, giving me the opportunity to rap him smartly upon the head.

I could hear a scuffle behind me. Then there was a sharp smack, and the midget rolled back down beneath my feet. I stepped over him and pushed the other man off the expensive carpet runner that protected my foyer. Blood is most difficult to get out of wool!

'Are you all right, Mrs. Hudson?' asked the young man.

'Quite well, Mr. Holmes. If you will retire to the upstairs, out of sight, I will summon the constable on duty. I have a whistle that will have him here at once.'

He moved out of sight, and I went into my lower rooms in order to find the whistle. As I rummaged about, I checked my apron pocket, and there was the envelope Mr. Holmes the elder had left in my hand. Surely he had intended that I open it!

I unfolded the crisp page, and another fell out of the protective wrapping. I stared down at it. Then I went to the door and blew the whistle shrilly into the damp night.

Of course, the envelope that Mycroft Holmes had sent was a note (how he put his hands onto it I probably do not wish to know) from Tinningsly to his secretary, asking him to come to the office in order to explain his recent activities with regard to the International Currency Market. While it did not directly accuse him of misdoing, the inference was plain, and the police saw that as quickly as I

241

had done.

I can only assume that Danvers's attempts against Sherlock Holmes were caused by his uneasiness at the thought that the great detective might take a hand in proving the innocence of his nephew, and in so doing would uncover the plot and its participants. The police believe that, as well, though Mr. Holmes only smiled when I mentioned my theory.

I hope that you are now well enough to visit Mr. Holmes, who is again in his rooms, though unable, as yet, to get about much. If I have rambled at some length, you must understand that it is seldom that a respectable female has the opportunity to participate in such exciting and interesting affairs, and this has been a most enlightening experience for

Your respectful friend,
Martha Hudson

You have, no doubt, read the newspaper accounts of the affair. The police, of course, never apologized to Master Holmes, but that is something they seldom do.

I understand at last the irritation that Mr. Holmes must feel when his dangerous and difficult work is ignored, while the police take all the credit. It was I who captured Danvers and his midget accomplice. But what did the Times headlines say?

LESTRADE SOLVES TINNINGSLY CASE

The very idea!

From a Detective's Notebook

P. G. WODEHOUSE

We were sitting round the club fire, old General Malpus, Driscoll the QC, young Freddie ffinch-ffinch and myself, when Adrian Mulliner, the private investigator, gave a soft chuckle. This was, of course, in the smoking-room, where soft chuckling is permitted.

'I wonder,' he said, 'if it would interest you chaps to hear the story of what I always look upon as the greatest triumph of my career?'

We said No, it wouldn't, and he began.

'Looking back over my years as a detective, I recall many problems the solution of which made me modestly proud, but though all of them undoubtedly presented certain features of interest and tested my powers to the utmost, I can think of none of my feats of ratiocination which gave me more pleasure than the unmasking of the man Sherlock Holmes, now better known as the Fiend of Baker Street.'

Here General Malpus looked at his watch, said 'Bless my soul,' and hurried out, no doubt to keep some appointment which had temporarily slipped his mind.

'I had at first so little to go on,' Adrian Mulliner proceeded. 'But just as a brief sniff at a handkerchief or shoe will start one of Mr. Thurber's bloodhounds giving quick service, so is the merest suggestion of anything that I might call fishy enough to set me off on the trail, and what first aroused my suspicions of this sinister character was his peculiar financial position.

'Here we had a man who evidently was obliged to watch the pennies closely, for when we are introduced to him he is, according to Doctor Watson's friend Stamford, "bemoaning himself because he could not find someone to go halves with him in some nice rooms which he had found and which were too much for his purse." Watson offers himself as a fellow lodger, and they settle down in – I quote – "a couple of comfortable bedrooms and a large sitting-room at 221B Baker Street."

'Now I never lived in Baker Street at the turn of the century, but I knew old gentlemen who had done so, and they assured me that in those days you could get a bedroom and sitting-room and three meals a day for a pound a week. An extra bedroom no doubt made the thing come higher, but thirty shillings must have covered the rent, and there was never a question of a man as honest as Doctor Watson failing to come up with his fifteen each Saturday. It followed, then, that even allowing for expenditure in the way of Persian slippers, tobacco, disguises, revolver cartridges, cocaine and spare fiddle-strings, Holmes would have been getting by on a couple of pounds or so weekly. And with this modest state of life he appeared to be perfectly content. In a position where you or I would have spared no effort to add to our resources he simply did not bother about the financial side of his profession. Let us take a few instances at random and see what he made as a "consulting detective." Where are you going, Driscoll?'

'Out,' said the QC, suiting action to the word.

Adrian Mulliner resumed his tale.

'In the early days of their association Watson speaks of being constantly bundled off into his bedroom because Holmes needed the sitting-room for interviewing callers. "I have to use this room as a place of business," he said,

244

"and these people are my clients." And who were these clients? "A grey-headed, seedy visitor, who was closely followed by a slipshod elderly woman," and after these came "a railway porter in his velveteen uniform." Not much cash in that lot, and things did not noticeably improve later, for we find his services engaged by a stenographer, an average commonplace British tradesman, a commissionaire, a City clerk, a Greek interpreter, a landlady ("You arranged an affair for a lodger of mine last year") and a Cambridge undergraduate.

'So far from making money as a consultig detective, he must have been a good deal out of pocket most of the time. In *A Study in Scarlet* Inspector Gregson says there has been a bad business during the night at 3 Lauriston Gardens off the Brixton Road and he would esteem it a great kindness if Holmes would favour him with his opinions. Off goes Holmes in a hansom from Baker Street to Brixton, a fare of several shillings, dispatches a long telegram (another two or three bob to the bad), summons "half a dozen of the dirtiest and most ragged street Arabs that ever I clapped eyes on," and gives each of them a shilling, and finally, calling on Police Constable Bunce, the officer who discovered the body, takes half a sovereign from his pocket and after "playing with it pensively" presents it to the constable. The whole affair must have cost him considerably more than a week's rent at Baker Street, and no hope of getting it back from Inspector Gregson, for Gregson, according to Holmes himself, was one of the smartest of the Scotland Yarders.

'Inspector Gregson! Inspector Lestrade! These clients! I found myself thinking a good deal about them, and it was not long before the truth dawned upon me that they were merely cheap actors, hired to deceive Doctor Watson. For what would the ordinary private investigator have said to himself when starting out in business? He would have said, "Before I take on work for a client I must be sure that that client has the stuff. The daily sweetener and the little something down in advance are of the essence," and would have had those landladies and those Greek interpreters out of that sitting-room before you could say "blood-stain." Yet Holmes, who could not afford a pound a week for lodgings, never bothered. Significant?'

On what seemed to me the somewhat shallow pretext that he had to see a man about a dog, Freddie ffinch-ffinch now excused himself and left the room.

'Later,' Adrian Mulliner went on, 'the thing became absolutely farcical, for all pretence that he was engaged in a gainful occupation was dropped by himself and the clients. I quote Doctor Watson: "He tossed a crumpled letter across to me. It was dated from Montague Place upon the preceding evening and run thus:

DEAR MR. HOLMES, – I am very anxious to consult you as to whether or not I should accept a situation which has been offered me as a governess. I shall call at half past ten to-morrow if I do not inconvenience you.

Yours faithfully,
VIOLET HUNTER

'Now, the fee an investigator could expect from a governess, even one in full employment, could scarcely be more than a few shillings, yet when two weeks later Miss Hunter wired "PLEASE BE AT THE BLACK SWAN HOTEL AT WINCHESTER AT MIDDAY TO-MORROW", Holmes dropped everything and sprang into the 9.30 train.'

Adrian Mulliner paused and chuckled softly.

'You see where all this is heading?'

I said No, I didn't. I was the only one there, and had to say something.

'Tut, tut, man! You know my methods. Apply them. Why is a man casual about money?'

'Because he has a lot of it.'

'Precisely.'

'But you said Holmes hadn't.'

'I said nothing of the sort. That was merely the illusion he was trying to create.'

'Why?'

'Because he needed a front for his true activities. Sherlock Holmes had no need to worry about fees. He was pulling in the stuff in sackfulls from another source. Where is the big money? Where has it always been! In crime. Bags of it, and no income tax. If you want to salt away a few million for a rainy day you don't spring into 9.30 trains to go and see governesses, you become a master criminal, sitting like a spider in the centre of its web and egging your corps of assistants on to steal jewels and naval treaties.'

'You mean . . .'

'Exactly. He was Professor Moriarty.'

'What was that name again?'

'Professor Moriarty.'

'The bird with the reptilian head?'

'That's right.'

'But Holmes hadn't a reptilian head.'

'Nor had Moriarty.'

'Holmes said he had.'

'And to whom? To Watson. So as to get the description given publicity. Watson never saw Moriarty. All he knew about him was what Holmes told him. Well, that's the story, old man.'

'The whole story?'

'Yes.'

'There isn't any more?'

'No.'

I chuckled softly.

247

SOURCES AND ACKNOWLEDGEMENTS

'The Martian Crown Jewels' by Poul Anderson, from *Ellery Queen's Mystery Magazine*, copyright © 1958 by Davis Publications, Inc.; reprinted by permission of A.M. Heath & Company Ltd/Scott Meredith Literary Agency, Inc.

'From the Diary of Sherlock Holmes' by Maurice Baring, from *The Eye-Witness* (November, 1911), collected in *Lost Diaries* (London: Duckworth, 1913).

'The Anomaly of the Empty Man' by Anthony Boucher, from *The Magazine of Fantasy and Science Fiction* (April, 1952(, copyright © 1952 by Anthony Boucher; reprinted by permission of Curtis Brown Ltd.

'The Adventure of the Paradol Chamber' and 'The Adventure of the Conk-Singleton Papers' by John Dickson Carr, first performed at annual meetings of the Mystery Writers of America, copyright © 1949, 1948 by Clarice M. Carr; reprinted by permission of David Higham Associates Ltd.

'The Adventure of the Snitch in Time' by August Derleth and Mack Reynolds, from *Ellery Queen's Mystery Magazine*, copyright © 1953 by Mercury Press, Inc., renewed 1962 by August Derleth.

'The Adventure of the Dog in the Knight' by Robert L. Fish, from *Ellery Queen's Mystery Magazine*, copyright © 1969 by Robert L. Fish; reprinted by permission of Robert P. Mills Ltd.

'The Adventure of the Three Madmen' by Philip José Farmer, from *The Grand Adventure* (New York: Berkley, 1984), copyright © by Philip José Farmer; reprinted by permission of the author and A.M. Heath & Company Ltd/Scott Meradith Literary Agency, Inc.

'Mr Montalba, Obsequist' by H.F. Heard, from *Ellery Queen's Mystery Magazine*, copyright © 1945 by H.F. Heard.

'A Trifling Affair' by H.R.F. Keating, from *John Creasy's Crime Collection 1980*, ed. Herbert Harris (London: Gollancz, 1980),